OBLIVION

THE WATCHER CHRONICLES
BOOK 3

BY
INTERNATIONAL
BESTSELLING AUTHOR

S.J. WEST

CONTENTS

COPYRIGHTS

Cover Design: coversbyjuan.com, all rights reserved.
Interior Design & Formatting: Stephany Wallace, all rights reserved.
Proof Reader: Kimberly Huther.

Published by Watchers Publishing March, 2013.
www.Sjwest.com

BOOKS IN THE WATCHER SERIES

The Redemption Series

Malcolm
Anna
Lucifer
Redemption

The Dominion Series

Awakening
Reckoning
Enduring

The Everlasting Fire Series

War Angel
Between Worlds
Shattered Souls

OTHER BOOKS BY S.J. WEST

The Harvester of Light Trilogy

Harvester
Hope
Dawn

The Vankara Saga

Vankara
Dragon Alliance

War of Atonement

ACKNOWLEDGMENTS

I would like to express my gratitude to the many people who were with me throughout this creative process; to all those who provided support, talked things over, read, wrote, offered comments, allowed me to quote their remarks and assisted in the editing, proofreading and design.

Thanks to Kimberly Huther, my proofreader for helping me find typos, correct commas and tweak the little details that have help this book become my perfect vision. Thank you to Stephany Wallace for creating the Interior Design of the books and formatting them.

Last and not least: I want to thank my family, who supported and encouraged me in this journey.

I apologize to those who have been with me over the course of the years and whose names I have failed to mention

CHAPTER 1

I had always heard going through the Tear was painful, but didn't realize how much of an understatement that was until now. I feel like my body has been stripped down to its finite number of atoms and sucked through a straw. Now I understand why tearers always look so shell-shocked when they arrive on our planet. In the back of my mind, I know I'll have to endure this torture one more time to get home. It's no wonder there aren't many people who ever return. Who in their right mind would willingly go through this twice if they didn't have to?

When we finally do arrive at our destination, Mason and I are still holding hands, amazingly enough. We find ourselves in a standing of trees with the only light coming from the low hanging crescent moon and Tear in the sky.

"I could have used a reminder about the pain," I tell

Mason, massaging my forehead to ease the sudden ache between my temples, and to reassure myself that my head is indeed still attached to my shoulders.

"Where's your sense of adventure?" Mason asks grimacing, obviously not immune to the effects of wormhole travel either.

"I must have left it back home," I reply, surveying the area we're in and seeing the glow of tall buildings in the far distance, slightly obscured by the trees.

"I think this is Central Park," I tell Mason, remembering the time Chandler and I spent here not so long ago.

"That would be my guess too," Mason says, making his own observation of our surroundings.

Multitudes of howls rip through the air around us, and I feel Mason's body tense beside me.

"Were those werewolf howls?" I ask, remembering all too well the Watcher child who took Faison's place when she went through the Tear.

"Yes," Mason says, holding my hand tighter.

I look over at him and watch as his expression changes from slightly worried to almost panicked.

"What's wrong?" I ask.

"I can't phase," he says, looking over at me. "This isn't our Earth, so I have no memory of places to phase to."

Letting go of Mason's hand, I quickly unstrap my plasma pistol from my thigh and hand it to him. Reaching behind me, I quickly pull my sword from its sheath and hear it sing against the scabbard for the first time.

"Well, I sure as hell didn't just travel through a worm-hole to be eaten up by a bunch of mutts," I grumble, the blade of my sword bursting into flames to chase away the darkness. "Will they try to eat you, or am I the only main entrée here?"

"Only you," Mason confirms, "but they'll have to get through me first."

In spite of the dire straits we find ourselves in, I smile at Mason.

"I like it when you get all protective of me, but you don't have to worry. Neither of us will die today," I tell him.

Mason narrows his eyes at me. "How can you say that with so much conviction?"

"Because I don't think God would send us here just to die. Not unless He has some wacked out sense of humor I need to know about."

"No," Mason says, realizing that I'm right. "He isn't one to find irony humorous."

I shrug. "Ok, then we shouldn't have anything to worry about."

"Since when do you have faith in anything He does?" Mason asks.

The question brings me up short. Why do I have faith that He didn't just send us here to die? It's a good question, but not one I exactly have time to ruminate over at the present time.

"So what do you suggest, run or stand our ground against these things?" I ask, choosing to ignore Mason's question about my faith in God for the time being. There are more pressing matters to deal with right now.

"Stand our ground. You would never be able to outrun them. They move too quickly."

I hold my sword with both hands out in front of me, preparing myself for what's coming.

The roar of an engine breaks the silence as a black jeep tears through the forest and comes to a stop behind us.

"Agent! What the hell are you doing out here? Why aren't you back at HQ by now?"

I turn and shield my eyes with one hand against the bright headlights of the jeep, only able to see the shadowy outline of the man with the gruff voice.

"Get your asses over here before those things are let out and rip you to shreds!"

Mason and I look at each other, realizing we don't exactly have a better option. The flames of the sword automatically extinguish, and I slide it back into its sheath on my back. Mason hands me my plasma pistol, and I drop it into the holster on my thigh as we run over to our rescuer. Mason climbs into the small backseat, and I take the passenger seat by the driver. When I look at the driver, I notice he's dressed similarly to me, in a Watcher agent uniform that's only slightly different.

Involuntarily, I gasp when I see the man's face, because I recognize him. Well, not this particular version of the man, but I know his doppelganger. It's Albert. Back home he's in charge of the front desk at the Watcher station in Tunica.

Many of the other Watcher agents call him Fat Albert because of his girth. But the Albert sitting next to me is anything but overweight. This Albert is slim with a muscular build, presumably honed from hours of working out with weights. I sit amazed at the difference in his appearance.

"Thanks, Albert," I say.

Albert slams the accelerator down to the floorboard, and the jeep lurches forward.

"Do I know you?" he asks me, chancing a glance in my direction as he deftly maneuvers the jeep through the line of trees and onto a paved path.

"I know your counterpart on my Earth," I tell him.

"Shit, you're travelers?" he asks in disbelief. "Guess that explains the sword; not exactly Watcher regulated weaponry around here. I should have known you weren't one of our agents. If you were, you would have known better than to stay out here while they're playing."

"Playing?"

"The Watchers. They like to pit their kids against each other to see whose little monster is strongest. It's a game they like to call 'Bait' here. You're lucky I came along when I did. This was my last sweep of the area before they let them loose."

"Let them loose on what?" I ask, fearing I already know the answer to the question.

The jeep passes through the gate of a twenty-foot-high chain-link fence with rolls of barbed wire welded to the top. We find ourselves racing down a crowded New York City thoroughfare. The gate automatically closes shut behind us as Albert brings the jeep to a complete stop, in front of a chrome and glass skyscraper a little ways down the street.

"My guess would be humans," Mason says from his seat in the back.

"And your guess would be right," Albert confirms, turning the key to shut off the jeep's engine.

"You didn't happen to come across a redheaded female traveler on your sweep of the area, did you?" I ask.

"No, you were the only fools out there besides the ten we brought in to act as bait for the game."

I sigh. I'm relieved Faison wasn't in the park, but I also feel a sense of guilt for that relief. I know I can't help the ten poor souls certain to face a gruesome death at the hands of the Watcher children. But what if Faison traveled to the holding pen where the werewolves were being kept? I decide not to entertain that possibility. Besides, Albert would have heard about such an incident occurring and mentioned it.

Albert turns to look at first Mason and then me. I can tell he's sizing us up, trying to determine if we're going to be a problem or not. It's what I would do in his situation. Watcher agents are trained to make snap judgments about Tearers in just one glance. Though, I guess on this version of Earth they're called travelers. I don't even have to ask Albert what his conclusion about us is because I know what I would classify Mason and me as: trouble.

"You two need to come inside with me. We should go ahead and get your information processed into our database. I'm pretty sure the Chancellor will want to speak with you as well."

"Chancellor?" I ask.

Albert's eyebrows lower. "Don't you have Chancellors on your Earth?"

"I don't have a clue what you're talking about, to be completely honest."

"You have Watchers," Albert says, pointedly looking at my uniform. "You must have one in charge of your sector."

"Which Chancellor is in charge of this sector?" Mason asks, subtly digging for more information.

"Chancellor Malcolm is in charge of the Northeast sector. We all answer to him."

"When you say in charge," Mason says, "do you mean he's in charge of the agents here, or something else?"

"He's in charge of everything from Maine to Florida and over to Illinois. Didn't the Watchers take over after the Tear opened on your Earth?"

"Take over?" I ask, feeling sure I understand what Albert is saying, but having a hard time believing what the evidence is pointing to.

"Yeah, you know, they took over the world," Albert says slowly, realization dawning. "They didn't do that on your Earth, did they?"

"No," Mason answers crisply, clearly troubled by what Albert has told us. "The Watchers on our Earth only help the governments, not run them."

"Well, they pretty much took over everything here. No

country has an elected government anymore. We're all divided up into sectors, with our own Watcher calling all the shots. You guys lucked out, though. This sector is one of the less strict ones."

"Why do you say that?" I ask.

"Chancellor Malcolm isn't as harsh as some of the other Chancellors. He gets a little preoccupied with the female agents on his detail, if you get my drift."

"Yes," Mason says knowingly, "our Malcolm is similar in that regard. At least, he used to be."

"Do the two of you happen to be married?" Albert asks, a question which seems completely out of the blue.

"Why do you ask?" Mason is quick to say before I have a chance to answer the question truthfully.

Albert looks me up and down. "The Chancellor will probably put you on his detail if you aren't. He might do it even if you are, but he tends to steer clear of married agents. He doesn't like complications."

"Been married a year," I lie smoothly.

Albert looks down at my left hand. "No wedding ring?"

"Not allowed to wear one while in uniform," I answer, amazed with how deftly the lies seem to be flowing out of my mouth.

"I would get a ring," Albert advises, "*if* you don't want to be put on his rotation. Though, from what I've heard, it's an easy gig. The girls don't do much real work."

"I like to work," I say, smiling grimly. "Not much for lounging around."

"Well, you'll have some time to decide," Albert tells us. "I heard he's locked himself in his penthouse tonight for some reason and isn't seeing anyone. But, we still need to put your information into our database of travelers. After that, you'll get an assigned room for the night."

"Does the Chancellor meet with all the new travelers in his sector?" I ask.

"No, but you're the first Watcher agent who's ever come through. It's a safe bet he'll want to meet you. Follow me into HQ, and I'll get you guys situated."

When we step out of the jeep, Mason takes hold of one of my hands, and I'm thankful for the contact. I feel like I'm Alice and have stepped through the looking glass into Watcherland. The mere idea of the Watchers taking over the world has my mind swimming in a sea of confused turmoil. How could the Watchers on this Earth be so different?

As we walk into the building Albert parked in front of, I feel as though I've stepped back in time, and not to a particularly good point in history.

Covering the walls are black and white propaganda posters prominently featuring Chancellor Malcolm. He's dressed in a crisply tailored black leather uniform and billed hat with a pair of silver angel wings attached to the front of it. Malcolm's style of uniform and austere posture brings to mind pictures of Nazi soldiers I've seen in history books.

In one of the posters, Malcolm is handing a white lily to a girl of about eight. Under the picture, the caption reads *In*

Malcolm We Trust. It soon becomes apparent you can't turn your head without seeing a picture of Malcolm staring back at you. I begin to wonder if Malcolm's image is embossed on the money here too. I always thought Lilly's protector was a bit on the vain side, with his never-ending supply of unbuttoned shirts, but his counterpart in this reality has taken it to an entirely new and disturbing level.

There are a few Watcher agents milling about, trying to comfort the people who just came through the Tear. Some of the agents openly stare at us as we walk down the black carpeted hallway, making me feel a bit conspicuous. Most of them seem interested in the sword strapped to my back, but the vast majority of female agents let their gazes linger on Mason longer than necessary. I find myself glaring at the ones who seem a bit too interested in him for my peace of mind. Out of the corner of my eye, I notice Mason smiling.

"Do you like being the center of attention?" I ask him, raising an eyebrow at one perky little blonde Watcher agent who seems determined to devour Mason with just her eyes.

"No," Mason says, still smiling. "But I like it when you're overprotective of me too."

"I just want to make sure they understand you're off limits. I don't share," I reply, staring daggers at a pretty brunette who passes by us, trying her best to look coyly at Mason. She seems to get the hint and scurries away quickly.

"Neither do I," Mason says ominously.

"You sound worried," I say, returning my full attention to him. "Why?"

"Malcolm used to be quite different before he met Lilly," Mason tells me, a warning in his voice. "Considering what's happened on this Earth, I have to assume this version of Malcolm has probably never met her."

"I don't understand how things can be so different here. What do you think happened?"

Mason shakes his head. "I don't know, but I think the sooner we find Faison the better. This isn't our reality, and I'd rather not make things worse with our presence."

Albert escorts us up to the tenth floor of the building, and into a nondescript office with a glass wall facing out towards a completely fenced in Central Park. He asks for our personal information and enters it into the computer. Mason has to lie about almost everything, but he seems to be rather good at conjuring up a false identity for himself.

"Could you look to see if you have a Faison Mills in your database?" I ask Albert. "She went through the Tear tonight too."

Albert seems to punch her name into the computer and shakes his head. "No, she's not in here. Could be she just hasn't been found yet."

I nod, knowing this is probably the case. Not all Tearers are found the first night they come through. Some hide out where they can, too frightened of their new circumstances to seek help. Most are found within the first month, but there are some, mostly of the criminal persuasion, who aren't located until they're caught doing something they shouldn't be.

I have no way of knowing what Faison's mental state is right now. For all I know, she could be stranded on a street corner somewhere, crying. I do know I need to get out and start searching for her as soon as I can, though.

"Hmm," Albert says as he stares at the screen, a confused expression on his face. "Neither of you seems to have a double here on this Earth."

"That's not unusual," I say. "We might have doppelgangers here, but their names might be different. Or, we just don't exist here."

"Eighty percent of the people who come from different Earths have doubles here," Albert says, and I know his statistical analysis is correct. It works out to that much on our Earth too. "It's just odd that neither of you has one. I would have thought at least one of you would."

"I guess that just makes us unique," I reply, trying to play off the odds.

If one of us didn't happen to be an angel, the odds would lean more towards our favor. I have no way of knowing if I have a counterpart here or not. The other Jess might not have my name, due to her specific life circumstances.

The phone on Albert's desk rings.

"Agent Washington," Albert says as he answers it. Albert's posture suddenly changes from relaxed to tense. His eyes shift to us nervously as he listens to the person on the other end of the line. "Yes, Chancellor, I understand."

Albert hangs up and stares at the phone for a moment, as if he's trying to decide something.

"That was Chancellor Malcolm," Albert tells us. "He wants to see the two of you immediately."

"How did he even know we were here?" I ask.

"Someone informed him we had a Watcher agent come through the Tear. Apparently, he wants to ask you for information about your world."

From the worried expression on Albert's face, I get the feeling being summoned to appear in front of Malcolm on this particular night isn't a good thing.

"Where is he?" I ask.

"Penthouse," Albert informs us. "We'd better go. He doesn't like to be kept waiting."

When we get into the elevator, Albert pushes the 'P' on the control panel.

"Please place your right eye directly in front of the retinal scanner," a disembodied female voice directs.

Albert leans forward towards a small lens above the buttons on the control panel.

"Thank you, Agent Washington."

The elevator begins to rise.

I reach out for Mason's hand, because I have no idea what will happen when we come face to face with Malcolm.

I watch the numbers light up on the control panel until the doors of the elevator open. We find ourselves in an antechamber with one set of black double doors embossed with a 'W' and an 'A' directly across from us. Two female

Watcher agents, both stunningly beautiful, are stationed on either side of the door.

When we walk up to them, one of them presses her hand on a scanner embedded in the wall, and I hear the lock in the doors disengage. One of the doors automatically swings inward.

Albert sweeps his hand in front of him, indicating we should walk into the room.

"He only wants to speak with the two of you," Albert tells us.

I squeeze Mason's hand even tighter, and we walk into Malcolm's lair together.

The room is dark except for the glow from the fire in the giant stone fireplace in the living room area. The fireplace is so large you could fit a cow whole on a spit inside it. As we stand on the polished dark wood floor of the entrance, my eyes are drawn to the glass wall in the room. I realize this one room is as big as my house. I see the silhouette of a tall muscular man standing in front of the glass wall and know it must be Malcolm. He's looking out over the city he controls with his hands clasped loosely behind him. He's shirtless, with his long black hair covering most of his bare back. He only seems to be wearing a pair of red silk pajama bottoms.

"We've never had a Watcher agent come through the Tear before," he says, not bothering to look our way as he addresses us.

"First time for everything, I suppose," I reply.

Malcolm slowly turns around. His face is hidden in the

shadows, making it virtually impossible to read his expression. He stares at us for what seems like forever before finally walking in our direction with an unhurried gait. When he reaches us, his gaze remains steady on Mason. Unlike the Malcolm on our Earth, this Malcolm's blue Watcher aura is tainted with a tinge of black, as if it's corrupted.

"Odd to see you again, Samyaza," Malcolm says to Mason, a look of confusion on his face. "You should be dead."

CHAPTER 2

"Dead?" Mason questions. "Why would I be dead?"

"You died in the war against Lucifer in my reality," Malcolm reveals.

"The war in Heaven?" I ask, needing clarification on which battle with Lucifer he's talking about.

"Yes," Malcolm confirms, staring openly at Mason's scar. "Why did the old bastard do that to your face? What sin did He think you committed to deserve the mark of His wrath?"

"I did nothing to stop the Watchers under my command from taking human wives and having children with them. This is my reminder of that failure."

"You commanded the Watchers on your Earth?"

"Yes."

Malcolm snorts derisively. "Knowing you, I doubt you

led your Watchers to take the Earth over when the Tear appeared."

"No, I didn't."

"Too bad." Malcolm smiles wickedly. "It's been a lot of fun so far."

"Our father asked us to find a way to seal the Tear, not control the humans."

"Must be nice to have Him talk to you directly," Malcolm says. "He's pretty much abandoned us on this Earth."

"Why would He do that?" Mason asks.

"Probably because almost all of us follow Lucifer now."

"Why?" I ask, wanting to understand what went wrong here to make the Watchers willingly follow Lucifer.

My question brings Malcolm's full attention to me, and I immediately wish I had kept my big mouth shut. Malcolm's eyes rake my body in one long sweep. A lascivious smile creeps onto his face. It doesn't take a genius to know what he's imagining us doing together in his mind.

"Agent Riley, isn't it?" Malcolm asks, his tone of voice becoming more of a murmur as he addresses me.

"Yes."

"I have a very important question for you, Agent. How does the agency on your Earth usually handle the child of a Watcher if they travel to your reality?"

"Why do you ask?" I question instead of answering.

"Just answer the damn question!" Malcolm roars, a glint of madness entering his eyes.

"I guess it would depend on whether they were in their human form or werewolf form," I reply cautiously, knowing this conversation could easily head into a downward spiral rather quickly if I'm not careful.

"And if they were in their werewolf form?"

"I would imagine if they started to attack people they would be shot."

Malcolm grimaces slightly at my answer.

"Why are you asking Jess these questions?" Mason says. "What's happened?"

Malcolm closes his eyes and runs both of his hands through his hair, looking haggard all of a sudden.

"My son went through the Tear tonight," Malcolm tells us.

All at once, I feel frightened and excited. If Malcolm's son was the werewolf who took Faison's place, I fear what he will do to me once he learns that I killed him. But, if it *was* Malcolm's son, then I have a lead on where Faison is now.

"Did someone from our world take his place?" I ask cautiously.

Malcolm opens his eyes and looks at me.

"That's usually the way it works, isn't it?" he asks sarcastically.

"Yes, of course it is. Would you happen to know where that person is now?"

"Why are you so interested?"

I shrug, trying to act nonchalant. "We were told some

Watchers were playing Bait in the park with their children. I was just wondering if your son was one of them. If he was, the human from our world probably didn't live long if your son was grouped with the other Watcher children."

"I've never allowed Sebastian to play in those games. He's never been allowed to taste human flesh."

"You've protected him all this time?" Mason asks, surprise in his voice.

Malcolm looks at Mason. "I didn't want him to lose his soul like I did. I wanted him to have a chance of reaching Heaven one day. I just hope he didn't attack someone when he traveled to your world. And if he did, I hope he was killed before he took a human life."

I feel torn. I'm fairly certain now Malcolm's son was the werewolf I killed. But how do I tell a grieving father that news and not lose my head in the process?

"So where is the traveler who took his place?" I ask.

Malcolm narrows his eyes on me, and I know he suspects something is out of place.

"Why so curious?" he asks. "Odds are you don't even know them."

"They're probably scared," I answer. "They might like to be with others from their own reality. I'm trained to take care of travelers. I might be of use."

"As far as I know, the girl was taken to the Watcher station near my son's home."

"And where is that?"

"Again," Malcolm says, crossing his arms over the large

expanse of his chest, spreading his legs in a defensive stance, "why so curious?"

"We just want to know if we can help this girl," Mason replies, trying to divert Malcolm's attention away from me.

Unfortunately, Malcolm isn't stupid.

"What aren't you telling me, Samyaza? Why is this girl so important to the two of you?" Malcolm's eyes wander from my face to the sword hilt peeking out from behind my back. "That sword. Pull it out so I can see it more clearly."

"Why?" I ask.

"Don't question me, and just do as you're told!"

I feel the bracelet JoJo and Chandler made for me become warm, and I know Malcolm is reaching a point where he's becoming a danger to me. Not wanting to anger him further, I reach behind my back and pull the sword from its sheath.

As the blade leaves the scabbard, it instantly begins to blaze; the flames flicker along its edge, chasing away the hopelessness of the Earth we're on. I hold the sword in front of me with one hand, letting the point of the blade angle towards the floor.

Malcolm's eyes grow wide at the sight of my weapon.

"How did you get Jophiel's sword?" he demands.

"It was a gift," I tell him.

"A gift from whom?"

"God."

Malcolm's eyes darken. "You're no ordinary Watcher agent. Who the hell are you?"

"Would you believe a messenger from God?"

Malcolm snorts. "And just what sort of message do you have for me?"

"That you need to change your ways before it's too late."

Malcolm stares at me as if he didn't understand a word I just said, and then he starts to laugh like what I said is the funniest thing he's heard in the last century.

On instinct, I reach out and touch Malcolm on the arm with my free hand, which instantly makes him stop laughing.

The bracelet allows me to feel his pain. The pain of losing his one and only child is ripping his heart to shreds. The uncertainty of not knowing whether or not his son is alive or dead is slowly killing him like poison in his bloodstream. I'm not even sure how he's standing and talking, considering the amount of grief he feels. It shows me Malcolm has a strength I can admire, even if this version of him has been corrupted by working for Lucifer.

Yet, his soul isn't completely lost. There's a small spark of hope that his father will forgive his sins one day. But that hope is slowly dwindling. He feels like his soul is almost to the point where it will be unredeemable.

Malcolm snatches his arm away from my hand.

"What the hell are you doing?"

"Don't give up hope," I beg him. "And stop being Lucifer's henchman. It's killing your soul."

"You're rather impertinent for a human," Malcolm says, eyeing me like I'm a curiosity.

"So I've been told."

"You still haven't answered my question," Malcolm says tersely. "Why are you so interested in this girl from your Earth?"

I look over at Mason because I know he isn't going to like what I'm about to do. Mason gives an imperceptible shake of his head, warning me not to tell Malcolm the truth.

But I know I have to tell Malcolm what's happened to his son. It might be one of the stupidest things I've ever done in my life, but I can't, in good conscience, let him live with his doubt.

"She's important to me because she's my sister," I say.

Malcolm grabs the tops of my arms and squeezes. I see Mason about to pounce on Malcolm, and I furiously shake my head at him. Reluctantly he stops, trusting me to know what I'm doing.

"What happened to my son?" Malcolm demands, his face so close to mine I can feel his warm breath on my face.

"He didn't give me any choice," I say, wanting to make sure Malcolm understands why I did what I did. "I had to kill him to protect myself."

Malcolm squeezes my arms so tightly I fear he might pinch them off. Suddenly, he pushes me away from him, but I know he didn't use his full strength, because my back doesn't break when I slam against the far wall.

Instantly, Mason is at my side, helping me get back on

my feet.

"Are you all right?" he asks worriedly, looking me up and down to check for injuries.

"I'm fine," I say, kneeling to the floor for a moment to fetch my sword.

"Is that what you used?" Malcolm asks, staring at the flaming sword in my hand.

"Yes. He lunged at me and impaled himself on its blade." I say, not wanting to elaborate any further on the death of his son.

Malcolm closes his eyes and is silent for a long while. Eventually, I see a twin trail of tears course from the corners of his eyes and down the sides of his face.

"So he didn't bite you?" Malcolm questions, his eyes still closed, voice quivering slightly. "He never tasted your blood?"

"No. He didn't taste human blood. And, if it's any consolation, I don't think he suffered. He died instantly."

Malcolm nods that he heard my words, but doesn't make a reply.

I look up at Mason for reassurance that I made the right decision in telling Malcolm about his son's fate. Mason caresses the side of my face and nods, silently telling me that, against his better judgment, I did the right thing.

"Thank you," Malcolm whispers. "Thank you for killing him before he lost his soul."

Malcolm suddenly opens his eyes wide like someone just hit him in the gut.

"You need to leave. He's coming."

"Who's coming?" Mason asks.

"Lucifer. I told him I would interrogate you for information about your world. If he finds you here, Samyaza, he *will* kill you without blinking an eye, and I don't have to tell you what he will do to her."

"Where is my sister?" I demand, not wanting to leave before I have the information I need.

"Run!" Malcolm shouts.

Mason phases us to the sidewalk outside the building.

"Damn it!" I scream at Mason. "Why did you do that? He's the only one who knows where Faison is!"

The people passing by us openly gape at me. I'm not sure if it's the flaming sword I'm holding or my public display of annoyance with Mason that's drawing their attention, probably a little of both.

"Jess, we've got to go," Mason says urgently, grabbing me by the arm and pulling me down the sidewalk to get lost in the crowd of people around us.

"No, we have to go back!" I say stubbornly, ripping my arm out of his hold and turning around, determined to get the information I need from Malcolm.

Mason grabs me around the waist and pulls me back roughly against his chest.

"Jess, listen to me," he whispers desperately in my ear. "Now is not the time. Lucifer will kill me and torture you. We will get the information another way."

I know in my heart Mason's right, but I'm hardheaded,

and leaving the one person who knows where Faison is goes against every fiber of my being. I take in a deep breath, trying to let Mason's reasoning clear my head.

My body relaxes and Mason lets me go because he knows I won't try to run back into the building. My sword loses its flames just as I lose my will to fight. I turn around to face Mason while sheathing my sword.

"What do we do now?" I ask.

Unfortunately, the answer to that question ends up not being our decision.

A black van comes to a screeching halt beside the sidewalk we're standing on. Two men dressed in black, with ski masks covering their faces, jump out and grab me. Before Mason can attack them, a man I recognize phases in beside Mason, grabs his arm, and phases him away.

The two hooded men pull me towards the van easily because they are much stronger than I am. But, that's no surprise to me since I see the blue auras surrounding them, marking them as Watchers. Unceremoniously, they dump me, still struggling, inside the van, jump in, and close the sliding door behind them.

"Go!" the one crouched directly in front of me yells to the driver.

The van's wheels squeal as the driver hits the accelerator, and we're off like a shot down the street.

I don't know what the hell is happening, but I do know one thing.

Brand has Mason.

CHAPTER 3

One of the men pulls my plasma pistol out of its holster on my thigh. The other reaches towards me like he's going to try to pull my sword out of its sheath, but I kick him in the groin before he has a chance. With a howl of pain, he doubles over, cupping his family jewels.

I reach back and pull out my sword, swinging it towards the second man, which makes him rethink lunging at me.

"Who the hell are you people, and where has Brand taken Mason?" I demand.

The second man holds up his hands, as if he surrenders. "Look, all we want to do is talk to you."

"So that's why you're trying to disarm me and play the divide and conquer routine? It doesn't seem like all you want to do is talk," I counter heatedly.

"Mind if I take the mask off?" the man asks.

"Sure."

When the man peels off his mask, I instantly jab the point of my blade smack dab in the middle of his throat.

It's Baruch.

"I take it from your reaction to me that you and I don't have a particularly good relationship on your Earth."

"I helped kill you," I answer.

Baruch's eyes widen in surprise. "Well, I can't say I saw that answer coming. Was I that bad there?"

"Bad's a relative term. More like desperate," I reply.

"I assure you that you're safe with this version of me. I'm not sure why my counterpart on your Earth did the things he did to deserve death at your hands, but please keep in mind that I am not him."

"Who are you then? Who do you work for? The Baruch I killed worked with Lucifer."

"I work against Lucifer here, can't stand the slimy S.O.B. to tell you the truth. That's why I'm part of the resistance."

"Resistance?"

"We're a faction of Watchers who are trying to help the humans take back their world."

"So not all of the Watchers here are working for Lucifer?"

"No. Most do, but there are about forty of us who don't."

The man I kicked is finally able to sit up straight, though he's still holding onto his groin for dear life, and seems to be having trouble breathing steadily.

"You might be able to breathe easier if you take that mask off," I tell him.

The man keeps one hand on his bruised ego and uses the other one to strip his mask off.

I instantly feel guilty.

"Sorry, Isaiah," I say lowering my sword from Baruch's throat.

"I take it we know each other in your reality?" Isaiah asks with a grimace.

"Yes," I say, sheathing my sword. "You were my boss when I first became part of the Watcher Agency. We're friends now."

If Baruch is with both Isaiah and Brand, I have to assume he's ok. Plus, he doesn't have a corrupted blue aura like Malcolm's. Maybe whatever happened in our world to make him evil didn't affect him in this reality. Either way, I know Isaiah. In any reality, he would be someone who remained a true friend.

"Why the divide and conquer maneuver?" I ask them again.

"Brand wanted to speak with Samyaza privately. We needed it to look like we were taking you both against your will."

"For what purpose?"

"This way no one will think you came with us voluntarily," Isaiah tells me. "If you decide you don't want to have anything to do with us, your reputation won't be tainted by associating with known criminals."

I grin at Isaiah's statement. Isaiah being a criminal is an amusing concept.

"Where are you taking me?" I ask.

"We have a hideout here in the city," Baruch answers.

"Is that where Brand took Mason?"

"Yes, they'll both be there."

Isaiah finally takes his hand from where I kicked him, but winces as he shifts his weight and leans his back against the van's sliding side door.

"Sorry about the kick," I tell him, truly meaning it.

"No, you had every right. Just lets me know you can handle yourself in a fight if you have to."

"Isaiah," I say, "what happened here? Why did the Watchers take over?"

"They didn't do that on your Earth?" Isaiah asks in surprise.

"No. That's why I'm so confused. The Watchers in our reality are all helpful." I let my eyes slide back over to Baruch. "Well, almost all of them anyway. There are a few who have sided with Lucifer, but it's fewer than twenty Watchers now."

"It would probably be better if we waited until we're with Brand and Samyaza to continue this discussion."

"Why don't we just phase to them?"

"Don't want to leave the kid."

"I'm not a kid," I hear a familiar voice say from the front of the van, hidden behind a metal divide with only a small grate to talk through.

"Joshua?" I question.

"Uh, Josh. Do you know me?"

"I know the Joshua from my Earth." I look at Isaiah. "How did he get involved with you guys?"

"We saved the kid a few years ago," Baruch says. "He was put into a game of Bait, but we were able to get him out before he became puppy-chow."

"Now I'm their indentured servant," Josh says good-naturedly from the driver's seat.

"But you're such a good little errand boy," Baruch teases. "Kind of like our pet human. Who else would make our coffee?"

"It's true," Isaiah agrees, grinning. "The kid does make a good cup of coffee."

"Glad my talents are appreciated," Josh replies with a touch of sarcasm.

"How many humans are there in this resistance of yours?"

"Thousands across the world," Isaiah tells me. "We're just waiting for the right moment to attack. It's going to have to be swift and unexpected if we want it to work. Plus, it's hard to turn the Watchers who are sector Chancellors to our side. After being under Lucifer's influence for so long, most of them don't want to give up their power."

"Have you approached Malcolm?"

Both Baruch and Isaiah are stunned into silence by my question, and then they both begin to chuckle.

"That narcissistic ass?" Baruch says derisively. "He'll

never give up the power he has. He revels in being the center of attention too much."

"You're wrong about him," I say, bringing their laughter to a halt. "He's more than he appears."

"There's no way he would help us," Baruch says with a shake of his head. "He and Brand have hated each other for millennia. Even if Malcolm did finally want to fight against Lucifer, he would never work under Brand willingly."

"If I were you, I wouldn't write him off so readily. If you approached him the right way, I think he would help you. He just needs something to believe in. He needs someone to put a little faith in him."

"Don't confuse our Malcolm with the one on your Earth," Baruch warns me. "You don't know what the one in this reality has done."

"I know he's done things he's ashamed of," I answer, feeling an odd need to defend Malcolm. "There's more to him than he's let many people see. If there wasn't, why would he let Mason and me go before Lucifer showed up at his place tonight?"

"He did?" Isaiah asks, surprise in his voice.

"Yes, he did. I think if you handled him correctly he could become a valuable ally."

Isaiah and Baruch fall silent as they each contemplate my words.

"We can discuss this further when we're with Brand. He'll have to be the final judge on any communication with Malcolm."

31

"Is Brand the leader of your resistance?"

"Yes," Isaiah tells me. "He held us together when Lucifer tore the Watchers apart."

The van comes to a stop.

"We're here," Josh says.

Isaiah leans forward, holding his hand out to me.

I place my hand in his and suddenly find myself standing in a large cement room, which has been converted into living quarters. I get the feeling we're underground in the windowless space. The room is comfortable-looking, with secondhand furnishings. It reminds me of my father's study, with its walls lined with bookshelves. There's a comfortable sitting area with a couch and some chairs. A dining area complete with table and chairs sits next to a large kitchen with dark wood cabinetry and stainless steel appliances and fixtures. A set of stairs leads up to a cement platform, where the only door to the room is located.

Mason and Brand are sitting at the dining table, with cups of coffee in front of them. When Mason sees me phase in with Isaiah, he immediately stands from his chair and walks over to me.

Mason envelops me in his arms, and I hear him sigh in relief. For the first time since we traveled to this reality, I feel safe.

"If you gentlemen would excuse us for a moment," Mason says to the others before phasing us to what I have to assume is the hallway just outside the room we were in.

The long corridor is made up of cement blocks. Low-hanging, naked light bulbs line the ceiling. I feel like I'm in a fallout shelter or an abandoned wing of a subway tunnel.

Mason pulls away from me slightly.

"Are you all right?" he asks, his eyes examining every inch of my face to check for damage.

I nod. "I'm fine now."

Mason leans his head down until our foreheads touch; taking a much- needed steadying breath. I reach up and cup his face before tilting my lips in towards his. Mason doesn't need much coaxing and crushes his lips to mine, each of us desperate to feel the other, confirming that we're both still alive.

I wrap my arms around Mason's neck, pulling him as deep as I can into me. His silky smooth tongue is demanding of mine, telling me he wants more than just a kiss. I wrap one leg around his hip. Mason slides his hand against my thigh and easily lifts me until both my legs are wrapped around his waist, and he has me firmly wedged between him and the cement wall behind me. I feel his manhood grow large against me, and smile against his lips, savoring the knowledge that the man I love can be affected by me so quickly. I don't dare lift my mouth from Mason's even though I'm desperate to take a real breath. I don't want to lose this moment.

We hear someone clear his throat.

I know Mason heard them too, but he refuses to let me go instantly. Instead, he slows the kiss and reluctantly pulls his lips away from mine. When he looks at me, his eyes are glazed over with pent-up desire, and I know if we had remained alone for just a little while longer, we would have finally consummated our love for one another.

Strangely enough, the thought of us finally making love in the middle of a rather- unromantic concrete hallway is just fine with me. I realize I don't need the flower-strewn bed with silky sheets and candlelight. I don't need a romantic setting to make the moment special. All I need is Mason.

"Sorry to interrupt," Baruch says, with Josh standing by his side, shuffling his feet nervously. "But I didn't think the boy needed a firsthand demonstration of the birds and the bees."

I feel myself blush under Baruch's knowing gaze. And poor Josh just looks embarrassed.

"Joshua?" Mason questions staring at the double of our young friend from back home.

"Josh," he corrects. "Just Josh here. How do we know each other from where you come from?"

"I saved Joshua from a game of Bait a few years back," Mason says, and I realize this is the first time I've heard this story. "Ever since then, he's lived and worked with me because he didn't have any other family. Most of the time, the Watchers from my world pick on the homeless to use as bait in their games, since no one would notice their disappearance."

"Sounds kind of like the way I ended up here," Josh

says, realizing he and his counterpart on our Earth have very similar histories.

"We should probably go in," Baruch suggests. "I think we have a lot of information to exchange with each other."

Mason takes my hand, and we follow Josh and Baruch back into the room.

Brand stands when we approach. This version of Brand still has the same easy smile of the one I know from our world, and it reminds me of how comfortable I've always felt in Lilly's husband's presence. Yet, unlike the Brand I've met, this Brand looks younger, somewhere in his early twenties would be my guess.

"Brand, this is Jess," Mason says.

Brand holds out his hand. "I'm sorry for the subterfuge earlier. I hope we didn't startle you too much."

I hear Isaiah cough from his position behind the kitchen island.

I smile.

"I can usually take care of myself," I say confidently.

"Yes, that's what Isaiah was just telling me," Brand replies, watching his friend's slow progress to the table with an amused twinkle in his eyes.

"Please sit down," Brand says to us. "We have a lot to discuss."

Mason and I sit beside each other across from the three Watchers. Josh makes his way to the kitchen area and starts a new pot of coffee.

Mason keeps hold of my hand and rests it on his thigh. I

smile and look over at him. He looks at me and winks. I wink back. I feel safe in the knowledge that as long as we're together there's nothing we can't handle.

"So I take it you two are a couple," Brand says.

Baruch clears his throat, reminding me he's seen this statement played out as fact.

"Yes," I answer, attempting to ignore Baruch. "Speaking of couples, where's Lilly?"

Brand looks confused by my question. "Who's Lilly?"

"You don't know who Lilly is?" I ask, sure I look just as confused as Brand now.

"No, I have no idea who you're talking about," Brand says, his eyebrows lowering in concern. "Is she someone important to me in your reality?"

Mason and I look at one another.

"How can Lilly not exist here?" I ask him. "I thought she would be important in every reality, considering what she did."

"I'm not sure why she's not here," Mason tells me, looking just as confused as I am before returning his attention back to Brand.

"I'm going to name some people," Mason tells Brand. "Let me know if any of them ring a bell. Caylin, Will, Tara, Malik, Utha Mae. Do you know any of those people?"

"I know a Will," Brand answers. "He's a rebellion angel who works for Lucifer. And I know a Malik. He's the leader of the Fae here. The others don't sound familiar to me. Should they?"

Mason's eyes become hooded, and I know this new information troubles him.

"Can you tell me how the Tear was made on this Earth?" Mason asks Brand.

"What do you mean 'made'?" Brand asks back, looking between Mason and me. "It just appeared in our sky one night. No one knows where it came from."

Mason looks down at the table, contemplating Brand's answer. I watch as he closes his eyes, and shakes his head as if he is just now realizing something very important.

"I never knew," Mason whispers, as if talking to himself.

I squeeze Mason's hand, making him look at me.

"Never knew what?" I ask, not liking the way he's reacting to whatever conclusion he's come to. "What's wrong?"

Mason looks at me, and I can tell he's in a state of complete and utter shock.

"The Earth we live on," he says, measuring his words carefully. "The reality we exist in… it's the Origin."

I feel more than see the other three Watchers in the room tense at Mason's statement.

"The Origin?" Baruch questions. "How do you know that for certain?"

"It's the only explanation that makes sense. We know how the Tear was made because it was made in our reality. It explains why Lilly doesn't exist here. She wasn't needed in this reality, only ours."

"Does that mean I don't exist here either?" I ask.

"That would be my guess," Mason says. "Albert couldn't find you in the database. Odds are you don't have a counterpart here. You're not needed here. You're only needed in our reality."

"You still haven't told me who Lilly is, and why you expected her to be here with me," Brand says. "And if you could throw in an explanation of how the Tear was made, we'd appreciate it."

"Lilly is your wife in our reality," Mason says, not trying to sugarcoat the facts no matter how surprising they might sound to this Brand. "She is the human child of Michael. In our reality, she stopped Lucifer from destroying the universe, but while he was trying to collapse the veils, he tore a hole between them instead, which formed the Tear."

"We always wondered what happened to make it just appear one night. It never occurred to me that an event in the Origin was the cause. So this Lilly, my wife in your reality, is the child of an archangel?" Brand asks, as if such a possibility is a foreign concept to him. "I've never heard of such a coupling being allowed to happen."

Mason looks over at me, silently questioning if he should say what I am too. I nod, seeing no reason to hide the information from the three sitting across from us.

"In our reality," Mason begins, "God has sent the seven archangels to our Earth. They melded their souls with human ones. Jess' soul is bonded to Michael's soul." Mason pauses to let that information sink in before he continues. "At some point on our Earth, they're meant to fight Lucifer and the Princes of Hell, to stop them from doing something. We haven't quite figured out what that something is yet, but we're pretty confident it won't be pleasant for any of us."

"Then why are you here?" Brand asks. "If Jess is needed in the Origin, why come to our reality?"

"My sister traveled here," I tell them. "Apparently, she and Malcolm's son traded places when the Tear opened earlier this evening. We came here to get her and take her back home."

"And how do you plan to get back to your Earth?" Baruch asks.

"God will open the Tear for us when the time is right," I say.

"You speak directly with Him?" Isaiah asks, eagerly leaning forward in his chair to hear my answer.

"That's a recent development," I say. "To be honest, I just started to believe in His existence."

I almost laugh at the expressions on the faces of the angels across from me. Confused was too small a word to explain their reaction to my blunt honesty.

"But you carry Michael's soul," Brand says, voicing what I have to presume they're all thinking. "Why haven't you believed in Him before now?"

"It's a long story," I say.

"One that isn't exactly pertinent at the moment," Mason tells them, saving me from having to go into any details about my life thus far. "But I have a few questions which are."

"You can ask us anything," Brand says openly.

"Malcolm told us I was killed in the war with Lucifer in this reality."

"Yes, that's correct. Lucifer killed you himself, actually."

"If I'm dead here, who became the leader of the Watchers when you were sent to Earth?"

"Justin was our leader." Brand says the name with undisguised loathing.

"What happened when you came to Earth under his command?"

"At first, things were fine. We were teaching the humans what they needed to know, as we were meant to. But many of us ended up falling in love and taking human wives. In fact, Justin encouraged it. He said our father would understand. But, of course, He didn't. When God cursed us and our families, Justin urged us to give into what our father made us into. It was an extremely dark period in our history. Most of the Watchers followed Justin, not seeing any point in trying to fight against the need to drink human blood and let their children feed on the corpses. After a while, Lucifer seemed to think the Watchers who became vampires were drawing too much unwanted attention to themselves with the trail of bodies they were leaving in their wake. I'm not sure what happened between him and Justin, but Lucifer must have grown tired of trying to reason with him, because he killed Justin. After that, Lucifer reined in the vampire Watchers and took control of them. They remained in the shadows for thousands of years, just legend to the humans here. That is, until the Tear appeared. Lucifer seemed to take it as a sign of some sort and used the confusion the humans were in to take this world over, under the guise of trying to help. I take it this isn't the way it happened on your Earth."

"No," Mason says. "I was the leader of the Watchers on our Earth; not Justin."

"Did the majority of the Watchers turn to vampirism after the curse?"

"No. Most of them abstained from it like I did."

"Then I wish you had been our leader here too." Brand sighs over the missed opportunity. "Maybe we wouldn't be in this mess if you had survived the war and led us like you were meant to."

Mason becomes still and quiet, letting what Brand has said sink in.

"Could you guys give us a minute alone?" I ask, knowing Mason needs some time with his thoughts.

Isaiah mumbles something about Josh and coffee. Brand and Baruch follow him into the kitchen area.

I turn to Mason and bring his hand to my lips to plant a small kiss, gently bringing him out of his troubled reverie.

"Are you ok?" I ask, worried about him because he hasn't moved since hearing how different the Watchers' history is on this Earth. I'm not even completely sure he's taken a breath since learning what would have happened on our Earth if he'd never existed.

"I always thought I did something wrong to make the

Watchers go against God's law," he finally says. "But it doesn't look like it would have mattered who their commander was. They would have done it anyway."

"How many of the Watchers gave into the hunger for blood on our Earth when He cursed you?"

"Forty-four."

I'm not surprised to hear Mason recite an exact number. He had carried the guilt of their turning into vampires from the beginning.

"Forty-four out of about two hundred? Sounds like you had a greater influence on them than you thought. If you had given in like this Justin and encouraged the others to do so too, it's possible our reality would be similar to this one. But you didn't give into your hunger like he did. You set a better example for your Watchers."

Mason finally looks over at me. "For so many years, I thought I let them all down."

"Well, the ones who did turn into vampires didn't help your guilt issues. To be honest, I think they were just jealous that the rest of you had so much more self-control than they did. Plus, you still had hope that God would forgive you one day if you didn't give into your urges. That hope was lost to them the first time they drank human blood. They even got a second chance directly from God, Mason. They could have earned forgiveness after the Tear was made, but they chose not to work for it. You have nothing to feel guilty about. You can't control what others do with their lives."

Mason sits and contemplates my words. Finally, he nods.

"You're right. I'm not responsible for the way their lives turned out. It never even occurred to me that I wouldn't exist in other realities."

"You've been feeling accountable for all the Watchers in every reality?" I say, fully realizing for the first time what Mason has been living with for all these years. "No wonder you have guilt issues."

I let Mason sit quietly for a moment to let his self-realization sink into his psyche. I now understand why God wanted Mason to come with me to this reality. If he hadn't, I'm not sure he would have ever found a way around the guilt he's been carrying inside his heart for all these years.

"Can I ask you something?" I ask, needing clarification about a couple of things that were said.

"You know you can ask me anything."

"What did you mean by our reality being the Origin? What's the Origin?"

"We come from the first of everything: the first universe. In Heaven, it's called the Origin. All of the other realities branch off from what happens in the first universe. Think of the different realities like a tree. We're the trunk, and every different reality is a branch sprouting off that trunk. Each of those branches sprouts smaller branches. Each branch is a different reality. The events that happen in our reality end up causing a ripple effect on all the other realities, like a pebble dropped in a pool of water. We're the pebble."

There's an urgent pounding on the door.

Brand hurriedly walks over and opens it.

"Brand, I need your help," a male voice says, filled with desperation. "She did it again! Could you *please* talk to her? She won't listen to me, but maybe she'll listen to you."

"I can try, Remy, but I'm not sure it will do much good. Why don't you come in and get some coffee? Maybe we can figure out a way to stop her from burning down half the city."

The man Brand was talking to steps into the room, and I'm able to see him clearly for the first time.

Surrounding him is a golden glow just like the one my father has.

When our eyes meet, he seems startled by my presence. He's a tall man with bushy brown hair and a shaggy matching beard and mustache, which both look in need of a good trim and wash. He's wearing wire-rimmed glasses which are smudged with fingerprints. I'm not even sure how he can see out of them.

Remy smiles with delight as he bounds down the steps and walks up to me like he's going to rush me. I automatically stand, preparing to defend myself. Instead of attacking me, he gives me a big bear hug like we're long lost friends.

He pulls away from me, and I see the excitement in his eyes as he asks, "Did God send you to bring us home?"

CHAPTER 4

I know what the man is, a Guardian from The Treasury of Souls, like my father, but I don't understand why he's here.

"Us who?" I ask.

The man named Remy looks confused. "God didn't send you to get us? But you're a vessel, right?"

I gently push Remy to arms-length away from me.

"Yes, I am," I answer. "But no, God didn't say 'by the way could you pick up the lost Guardian that's in the reality you're going to'. Sorry, I didn't get that memo."

"Then, why else are you here?"

"I'm here to get my sister. Why are you here?"

"The vessel I was sent to protect was transported here. I came with her."

"Leah's a vessel of an archangel?" Brand asks, apparently hearing all this for the first time.

"Why is she here?" I ask. "She's supposed to be in my reality."

"Long story that," Remy says, scratching his beard nervously. "But I'll give you the Cliff's Notes version. Her mother is the one who actually came through the Tear. She just happened to be pregnant with Leah at the time."

Remy grabs me by the arms, desperation in his eyes. "You have to take her back with you."

"Could you stop touching me?" I ask, gently removing my arms from Remy's hold. "I'm not exactly a touchy-feely kind of person with strangers."

"Oh, sorry," Remy says, stuffing his hands in the pockets of the threadbare brown coat he's wearing. "But Leah needs to go back. She doesn't belong here. She never has."

"Where is she?" I ask.

"Back in our room, sulking because I yelled at her."

"What did she do this time?" Brand asks.

"Burnt down another abandoned Watcher complex."

"She *does* realize she's just doing them a favor, right?" Brand asks. "Saves them the hassle of completely demolishing the buildings themselves."

Remy turns to me. "Her power is partially awakened."

"How?"

"A Watcher attacked her, and she used it on him a week or so ago. Now she feels like she's invincible. You have to take her back to your Earth before she gets herself into trouble here."

"What is her power?"

"Fire."

"Yeah, that's not telling me much, Remy. Explain."

"She's able to conjure a flame in the palm of her hand. Now she's going around setting everything on fire like some pyromaniac."

"I need to see her," I say.

"Come with me."

Mason comes to my side and takes my hand as we follow Remy out of the room. I'm faintly aware of Brand following us.

For someone his size, Remy walks rather quickly down the concrete hallway. His urgent gait makes me feel like I'm in a race against time. He opens one of the many grey metal doors which branch off the corridor, and stands completely still in the doorway.

I hear him curse, and find myself surprised an angel has that particular four-letter word so readily available in his vocabulary.

"What's the matter, Remy?" Brand asks.

"She's gone! Damn it, damn it, damn it! I knew I shouldn't have left her alone."

"Calm down," Brand says soothingly. "Let me go speak with Josh. He'll probably know where she is." Brand looks at Mason and me. "I'll be right back."

After Brand phases, Remy huffs and crosses his arms in front of him. "That girl has been nothing but trouble since the day she was born."

I feel my temper flare.

"You made her," I remind him. "Why don't you look at yourself before cursing her again? And for God's sake stop cussing so much! You're not setting a very good example. You're supposed to be an angel, not a foul-mouthed heathen. Leave that to us humans."

Remy sighs and lets his arms fall to his sides.

"I just love Leah too much, is all," he says. "Ever since her mother left her with me, I've tried my best to raise her, but I just wasn't cut out to be a father."

I have to agree with Remy on that point. From what I've seen so far, he is not what I would call father material.

"What do you mean her mother left her?" I ask.

"As soon as Leah's mother gave birth, she just up and left us. We haven't seen her since. It didn't help that we ended up on a planet where the Watchers had taken over. I've tried to keep us under their radar for the past few years, moving from sector to sector. When I caught up with Brand and his renegade angels, I hoped she would straighten up. I thought it was working up until she awakened her powers. Now she thinks she can do anything she wants. It's going to get her killed!"

Brand reappears with Josh at his side.

"Josh thinks he might know where Leah is," Brand tells us.

"Yeah, she was talking about checking out that Watcher supply depot on Hemingway Street," Josh tells us. "If I were to bet, I would say she went there to blow it up."

"It's not far. She might even already be there," Brand

informs us. "Remy and Josh, you stay here in case she comes back."

Brand holds out his hands to Mason and me. He phases us, and we find ourselves standing on a lonely deserted street in what looks like a not-so-good part of town. My eyes are drawn to a lone figure standing a couple of hundred feet down the sidewalk from where we are. The blustery wind blows Leah's long dark hair behind her, giving her figure a ghostly appearance. I know it's Leah, without even having to see her face, because I instantly feel our archangel connection to one another ignite. She turns in my direction, and I know she feels it too.

"Would the two of you mind staying here?" I ask Brand and Mason. "I need to speak with her alone."

"We'll be here if you need us," Mason tells me, squeezing my hand before letting it go.

I walk over to Leah, feeling our bond grow stronger the closer I get to her. When I reach her, I see the face of the beautiful Asian girl from my vision. She's wearing the same old green coat and threadbare green knit cap. Her long black hair floats around her on the current of the wind, giving her beauty an ethereal quality. Her face isn't streaked with soot this time, but tears. Before I know it, she's in my arms, crying on my shoulder. I just hold her, content in the fact that she feels safe with me.

"You came for me," she cries. "I didn't think you would."

I'm not sure if it's the right time to tell her I didn't even know she existed in this reality, and decide to keep that small fact to myself for the time being.

"I'm here to take you home," I tell her instead.

It's the truth. Nothing in my life has ever happened without a reason. It's now clear to me that Faison went through the Tear to force me to follow her and find the fourth vessel who, unbeknownst to any of us, was stranded in this alternate reality. My destiny had struck again, but this time it had taken a life to correct its own course.

Had John Austin been a necessary sacrifice in the fight with Lucifer? Or had his death already been preordained, and it was just a coincidence that he died right before the Tear opened to this alternate Earth? An Earth that just happened to contain one of the archangel vessels. Seems like too much of a coincidence for me to believe God didn't have a hand in his death to force me to come here. I make a mental note to bring it up with Him the next time we see each other.

Spent of her tears, Leah raises her head from my shoulder and looks at me. I loosen my hold of her so she can wipe the wetness from her cheeks.

"Remy always said when the time was right someone would come for us," she tells me. "When I got my powers, I knew it wouldn't be too much longer. I'm ready to go."

"We have to get someone else too while we're here."

"Who else would be here that you know?"

"My sister came through the Tear tonight. I need to find her and bring her back home with us."

"Your sister?" Leah asks, instantly realizing why I'm actually here. "You came here to get her, not me."

"I was sent here to get both of you," I tell her. "How I came to be here is irrelevant. We've been looking for you, Leah. If I hadn't followed Faison here, we would have never found you."

"We?"

"You're the fourth archangel vessel I've found. We saw you in a vision, earlier tonight. You were burning down a Watcher-owned building. In the vision, you heard sirens and ran down a street to get away from them. Honestly, I think you're the whole reason I was brought here."

"Then God *did* send you?"

"Yes, He opened the Tear so only Mason and I could go through. He'll open the Tear again when it's time for us all to go home."

"Then we need to find your sister," Leah says with conviction. "If He only meant for you to find me, the Tear would be opening. He must want you to find her too."

"I hope you're right," I say, wondering to myself how hard it will be to get Faison to agree to come home with me.

"Well, well, well, who do we have here?"

I look over Leah's shoulder and see Lucifer standing a short distance behind her. I know it's him because he looks the same here as he does in my reality.

Instinctively, I draw my sword and place myself between Lucifer and Leah.

I hear the sound of running behind us, and know

Mason and Brand are heading to our location. Lucifer looks over my shoulder and smiles. Almost instantly the running stops, and I hear cries of pain.

I point my sword towards Lucifer.

"Stop torturing them," I tell him. I feel like a mother telling her son to stop using a magnifying glass to burn ants with the sun's rays just to see what will happen to them.

"Who are you?" Lucifer asks, completely ignoring what I said.

"No one you need to know," I tell him. "Now... *let... them...go.*"

"No, I don't believe I will. Not until you at least tell me your name."

I feel like just stabbing Lucifer in the chest with my sword, but I have no idea if it will even faze him. Odds are it will just piss him off.

"Jess," I answer.

"Jess what?"

"Jessica Michelle Riley. Need to know anything else?" I ask not hiding my irritation.

Lucifer smiles, and I know that's not a good sign.

"Why aren't you cowering in my presence?" he asks, eyeing me up and down. "Most humans do, unless I'm working my charms on them. Though, I mostly only do that to the females I want in my bed."

I realize I'm having the same conversation with this Lucifer as I did with the one on my Earth once upon a time.

"Listen, I really don't feel like having this conversation

twice in my life. I've already had it with the Lucifer on my Earth. It's getting kind of old."

"So you *are* the agent Malcolm had in custody. He said he wasn't sure how you escaped." Lucifer smiles. "I'm not sure why he thought he could lie to me, but I think I made it crystal clear to him before I left his apartment this evening that it's never a good idea."

"What did you do to him?"

"I don't believe that's any of your concern, Jessica. Though, I did get some interesting information from him before he blacked out from the pain. He mentioned a sister…"

I remain silent. Do I admit I have a sister or not? He seems to be baiting me. I decide to not say anything and see where he leads this conversation.

"Faison, isn't it?" Lucifer says.

Crap. He does know about her.

"She doesn't seem to like our reality very much," he comments dryly. "I assume you followed her here to take her back home?"

I try to remain calm.

"What do you want?" I ask him.

"A simple conversation in private, nothing more."

"And after this simple conversation?"

"I promise to let you go."

"Do you keep your promises?"

"Sometimes," Lucifer says, smiling grimly.

"Don't trust him," Leah advises me.

"I never have," I tell her, lowering my sword. "Fine. We can talk if that's what you want. Then I want my sister back."

"We'll see," Lucifer says. "It all depends on you, Jessica."

"Stop torturing them first," I say, chancing a glance in Mason and Brand's direction.

Both men are on the sidewalk holding their heads in their hands. Almost instantly, it appears their pain stops. Slowly, they get to their feet.

"Go to them," I tell Leah.

She runs over to Brand and Mason without asking any questions. Yep, smart girl. Unlike me, because I'm about to put a little faith into a Lucifer I don't even know.

Lucifer holds his hand out to me.

"I guess you want to go somewhere private for this talk of ours?" I ask.

Lucifer grins. "You assume correctly."

"Jess, no!" I hear Mason scream, but it's too late.

I've already put my hand in Lucifer's.

Lucifer phases us a few times. I have to assume he's trying to cover his tracks so Mason and Brand don't follow us. We end up at the top of the Empire State Building. I only recognize where we are because Chandler and I came here on the day we acted like tourists. The wind is biting cold at this elevation, but Lucifer doesn't seem to be affected by it. Color me not surprised. I sheath my sword so I can wrap my arms around myself to ward off the chill.

"Who are you really?" Lucifer asks. "I know you're more

than human, but I can't quite put my finger on what's different about you."

"Neither can your counterpart on my Earth, so don't feel bad. You're ignorant on two worlds."

Lucifer scowls at me. "You're rather insolent for a human."

"Yeah, I've been told that tonight already. Why don't you tell me something useful like where my sister is?"

"In a safe place. If I get the answers I want, I'll give her to you."

"Alive?"

Lucifer grins. "Smart question for a monkey. Since you asked it, yes, I'll give her back to you alive."

"Jessica."

I look to my right and see Michael.

"Tell him what you are," Michael says.

"Are you crazy?" I ask.

"I'm beginning to think *you* might be," Lucifer says, staring at the empty space I'm talking to.

I choose to ignore him.

"Think of it as a trial run," Michael says, eyeing this alternate version of Lucifer warily. "Let's see what he'll do."

"He might kill Faison," I argue.

"I don't think so. I don't even think he has her."

"How can you be so sure?"

"Because if he did, he would have her here and torture her in front of you to get the information he wants."

It made sense. It felt strange to be counting on Lucifer's

penchant for cruelty as a tool with which to measure his truthfulness. But Michael was right. If this Lucifer had Faison, he would have shown her to me by now.

"Why do you want to tell him the truth?" I ask Michael.

"Because it might give us an idea of how our Lucifer will react if you tell him."

"What does that gain us?"

"It will let us know if we shouldn't do it with our Lucifer. If it goes badly here, then we'll know what not to do back home."

"Not much of a plan," I complain.

"Don't worry. You're in no danger. I might have to take you over for a moment if things do go wrong, but I'll only do it if I think your life is in peril."

"All right," I say, not wholeheartedly believing what we're about to do will work in the slightest, but placing my trust in Michael's judgment.

I look at this Earth's Lucifer, who is still looking at me like I may have completely lost my mind.

"You want to know what I am?" I ask him.

"Yes, I believe that's what I've been asking, isn't it?"

"I'm a human vessel whose soul is bound with an archangel's soul."

"Which archangel?"

"Michael."

Lucifer stands completely still. If he wasn't breathing, you could have mistaken him easily for a statue.

"You're lying."

"No," I say, "I'm not."

"Yes... you are."

"I refuse to say 'no, I'm not' again. Otherwise, we're going to start sounding like a couple of five-year-olds. You can either believe me or not."

"I suppose you were talking to Michael just now?" Lucifer asks snidely, completely convinced I'm lying to him in some game of wits.

"Yes."

"If you're telling the truth, have him tell you what the last word I said to him was."

I look over at Michael and raise an eyebrow at him, because I know he heard the question for himself.

"He said 'Go'," Michael answers, looking at his onetime best friend with pity.

"The last word you said was 'Go'."

Lucifer stares at me like he's trying to find his best friend in the depths of my eyes.

"Michael?"

"Tell him I've missed him," Michael says to me.

"He misses you," I tell Lucifer. "He misses your friendship." I take in a deep breath. "I can feel his pain."

"Pain?" Lucifer questions incredulously. "What could he know of pain? You just left me here," Lucifer says, his eyes growing even darker than usual. "You're no friend of mine. If you had been, you wouldn't have left me to rot with the monkeys. You would have found a way to protect me from our father. He might have listened to you if you had begged Him to give me another chance."

"There was no chance to beg for," I tell Lucifer, relaying what Michael tells me. "You went too far. Too many lives were lost because of you. God wouldn't have allowed you to stay in Heaven even if Michael had begged on your behalf."

"But you didn't even try!" Lucifer storms.

"Michael couldn't beg God to have mercy on you," I tell Lucifer.

I look at Michael, lifting both my eyebrows this time to make sure he truly does want me to say his next words.

"Seriously?" I ask Michael, knowing if I say what he wants me to I might as well just jump off the building for a quicker death than what Lucifer will do to me. "You're sure you want me to say that to him?"

Michael nods.

I shake my head, not agreeing with his decision but trusting that he knows what he's doing.

"Michael couldn't beg God to show you mercy because he didn't believe you deserved it. He thought you needed to spend time with humans, if for nothing else than to teach you a lesson."

Lucifer's hands ignite with blue flames, and he lunges for my throat.

The next few minutes move in slow motion for me, mostly because Michael takes control of my body. I watch as he spins my body away from Lucifer's grasp and catapults us up the guardrail, which is meant to keep people from falling off the top of the building. Michael stands on the railing completely balanced like a cat on a fence, and looks down at Lucifer.

"Stop, Lucifer. She only said what I told her to say."

Lucifer stops abruptly as if he suddenly hit a brick wall. "Michael?"

"Yes, it's me. Don't harm Jess."

"If I kill her, I kill you! It's a win-win situation for me." Lucifer smiles maliciously.

"Do you really want to kill me, old friend?"

Lucifer looks emotionally torn.

"You were my only friend," Lucifer says. I feel Michael's pity for his friend inside my heart. "How could you just leave me? You never once came to see me or even tried to contact me. Why?"

"I hoped you would ask our father for absolution, Lucifer. There were so many times I yearned to speak with you and urge you to ask for His forgiveness. I hoped your time on Earth would lead you to realize on your own what a mistake you made instigating the war against our father. I still have hope you will do that one day."

"If anything, my time here has shown me how right I was," Lucifer says scathingly. "The monkeys don't need to be worshiped and protected. They need to be destroyed before they destroy *everything* He created."

"That's an old argument between us," Michael says tiredly, "one I thought you would have out grown by now."

"Old habits die hard, I guess. What are you worried

about? You won't really die anyway. Your soul will just go back to Heaven, along with this human's."

"But she deserves to have a life before she's asked to give it up."

"No, she doesn't. She deserves to die."

Just as Lucifer phases beside me and reaches for my arm, Michael jumps off the guardrail, and we begin a freefall to the street below.

CHAPTER 5

Yeah, jumping off the Empire State building....this is a good plan.

Note to self: Do NOT trust Michael the next time he says I should.

I want to scream at Michael, but oddly enough he seems to be enjoying our death- knell swan dive. He has my arms spread out like we're a bird and is whooping it up like we're on a joy ride. Just as I think my body is going to smash head-long into the pavement, I feel my body begin to glide, and I realize I'm flying.

Michael puts my arms out in front of us, and I wonder if I look like Superman as he flies us between the skyscrapers of New York City.

"*How?*" I ask him, though our communication is restricted to being completely mental.

"It's one of my powers," he tells me. *"I felt it awaken when we joined with Leah."*

"You could have told me," I accuse.

"Sorry, I wasn't sure how you would react to flying. Are you ok?"

"Yes, I love it! Though, a little warning would have been nice. Will I be able to do this without you being in control?"

"Yes. I just wanted to show you a few moves that might come in handy."

Michael shows me how to ricochet between objects, in this case buildings. I feel like a pinball as we bounce off each structure. He shows me how to land gracefully in a spinning roll, which I have to admit looks pretty cool. He makes sure I understand the basics of taking off, turning, and landing. It's one of the best times of my life.

"Can I phase?" I ask him.

"No, you're still human. Phasing is reserved for angels only. Your body can't handle going through folds in space too often."

"Is that what they're doing? Folding space?"

"Yes."

Michael flies us over a street I recognize. A solitary figure stands on the sidewalk: Mason.

"He's waiting for you," Michael tells me. *"Do you feel up to trying to land by yourself?"*

Not at all sure I can, but having to try at some point, I tell him I think I can.

"Ok, I'm going to let go now."

Michael turns control back over to me, and I attempt to angle down towards Mason. He must sense me because he looks up. I smile at the surprised look on his face and attempt to land in front of him in the elegant rollout spin Michael taught me, but it doesn't come out quite as I planned. Instead of landing lightly on my feet, I end up losing my balance and spinning into Mason, knocking him to the ground with me sitting on top of his face.

I quickly move down so I'm not on his face, but sitting around his waist.

"Sorry," I say, but don't get a chance to say anything else because Mason pulls my face down to his, kissing me like there might not be a tomorrow.

Considering our luck, he might be right.

Mason sits up with me straddling his hips.

He pulls his lips away from mine to look at me.

"Why do you keep doing that to me?" he asks, planting small kisses all over my face, making me smile.

"Keep doing what?"

"Making me worry."

"Well, I hate to admit it, but it was a pointless thing to do. Lucifer didn't have Faison."

Mason stops kissing me to look into my eyes. "You're flying now. That's new."

"Michael said it was one of his gifts."

Mason nods. "Yes, he needed it to oversee the war."

"That's two powers of his that I have because of the war in Heaven: seeing auras and flying."

"What happened with Lucifer?"

I tell him.

"Michael shouldn't have done that," Mason says, glowering. "He put your life in danger unnecessarily."

"But it gives us a good idea of how our Lucifer will react when he learns the truth about me."

"Still, he put your life in danger. That's not something I'll ever condone no matter what information you might have gotten from it."

"Don't you remember what I told you earlier?"

"What?"

"That neither one of us would die today."

"You never did answer my question. Since when do *you* have faith in anything God does?"

I sigh. "It's a hard question for me to answer because I'm not sure. It just seemed illogical to send us here just to die. It wouldn't make sense. Now we know the main reasons He let us come here: To find Leah and to make you realize what might have happened if you had never led the Watchers."

"Now we just need to find Faison and go back home."

"I know you don't want to, but we need to go back to Malcolm's. If Lucifer doesn't have Faison, Malcolm has to have her. Lucifer said he passed out from his torture after we left. He might be hurt."

"Malcolm would have regenerated by now. And I don't agree with going to his penthouse again. It's just too dangerous, especially now that Lucifer knows what you are. Let's go back and talk to Brand and the others. They might know where Malcolm's son used to live. I would rather try to find her on our own if we can."

"All right," I say. I've put Mason through enough for one night. I don't intend on badgering him into taking me to Malcolm's tonight. Not until we've exhausted all of our other options.

Mason phases us directly into Brand's living quarters.

Brand is sitting at the dining table alone, with a cup of coffee, which doesn't look like it's been touched, between his hands. Remy is sitting on the brown leather couch in the room, with his head knocked back, snoring. Leah has her head in Remy's lap, peacefully sleeping.

"Glad to see you made it back in one piece," Brand says to me from his seat at the table.

Mason and I sit down across from him. I tell Brand what happened during my time with Lucifer, and I ask him about finding Faison.

"I'm not sure where Malcolm's son used to live, but I can try to find out. Josh is excellent with computers. He can probably find the information you need fairly quickly."

Brand grows quiet and stares down at his coffee. I get the feeling he wants to ask us something but doesn't know how or possibly if he should. Finally, he sighs and looks back up at us.

"Could you tell me about this Lilly from your world? What kind of life do we have together? Is my immortality an issue?"

"You're not immortal in our world," Mason tells Brand. "You're human."

"How?" Brand asks, completely caught off guard by such a revelation.

"When Lilly stopped Lucifer, Brand asked God to make him human so he could live out a normal life with Lilly. God granted his request. Lilly and Brand have three children now: Caylin, Will, and Mae."

"Three kids? Are they human?"

"Not completely. Caylin was conceived while you were still an angel, and of course Lilly is still half-archangel."

"Is Caylin cursed? Does she become a werewolf?"

"No, God took away the curse from all the Watcher children who never drank human blood."

"So Abby is human in your world?"

"Yes. She's actually married to Malcolm's son, and they have two children."

Brand laces the fingers of his hands in front of his face and rubs his temples with the pads of his thumbs. I wonder what he's thinking. I want to ask who Abby is, but I feel sure from Brand's reaction it's probably his daughter, still cursed in this reality to transform into a werewolf every night.

"You and Malcolm are friends, of sorts, in our reality," Mason reveals to Brand.

Brand lowers his hands and looks at Mason like he's sure he misunderstood him.

"Malcolm and I are friends?" Brand asks dubiously.

"At first, it was only for Lilly's sake," Mason says. "She

and Malcolm have been friends pretty much since the day they met. But since the Tear appeared, the two of you have become close because of your families. Our Brand trusts Malcolm to help keep his family safe. I don't think I could give Malcolm any higher praise than that."

"I suppose Baruch and Isaiah told you my thoughts about bringing Malcolm into the resistance?" I ask.

Brand nods. "I'm sorry but I just don't see that as a possibility."

"At least think about it," I urge. "He has good in him. It's just buried under a lot of bad baggage."

"I *am* surprised he let you go," Brand admits. "His only redeemable quality was his refusal to let Sebastian drink human blood. Mason told me you had to kill him when he traveled to your world."

"Yes. I killed him with my sword."

"At least it was a quick death then."

Brand stands. "I'm sure the two of you are tired. We made up a room for you to stay in while you're here. Was I right in assuming you would want to share the same room?"

Mason looks to me to answer the question.

"Yes, one room is all we need," I answer, reaching for Mason's hand, laying claim to my man.

We follow Brand out of the room, into the hallway. We end up not having to walk too far. Brand opens a metal door that is only a couple of doors down from his quarters.

The room is sparse, with one full-size bed covered in white cotton sheets and a thin black wool blanket. A small metal table with a small lamp sits on the right side of the bed. There is a narrow bathroom off to the left with a metal chair sitting by the entrance.

"We don't have a lot of visitors," Brand says by way of explanation for the lack of décor.

"It's fine," I tell him. "There's a bed. That's all we need."

Mason raises an eyebrow in my direction and tries to hide a smile.

"Well, I hope it's comfortable enough," Brand says, seeming to become uncomfortable around us all of a sudden. "I'll see you two in the morning."

I let go of Mason's hand and walk into the room, trying to unbuckle the belt of the baldric from around my waist as quickly as I can. I hear Mason close the door behind me. For some reason my fingers feel like they've gone numb, and my stomach suddenly feels like it's full of butterflies.

"Here," Mason says, coming to stand in front of me, "let me help you with that. You've had a rough night. You need to get some rest."

I look up at Mason, who is concentrating on working the leather strap through the buckle.

"I don't need rest," I say, hoping he gets the subtle hint without me having to spell it out for him.

A slow smile stretches his lips. "Should I be worried about my chastity tonight, Agent Riley?"

"Most definitely, Mr. Collier."

His smile grows wider but falters slightly, and he lets out a small sigh. I immediately know something is up.

"What's wrong?" I ask.

He shakes his head, "Nothing."

Mason walks around me and lifts the straps of the baldric from my shoulders. I turn around and watch him prop the sword against the metal chair by the bathroom entrance.

When he comes back to me, he wraps his arms loosely around my waist, and I loop mine around his neck. He leans his head down towards mine and kisses my lips softly. Not satisfied, I pull his head down even further to deepen the kiss, tugging at the bottom of his shirt until it's released from his pants, and running my hands up the bare skin of his back. Mason moans and lifts me easily in his arms to carry me to the bed.

Without breaking contact, he gently lays me on the mattress, following me down and laying partially on top of me. I feel his fingers nimbly undo the buttons of my blouse and realize he *does* have dexterous fingers. He tugs my blouse from my pants, and I lay there with my shirt open for his further exploration. He rests one of his large warm hands against my stomach.

Mason's lips leave mine to travel down the side of my neck, planting small, wet, maddening kisses along the way. He shifts slightly, peeling the left side of my shirt away from my chest to kiss the soft flesh over my racing heart. Tenderly, he kisses the tops of each breast peeking up from my bra, and makes a trail of butterfly kisses between them down to the sensitive skin surrounding my belly button.

In an effortless move, he straddles me and leans on his knees and elbows above me. I can feel his arousal, and yearn to strip off the rest of my clothes and finally be able to feel him fully against me without anything in the way.

Mason runs a finger against the side of my face as he gazes lovingly down at me, but I can still see something in his eyes that tells me not all is right. Plus, he's not kissing me, which just won't do.

"What's wrong?" I ask him. "Why are you stopping?"

"You're going to think it's silly," he says reluctantly, letting his finger trail down to my chest and tracing an outline of a heart where my real heart is beating ninety to nothing.

"Tell me," I urge, because I know if he doesn't say what's on his mind we'll never be able to get back to what we were doing.

Am I being selfish? Yes. But in the long run, I think we'll both gain satisfaction from my selfishness.

Mason looks around the room. "I just didn't imagine us making love for the first time in a place like this. I wanted to make it special for you."

I put my hands on either side of his face and make him look straight at me so he doesn't miss a single word I say to him.

"You're here. That's all I need. I don't need silk sheets. I don't need flowers. I don't need candles. All I *need* right now is *you*."

Mason grins. "But I want to give you the silk sheets, the flowers, and the candles. I *need* to give you those things, Jess. I can't believe I'm about to say this," he says, shaking his head. "I want to wait until we go back home. Please let me make our first time together beautiful for you, and not," he looks around the room again, "this."

With my hands still on his face, I make him look back down at me.

"*You...are...killing...me*," I say to him, reminding him of the words he has said to me on more than one occasion.

He smiles, and I instantly feel overwhelmingly loved. I know he wants to make love as much as I do. It's blatantly obvious by the predominant bulge pressing against me, but he loves me enough to stop so our first time together can be a magical moment, something we'll both look back on one day and smile about. I can't say I don't understand why he wouldn't want to make love in the room we're in. It does bring to mind a place where an inmate would have a conjugal visit.

"Can we at least keep kissing?" I beg, not willing to give up all contact just yet.

"For a while," Mason says, "until I need to go take a cold shower, or do you think you could work up some tears for me?"

I laugh and grab a fistful of the shirt he still has on, bringing his lips down to mine.

"I'll see what I can do," I say against his mouth.

Eventually, Mason does have to go take a shower. I watch him as he stands with his back to me and completely undresses in the room, except for his underwear, which is a bit of a disappointment.

"What?" I ask as I lay on the bed watching him. "I don't get to see all of you?"

Mason smiles. "I have to keep some element of surprise for our first time."

I sigh, completely disappointed my voyeuristic side isn't going to be satisfied.

"Would you like some company in the shower?" I offer, hoping for a yes but not counting on it.

Mason's smile grows wider as he looks over his shoulder at me, which makes my heart skip a beat.

"I believe that would completely contradict the purpose of the shower."

I sigh again, which makes Mason chuckle. He turns slightly, and I see the outline of the bulge peeking out from the front of his underwear.

I begin to chew on the inside of my bottom lip as I study what Mason seems to have to offer.

"What's wrong?" he asks, seeing my distress.

"Are men usually that...well-endowed?" I ask, not completely sure how my body is supposed to accommodate so much of him.

Mason blushes and grabs his shirt from the chair to hide himself from my eyes.

"Are you sure it will fit?" I ask him, not having to elaborate on where exactly it's supposed to fit.

Mason smiles and rolls his eyes at me, all the while growing redder by the moment.

"Yes, your body will adjust to me."

"Ok," I say, not completely convinced. I cock my head and blatantly stare at him, because the shirt is doing nothing but making him look even larger as it makes a tent shape against his member. "I don't see how, but I guess I'll have to trust your judgment on that."

"I'm going to take a shower now," he says, seeming desperate to get away from my open leering of his person. He tosses his shirt back on the chair before stepping into the bathroom.

Mason has to turn in the small confines to close the door behind him, and I feel my eyes grow larger from the full side and frontal views of him before he closes the door.

I shake my head and lay it back on my pillow, completely paranoid now that my body won't be able to handle all of Mason.

I do my best to stay awake, wanting to snuggle with Mason when he gets out of the shower, but my body has other plans. As soon as I close my eyes, the stress from the day's events crashes into me like an ocean wave, reminding me just how tired I am. My mind feels like a piece of driftwood floating out to sea as it searches for the land of nod.

At some point, I wake up and find myself wrapped in Mason's arms, facing his naked chest. Although I'm too tired to do much else, I plant a small kiss in the middle of his chest and snuggle in closer to his warmth, drifting back to sleep.

A bit later, there is a soft knock at the door. Mason gets out of bed and pulls his pants and shirt on before walking over to open it.

"Oh, hi. I didn't know you guys were still sleeping," I hear Leah say to Mason. "I can come back later."

"Wait, Leah," I say, sitting up. "Come on in."

I reach over and turn the lamp beside the bed on for some extra light.

"I'm going to go see if Brand is up," Mason tells me, grabbing his socks and shoes from the metal chair.

He walks over and gives me a kiss.

"Good morning, by the way," he tells me with a smile.

"Good morning," I reply, smiling back because I realize I want to begin every morning of my life with a kiss from Mason.

"Brand's up," Leah informs us. "I just came from his quarters. He's making breakfast."

"I'll see the two of you when you get finished then," Mason says, leaning into me for one more kiss before he goes.

When he walks out the door, Leah walks towards me. I pat a spot on the bed beside me, silently telling her to take a seat.

"Can I get one of those when I go to your Earth?" Leah says pointing to the open door Mason just walked out of.

I giggle.

"Sorry, there's only one Mason, and I don't share."

I touch one of Leah's hands and instantly feel her relax.

"Why does it feel so good when I'm near you?" she asks me.

I shrug. "Our archangels seem to be happy when they're close to one another. At least, that's the explanation we've been going with."

"Will I feel this way when I'm with the other two you've found?"

"Yes, though I should warn you we have a devastatingly handsome rock star in our midst."

"What's his name?"

"Chandler Cain. And JoJo Armand is a French fashion designer. You're going to love them."

"Do you think they will like me?" Leah asks, showing the insecurity associated with her age.

"Leah, they will love you, just like I do. It's pretty much hardwired into our systems."

Leah's uncertainty about how Chandler and JoJo will react to her prompts me to ask her a question.

"Have you had many people in your life? Except for Remy, of course."

Leah shakes her head. "No. Remy has pretty much been all I've had. My mother abandoned me when I was a baby. Remy's my family."

I put an arm around Leah's shoulders and bring her closer to me. She lays her head on my shoulder, and I feel a kinship with her beyond just our archangel bond. Unlike Leah, I at least had a mother who gave me seven years to be with her. Even though she ultimately abandoned me, I suddenly feel lucky to have been given that much time. I can't imagine what Leah has gone through, knowing her mother didn't want her. The heartache of such knowledge would weaken most, but Leah seems like a strong- willed young lady who hasn't let hardship corrupt her soul.

"Who will I live with when I go back with you?" Leah asks.

It's a question I hadn't thought too much about, but feel sure I know the perfect person to raise Leah. She raised me and Faison, after all, and we didn't turn out too badly.

"I think the woman who adopted me would love to have you as a third daughter."

"You lost your real mom too?"

"She left me when I was seven, but she picked Mama Lynn to be my mother after she was gone. Even if I tried, I don't think I could pick a better person than her for you to live with. Plus, my house is just down the street from hers. So I'll only be a short walk away."

"I hope she likes me."

"Trust me. She'll love you."

My stomach growls.

"Did you say Brand was making breakfast?" I ask Leah.

Leah sits up and nods. "Yeah. Sounds like you need it."

"I'm starving. Let's go eat!"

I finish getting dressed and strap my sword on, remembering God's chastisement about not just leaving it anywhere. When Leah opens the door to Brand's quarters, I smell the wonderful aroma of eggs, bacon, sausage, biscuits, and coffee. Isaiah, Baruch and Remy are already sitting at the table, digging into their meals. Brand and Mason are speaking to one another in the kitchen area.

All eyes turn our way as we take our first step into the room.

I'm just about to say how good breakfast smells when I see Isaiah and Baruch stand so quickly from their seats the chairs topple over onto the floor. Both men phase and I hear them threatening someone behind me with bodily harm if they attempt to move a muscle.

I turn to see what's going on, and feel my body begin to tremble.

Baruch and Isaiah have Malcolm pinned against the cement wall of the hallway. He's dressed in his black leather Watcher Agency uniform. Malcolm doesn't try to fight against the two angels holding him back. He allows them to restrain him, and I get the feeling he's amused by their reaction to his presence in their secret hideout.

But seeing Malcolm again isn't what makes me tremble.

Faison is standing off to the side, staring at me with startled eyes.

Before I know it, my sister is in my arms, crying, much like the last time I saw her.

"I'm so sorry," she sobs. "I'm sorry I left you."

If anyone knows the pain I've suffered from being left by those I love, it's Faison.

"It's ok. Everything is ok now," I say, hugging her tightly to me.

Mason and Brand walk into the hallway.

"How did you know where to find us?" Brand demands of Malcolm.

"Did you really think I didn't know where you were?" Malcolm counters. "I know everything that happens in my sector."

Faison lifts her head and looks at Malcolm.

"Why are you doing that to him?" she questions Baruch and Isaiah harshly. "He saved my life. Let him go!"

"Saved you?" I ask. "How?"

"The people at the Watcher station I was taken to were keeping me prisoner. They said Lucifer wanted me for something. Malcolm phased in and grabbed me just before Lucifer was supposed to arrive." Faison looks at Baruch and Isaiah fiercely. "*Let…him…go.*"

"Let him go," Brand reiterates.

Baruch and Isaiah take their hands off Malcolm, but watch him with undisguised suspicion.

Malcolm straightens out the leather jacket he's wearing.

"Why are you here, Malcolm?" Brand asks.

"I thought you could use my help in this little rebellion you're trying to cook up."

"Why would you help us, and what makes you think we would trust you to help?"

"Let's just say not all of us Chancellors are happy with the way things are going. It's time to shake things up a bit. I've never been too much on uniforms either," Malcolm says, unbuttoning his jacket. "I'm hot-natured. Clothing just makes it worse."

Well, that explains the constant open shirts of the Malcolm back home.

"So you want to return control of the world to the humans because of your keen fashion sense?" Brand asks skeptically.

"Do you need a better reason? I can tell you which Chancellors will help when the time comes, and which will stab you in the back. Do you have anyone else who can do that for you?"

"No," Brand admits reluctantly.

"There you go then," Malcolm says, like his offer is completely reasonable. "I can be of use to you."

"How do we know this isn't some sort of trap?"

"You can tell if I'm lying, can't you?"

"Yes."

"Am I?"

"Not that I can detect."

"Then have a little faith in me."

Malcolm looks directly at me. "Consider us even now, by the way."

"Even?"

"You saved my son's soul. I saved your sister from a gruesome death. I think that makes us even."

I nod. "Agreed."

"You should probably come inside so we can talk some more," Brand says to Malcolm.

I watch them enter the room, embarking in a tenuous détente. I wish them the best of luck because I have a feeling they will need it.

Mason comes to stand by my side as I turn to Faison.

"God will open the Tear soon for us to go back home," I tell her. "Please, Faison, come back with me."

"I want to," she says, hesitation in her voice. "But I want to know if John Austin is alive in this reality first."

I understand what she wants, but I have no idea if I can give it to her.

"I don't even know if he exists here," I say.

"Isn't there someone here who can find that out for me?"

"Maybe Josh can help with that," Mason suggests. "If he's anything like our Joshua, he can probably find out if John Austin exists here. Let me go ask him."

Mason steps back into Brand's quarters to find Josh and ask for his help.

"Do you think it's silly?" Faison asks me. "To want to find out about a John Austin I don't even know."

I place an arm around Faison's shoulders. "No, it's not silly at all, Fai."

Mason soon returns with Josh, who is licking something off his fingers which does nothing but remind me how very hungry I am. But there's no time to eat. I don't know how much time God will give me to convince Faison to come back home with me. Every second could be precious.

"Josh says he can find John Austin for us," Mason says.

"Where does he live in your world?" Josh asks.

"Tunica, Mississippi," I tell him. "He died a few days ago in our reality."

"Follow me," Josh says, taking a few steps down the hallway. "Let's see what we can find out."

I take one of Faison's hands, not willing to lose contact with my sister, because I need her to know I'm there for her. Mason follows behind us.

Josh takes us downstairs to a large cavernous space, and I realize we're in a set of subway tunnels. This space looks like it was once used as a subway terminal, with its green pillars delineating the platform from the tracks.

An impressive array of pieced-together computer equipment is set up in one corner, and Josh goes over to sit down in front of a rudimentary keyboard. It's a far cry from the high-tech computer system our Joshua has access to.

We provide Josh with as much information as we can about John Austin. It doesn't take him long to locate him.

"It looks like our version of him lives in small community near Tunica called Cypress Hollow," Josh tells us.

My heart sinks. If John Austin is alive here, what chance do I have of bringing Faison back home with me?

"He's alive?" Faison asks, filled with a new sense of hope.

Josh looks at his computer screen. "Yes, he's alive. He has a wife named Shelby and a daughter named Abigail."

"He's married to Shelby?" Faison asks, in complete shock. "Do I exist here?"

"Full name?" Josh asks.

"Faison Ann Mills."

Josh pulls up Faison's information.

"You also lived in Cypress Hollow at one time." Josh reads a little more. "Apparently, you were adopted by a Lynn Mills when you were a baby, but she died in a car crash when you were seven. You were sent to live with your only living relative, who was your mother's brother, Dan Mills."

I feel my heart race, and not in a good way.

"Where is this Earth's Faison now?" I ask.

"Hmm, it looks like your double committed suicide when she was fourteen," Josh leans in toward his screen to read something, "but the police suspected your uncle was abusing you and might have killed you himself. They weren't able to find any evidence to support their suspicions, though. Looks like your Uncle Dan died here a few weeks back, from complications due to pancreatic cancer."

We were in a world where Faison had lived alone with Uncle Dan for seven long years. They were seven years where he would have had constant contact with her. I felt like weeping for that little lost girl, but didn't. She was in a far better place now.

"I'm dead and John Austin is married to Shelby," Faison

says, trying to absorb all of the information at once. "We always said if we had a daughter her name would be Abigail."

Faison breaks down into sobs. I bring her into the circle of my arms and hold her close to me.

I look up at Mason and see his concern for my sister. I know he wants to help, but there's really nothing either of us can do. Faison will have to deal with the information she's received on her own terms.

There's a great pressure on my chest, just like I felt the first time I went through the Tear.

I put my hands on Faison's shoulder and make her look at me.

"The Tear is opening. Come home with me," I beg.

Faison catches her breath and nods. "I am."

After that, the only thing I feel is pain until we're all back home.

CHAPTER 6

It's morning time in Cypress Hollow. The birds are chirping. The grass is frosted over, making it glisten like snow against the rising sun.

We're home.

Chandler and JoJo come running out of my front door, almost toppling me over as they squeeze me between them like an archangel sandwich.

"God, Jess, we were so worried about you," Chandler says to me.

"*Oui*, so very worried," JoJo agrees, hugging me tightly and giggling with happiness to have me home.

As if sensing her presence, they turn in unison to where Leah is standing.

JoJo gasps, holding a hand to her mouth.

"You found her?" Chandler asks, squinting at Leah as if he's not sure he should believe his eyes. "How?"

"It's a long story," I tell them. "I'll tell you all about it over breakfast."

I suddenly remember it's Wednesday. I didn't get to eat the wonderful-smelling breakfast alternate Earth Brand made, but Beau's cinnamon rolls are suddenly calling my name.

JoJo and Chandler walk over to Leah and introduce themselves. I see Leah's eyes light up with joy, and I know she feels the bond we all share with one another.

I turn to Faison.

"How are you doing?" I ask her.

"I'm ok," she says, giving me a small, sad smile. "I really screwed up, didn't I?"

I shake my head. "No, it was meant to happen. If I hadn't followed you through, I wouldn't have found Leah."

"She's one of you?" Faison asks in surprise. "An archangel?"

I nod. "Yes, she's the fourth. She's been stranded in that other reality since before she was born."

"Then... maybe it wasn't for nothing."

"What wasn't for nothing?"

"John Austin's death here on our Earth," Faison answers. "If he hadn't died, I never would have wanted to leave here, and you would have never found her. It means his death wasn't meaningless."

I'm glad Faison sees it that way, but I still have a bone to pick with God about it.

I see Faison look off down the street towards Mama Lynn's house.

"I should go talk to her," Faison says. "I never should have blamed her for his death. It wasn't her fault. It was just his time to go."

"Do you want me to go over there with you?" I ask.

Faison shakes her head. "No. I need to do it alone."

Faison gives me a fiercely tight hug. "Thanks for coming for me."

I hug her back just as tightly. "I fight for my family, even if they don't want me to."

I hear Faison sniff. "I did. I just didn't know it at the time."

I watch as Faison walks down the sidewalk towards Mama Lynn's house.

"Is she ok?" Mason asks me, coming to stand by my side.

"She will be. She just needs some time." I turn to Mason and give him my best doe-eyed look. Hey, it's worked for Faison all these years. Why not me? "Could you do me a favor?"

Mason smiles down at me, obviously amused by my attempt at cajoling a favor out of him with my womanly wiles.

"You know I would do anything you asked," he tells me.

"Could you phase over to Beau's store and grab us some cinnamon rolls for breakfast?"

Mason leans down and kisses me. "Be right back."

When I look back at where Leah, Chandler, and JoJo are chatting, I notice Remy standing conspicuously off to the side of the group. He has a melancholy look on his face, and I see him wipe away tears from the corners of his eyes.

I walk over to him.

"Are you ok?" I ask Remy.

"I'm just happy to see her back where she belongs," he answers, sniffling. He wipes his nose on his sleeve and looks back over at me. "I'll need to leave now, you know."

"I figured as much."

"I don't want to tell her," he says. "I'm the only person she's had to count on her whole entire life. I hope she doesn't think I'm abandoning her too."

"I think she already knows you have to leave," I tell him, hoping the information will ease his guilt. "She asked me who she would be living with when we came here. She's smart. I think she realizes you can't stay with her forever."

"Who will be taking care of her? You?"

"We all will, but I think she would be in better hands if she lived with my mother."

"Could I meet her before I go?"

"When do you think you will need to leave?"

"Soon," a familiar voice says behind me.

I turn to see my dad. I can't help but smile.

He walks up to me and gives me a hug.

"Hey, Jessi."

"Hey, Daddy."

"Of course," Remy says, realization finally dawning. "I should have known you were Zeruel's daughter. I knew there was something different about you."

My dad holds his hand out to Remy.

"Good to see you again, Remiel. The six of us wondered what happened to you. We just assumed God sent you on a special mission we weren't supposed to know about."

"Special mission," Remy says, chuckling softly. "I guess that's a better way of putting it than saying we were stranded in an alternate reality with no way to get back home."

"So I was told," my dad says. "I'm here to take you back with me when you're ready."

"I need to do a couple of things first," Remy tells my dad, looking over at Leah. "I can't leave her just yet."

"Take your time. I know how hard it is to leave them."

My dad puts his arm around my shoulders, instantly letting me know that leaving me was one of the hardest things he ever had to do.

I hear the squeak of a rocking chair come from my front porch. No one seems to notice Lucifer's arrival except for me.

"Daddy, would you mind phasing everyone inside?" I ask, keeping my eyes on Lucifer as he studies the people standing on my front lawn.

My father follows my gaze and realizes why I've made such a request.

Without saying another word, he and Remy walk over to

my group of friends to phase them inside my home and out from under Lucifer's intense scrutiny.

I walk up onto the porch.

"I was waiting for your return," Lucifer tells me. "I wanted to make sure you got back in one piece. I've heard wormhole travel can be a bit painful."

"That's the understatement of the year," I tell him.

"So how was your trip? Successful, I hope, for your sake."

"Yes, I have my sister back."

Lucifer just stares at me.

"Was there something else you wanted to ask me?" I question, knowing what's coming.

"Why were two Guardians from the Treasury of Souls just standing on your lawn? Who are they to you?"

I contemplate how to answer the question. I could just tell the devil to mind his own damn business, but would that gain me anything besides antagonism? I mentally run through all of my options and decide on one. Is it the smartest option? Only time will tell me that, but it's what my heart says I should do, and I always follow my heart.

"One of them is my father."

Lucifer stops rocking. He looks completely floored. I get the feeling it's not because of what I said. I think he's surprised by my willingness to share such important information with him. It's something a friend would do, not an enemy.

"Which one: Zeruel or Remiel?"

"Zeruel."

"Why would you call him your father?"

"Because when he made my soul he infused it with part of his own."

Lucifer narrows his eyes at me. "Why are you sharing this information so freely with me, Jessica? You've never been very forthcoming before. Why start now?"

"Maybe I'm just getting tired of playing games with you. You and I keep going back and forth, but neither of us seems to be getting anywhere with it. And in the long run, maybe it doesn't matter what you know about me. I have a feeling when you learn the complete truth you'll just end up wanting to kill me anyway."

"I have no desire to kill you," Lucifer says, his face completely serious. "I've come to enjoy these little conversations of ours. Sadly enough, you're the closest thing I have to a friend on this planet."

I have no idea if Lucifer is trying to play on my sympathies, but I get the strange feeling he's telling me the truth.

"Why would you say I would want to kill you after I find out the truth about you?" he asks. "You say it with such certainty."

"I met your doppelganger while I was away."

"Did you now?" Lucifer grins. "Was he as devastatingly handsome as me?"

"Exactly."

"And what did he do to make you think I would want you dead after I learn the truth of what you are?"

"He tried to kill me."

Lucifer looks amused. "Did he? That's interesting. Do you mind me asking how you got away unscathed? Usually if I want someone dead, they die. Yet, here you are, still alive. How?"

"I think I've over-shared enough for one day, don't you?"

"One more question, if you don't mind," Lucifer says, leaning forward in his chair. "Those three humans I just saw. Who are they?"

"My friends."

"What kind of friends? There's something about them that's different, like you're different, but I can't quite put my finger on what it is I'm sensing from them either."

"Like I said, I've over-shared enough with you for one day. They're my friends. That's all you need to know."

Lucifer leans back in the chair and continues to rock.

"By the way," he says, "I've been meaning to ask why you're pretending to be that boy's girlfriend."

"I'm doing him a favor."

"Doesn't that bother you, Mason?" Lucifer says, looking past the porch rail to the sidewalk behind me.

I instinctively turn and see Mason holding a white cardboard box from Beau's store in his hands.

"The boy knows his place," Mason answers, walking up the steps to stand beside me on the porch.

"What, inside your girlfriend's mouth?" Lucifer laughs. "I saw the pictures of the two of you. It didn't look much like pretend from what I saw."

"Chandler made a mistake," I say. "He apologized afterward. He simply mistook friendship love for romantic love. He's human. It happens."

"Still, I'm surprised Mason didn't throw him through a wall or something worse."

"The thought did cross my mind," Mason admits. "But it wouldn't have made Jess happy, and her happiness is all I care about."

"She certainly has you wrapped around her finger."

"Maybe you should try looking in a mirror one day," Mason tells him.

Lucifer smiles grimly. "I suppose you'll want to go and share those delectable pastries with your friends inside."

I take the box from Mason's hands and open it, allowing the sweet scent of freshly baked sugar and cinnamon to permeate the air around us. I hold the box out to Lucifer.

"Would you like one?"

Lucifer looks surprised by my gesture. I get the feeling he isn't used to being included in things like sharing a meal. He hesitates, but finally succumbs to the call of the cinnamon rolls and picks one out of the box.

"Thank you," he says, frowning, like the words are foreign on his tongue.

"You're welcome," I tell him, unable to suppress a smile because it's the first time I've seen Lucifer act civilly.

"I should be going now," Lucifer says abruptly. "I will see you again soon."

"Ok."

Lucifer looks confused by my easy acceptance of his next visit, but phases before giving anything else away.

"I don't know how you can stand talking to him," Mason tells me.

I hear his disapproval of my relationship with Lucifer clearly in his voice.

I shrug. "I've gotten used to him, I guess. Is that strange?"

"Honestly? Yes, it is. I won't lie about that. He is evil in its purist form, Jess."

"I know that, but sometimes when we talk I get the feeling there's still a small sliver of good inside him, wrapped up in his own darkness. Maybe all he needs is someone to have a little faith in him."

"Faith?" Mason scoffs. "I have faith that he'll rip you from limb to limb one day just because he can. You can't trust him, Jess. Not now, not ever!"

I feel my temper start to flare, and realize a part of me does consider Lucifer something of a friend. A good one? No. One I can trust? Absolutely not. But one who has potential. There's a part of me, whether due to Michael or not I'm not sure, that yearns to bring Lucifer back from the dark. To make him see he doesn't have to be what he is.

"Even God said He still has hope Lucifer will come back to Him one day," I remind Mason. "Why should I think any differently? Or don't you trust God's judgment?"

"Of course I trust His judgment," Mason sighs, his shoulders sagging slightly. "But your safety is what has me worried here. Not only your physical safety, but emotionally you're allowing yourself to care for a creature who lost his ability to be concerned about someone else a long time ago. I know him, Jess. I fought against him in the war. If you had seen him do the things I have, you wouldn't trust him either."

Crap. I completely forgot all about that. Of course Mason wouldn't understand my feelings for Lucifer. They had been mortal enemies at one time after all. Once an enemy always an enemy seemed to be Mason's mindset. I can't blame him, though. I suppose I would feel the same way if I had been through what he had. Plus, we just learned that Lucifer killed Mason during the war in Heaven in alternate Earth's timeline.

I close the lid on the box and set it on the rocking chair. I wrap my arms around Mason's waist and feel his arms go around me too.

"I'm sorry," I say. "I'm sorry you had to go through something as horrible as that war."

Mason sighs, and I know he's reliving that period of his life in his mind. I want to wipe the visions of death and slaughter from his memory, but I know I can't do that. I can only hope to give him better things to think about.

I lift my head from his chest, and he looks down at me with haunted eyes.

"I love you," I tell him, leaning up to brush my lips against his, reminding him that there is beauty in the world. "I will always love you."

Mason buries his fingers in my hair as he deepens the kiss, but it isn't demanding. Passion is secondary in that moment because all either of us wants is for the other to feel how much we truly cherish one another. We end the kiss, knowing how blessed we are to have found each other.

We go into my home hand in hand, ready to face whatever happens next together.

CHAPTER 7

Before we tell Chandler and JoJo what happened to us in the alternate reality, I ask, "What did God need to speak with you about after Mason and I went through the Tear?"

Chandler shrugs. "He didn't say that much except that there would come a time when we would need to remember that our archangels are permanently connected. If you know what that's supposed to mean, I'm all ears."

I sigh. "No, I don't know why that's important to know. I guess we'll figure it out when the time comes."

"Mason," JoJo says, her eyes squinting at him. "You look different for some reason."

Chandler stares at Mason, which makes everyone stare at him. Mason shifts uncomfortably in his chair.

"I'm not sure what you're talking about," Mason replies.

"Your scar," Chandler says, as he continues to study Mason's face. "It's like almost gone."

I look closer at Mason and notice that Chandler is right. Why hadn't I noticed that before? I guess it was because I never really noticed Mason's scar that much in the first place.

Mason reaches up and touches the place where his scar is. Now, it's simply a slim line where the skin meets. Mason looks at me and I smile. He grins and shakes his head in disbelief. I don't think he ever thought he would be able to forgive himself enough for it to shrink so much. I feel sure after we seal the Tear, it will disappear altogether.

We spend a good hour telling Chandler and JoJo what happened to us on the alternate Earth. JoJo is exceedingly excited to learn I can fly.

"Told ya you were wicked cool," Chandler says, winking at me.

"Can you do it whenever you want?" Leah asks.

"I really don't know. I only did it the once. I still need to practice my landings, though."

"I don't know," Mason says, a corner of his mouth lifting in a half-smile. "I thought you landed rather perfectly the last time."

I roll my eyes at him, not even bothering to acknowledge his statement with one of my own. But the word 'incorrigible' comes to mind.

"Anyway, to answer your question, I don't know. I guess I need to try to fly again soon."

"But the rest of us will not get flight?" JoJo asks, looking completely crestfallen.

"Apparently, it's a Michael-only power," I tell her. "Sorry."

"Well, JoJo and I have been trying to fine-tune our powers while you were away," Chandler tells me, pulling out the pipe we retrieved for him in the Cave of Treasures from his back pocket.

He puts it up to his lips and begins to play a sweet tune that makes me instantly feel happy. When he ends it, we're all smiling, even Mason.

"I told you," Mason tells Chandler. "It's not the instrument, but the man who uses it that determines how it affects other people."

Chandler smiles shyly. It's the closest he's come to getting praise from Mason.

"Oh, oh! I made something for you," JoJo says to me, running into the living room and appearing quickly with her little black purse. From it she pulls out a black choker necklace made of braided silk with a silver star encrusted with crystals dangling from the middle.

"What does it do?" I ask, lifting my hair as she places it around my neck.

"It will stop you from becoming *enceinte*," she tells me rather proudly.

Mason almost chokes on the coffee he just sipped.

Chandler hits him on the back in an effort to help clear his airway.

"Dude, you ok?"

Mason clears his throat and nods.

"Yes, I'm fine. Anyone else need some fresh coffee?" he asks, quickly standing from the table and going into the kitchen like he's trying to escape from something.

I'm scared to ask what '*enceinte*' means now, considering how Mason just reacted. My father and Remy are looking at me funnily too. Apparently, they understand French. I decide to inquire about the meaning of the word later because I'm not sure I want it explained to me while everyone is staring at me.

"Thanks, JoJo. It's beautiful."

"Jessi," my dad says, and I immediately hear the concern in his voice, "could I have a word with you in private?"

I feel like a little girl who's about to get a talking-to from her father.

My father stands and I follow him into the living room. I see Mason watching me walk out of the room, a worried look on his face, which in turn makes me feel even more paranoid.

My father sits down on the couch, and I sit down next to him.

"I'm assuming you don't know what *enceinte* means," he says, a wistful smile on his face.

"No, I don't," I confess cautiously. "And from the way you and Mason are reacting, I'm not sure I want to."

My dad's smile turns into a full-fledged grin. "*Enceinte* means pregnant."

I feel blood immediately rush to my face. No wonder they started to act so weird.

I close my eyes and shake my head.

"Not exactly something you want your father to hear," I say.

"So are you and Mason…" my father lets the rest of his sentence hang in the air unfinished because we both know what he's asking.

"Not yet."

"I see," my dad says, nodding his head. "But I take it you will be soon?"

"Do I really have to answer that question or can I plead the fifth?" I ask, leaning my elbows on my thighs and burying my face in the palms of my hands. "And please tell me you aren't going to try to have 'the talk' with me now, because I'm pretty sure I know everything I need to know."

I hear my dad chuckle. "No, I'm not going to have 'the talk' with you, and I can see the answer to my question for myself without you having to say it."

I spread my fingers and peek over at him through the slits. He looks worried. I sit up and drop my hands to my lap.

"What's wrong?" I ask him. "Why do you look so worried? I'm not going to go to Hell for having pre-marital sex, am I? Because I really don't think I could take an eternity with Lucifer."

My dad smiles. "No. You're not going to Hell. It doesn't work that way. If it did, Heaven would practically be empty. Besides, you and Mason love each other. It's different. But, honestly, I just thought Mason might want to get married first. He seemed rather old-fashioned when we talked while you were recovering from what Asmodeus and Mammon did to you."

I sigh and slouch against the back of the couch.

"He does want to get married," I tell my dad. "But I don't know if I want to."

"Why not? You *do* love him, right?"

"With everything that I am."

"Then what's holding you back, Jessi? Why don't you want to get married?"

"I don't know," I admit. "Every time it's brought up, I get this panicky feeling in the pit of my stomach. I mean, do we really have to get married? As long as we love each other, I don't see why it matters."

"Marriage is a declaration of that love," my dad tells me. "It shows the world that you want to spend the rest of your lives together, through thick and thin. It's a way to show how committed you are to one another. I don't think Mason is a man who would be completely happy without being married to the woman he loves."

I know my dad is right. Mason would go through life unmarried if I asked him to, but could I really be that selfish? I sit and think, trying to filter through the reasons I don't want to get married.

. . .

1. *I don't really love Mason….*Hell no, definitely not it. I love him beyond all reason.

2. *I don't think we'll get along as a married couple…*No possibility of that ever happening either. We get along too well.

3. *I think he'll cheat on me….* I laugh. No chance of that ever happening either. Mason is as loyal as the day is long.

4. *I don't want to have to walk down the aisle in front of all our friends and family in a big poofy white dress and have them gawk at me….*My stomach churns, and I feel like I'm going to be sick. Yep, that's the one.

"It's the wedding," I tell my father. "I don't want the wedding."

"Oh," my dad says, suddenly looking disappointed.

"What? Why do you look like I just shot your dog?"

"Well, I was hoping, since I'm allowed to be in your life now, that I could give you away at your wedding."

Men. Sheesh.

Isn't it supposed to be me who wants the sweet romantic

wedding with all the bells and whistles? But no, it's the men in my life who get all mushy about it.

"Maybe there can be a compromise," I suggest, not wanting my dad to look like I'm going to make him miss one of those monumental moments in my life.

If my dad looks this disappointed, I can't imagine what Mason's reaction would be if I suggest just going to the justice of the peace for a quickie ceremony. A picture of Mason looking completely devastated appears in my mind, and I quickly squash it out like a bug running across the floor of my imagination. No, I can't have that. I'll think of something.

"He hasn't actually popped that particular question yet. We had a talk about it, and I basically told him I didn't want to get married," I say.

"You know he wants to."

I sigh. "I know. Don't worry. I'll think of something."

The gears in my mind begin to go into overdrive as a plan forms.

Remy walks into the living room.

"Hey, could I talk to you guys for a second?" he says to us, taking a seat in the chair by the couch.

"What's wrong, Remiel?" My father asks.

Remy scratches his beard like he's not completely sure how to start what he wants to say.

"It's about where Leah's crown is."

"Where is it?" I ask. "Can you take us to it?"

"Yeah," Remy says, drawing out the word, "see, therein

lies the problem. I don't really want to take Leah to where it is."

"Why?" I ask, suspicion creeping in. "Where did you leave it?"

"Where her mother worked," Remy whispers as if it's something he doesn't want to say too loudly.

"I take it by the way you said that she didn't work somewhere nice."

Remy looks toward the kitchen to make sure Leah is still at the table talking to Chandler and JoJo.

He leans in towards us and says, "She worked in a whorehouse just outside of Las Vegas."

"You left the crown of an archangel in a whorehouse?" I ask, attempting not to make it sound like I'm calling Remy a complete idiot. I'm thinking it but trying really hard not to say it to his face.

"I didn't have much choice," he says with a shrug. "There wasn't a lot of time to find a better spot."

"Did you at least hide it in a safe place there?"

"I think so. I put it in an air conditioning vent."

"So it's been sitting there for the past fifteen years?"

"I hope so."

"Then why don't you just go get it and bring it back?" I say. "You can carry the box."

"Oh," Remy says. "You know I forgot about it being in a box." Remy stands up "Be right back."

I turn to my father. "I thought all angels were smart. How the hell was he put in charge of making souls?"

"Jess," my father admonishes, "you shouldn't talk about him like that."

"Sorry." Now I feel like I'm five years old again. "But, come on, Dad, even you have to admit he's not the sharpest knife in the drawer."

"He used to be quite sharp, actually. I think being over in that alternate reality for so long had an adverse effect on him."

"How?"

"His body wasn't meant to be there. Anyone who travels between worlds ends up getting their molecules scrambled, and when they are in that world for a long time their body is forced to live at a different frequency."

"Is that why Tearers who come here glow red to me?"

"I always assumed so. You can see their bodies vibrating at a different frequency than people who normally live here."

Remy reappears.

"Yeah, so about that air conditioning vent," he says, scratching his beard nervously. "Looks like they recently renovated the place."

"What does that mean?" I ask. "Where's the box?"

"The box is gone."

"Where's the crown?"

"Sitting on the Madame's desk in her office."

I sigh. "Well, then we don't have any choice. We have to take Leah there to get it. She's the only one who can pick it up."

"Pick what up?" Leah asks, walking into the living room, looking between me and Remy.

"Your crown," I answer, not quite sure how I'm going to tell Leah her mother was a whore. How do you tell a kid something like that?

"Leah, your mother used to work in a whorehouse near Las Vegas," Remy says. "We're gonna have to go there to get it."

Well, I guess that was one way of doing it; not exactly tactful, but truthful.

"Ok." Leah says, not as upset about this revelation as I thought she might be.

"Hold on," I tell them. "Let me grab my sword. I'm going with you."

I look down at my dad.

"Don't say anything to Mason about you-know-what," I tell him. "I'm planning a surprise, so don't go spoiling it."

My dad smiles. "Ok, Jessi. Not a peep."

I walk into the hallway and grab my sword from off the top of the Bombay chest there.

"Let me help you put that on," Mason says, coming up behind me and taking the baldric from my hands.

I put my arms through the straps, and Mason spins me around so he can fasten the belt's buckle for me.

"What were you and your father talking about?" Mason asks, curious but not wanting to appear too curious.

"He told me what *enceinte* means."

Mason grins. "Yeah. JoJo surprised me with that one. Who *doesn't* know that we'll be making love soon?"

"Probably nobody now since my dad and I just had a long discussion about it."

Mason sighs. "Should I expect a lecture from him while you're gone?"

"No, he won't say anything to you about it ," I say, smiling at how uncomfortable Mason looks at the possibility of having such a conversation with my father.

"Well, since everyone seems to know about our soon-to-be sex life," Mason says, pulling me into his arms and looking completely irresistible, "would you like to go out with me tonight, Agent Riley, so I can completely have my way with you afterwards?"

I suddenly feel a little nervous, but I refuse to let it get in my way.

"Why yes, Mr. Collier, I would love to. What time?"

"Let's say five."

"How should I dress?"

"I'll speak to JoJo about it while you're gone. That way it will be a surprise."

"Ok. Since she's here, I seriously doubt she would let me dress myself anyway."

Mason chuckles. "Maybe after tonight you'll let me see you the way I've wanted to for a while now."

"Well, you could have seen me that way last night if you had taken me up on my offer to join you in the shower."

"True. But it just wasn't the right setting."

"And will you be arranging this setting while I'm gone?"

"Yes, after I speak to JoJo." Mason leans down and pecks me on the lips.

"That's all I get?" I question with a raised eyebrow.

"Until later," Mason promises sweetly.

"I plan to hold you to that promise," I say, walking past Mason towards the living room.

I suddenly feel a pinch on my butt and jump. I whirl around to face Mason.

"Sorry," he says, not looking the least bit sorry. "I couldn't stop myself. It's just so cute."

I narrow my eyes at him. "Have I told you that you're completely incorrigible?"

"Often," he says with a smile, not looking sorry about it one little bit.

CHAPTER 8

Remy phases us, and we soon find ourselves standing outside what I assume to be the whorehouse. Surprisingly enough it looks rather normal, considering what goes on within its walls. The house was your basic two-story farmhouse, replete with white clapboard exterior and wraparound porch.

Leah presses her hand into Remy's as we walk up the wooden steps to the front door.

Remy rings the doorbell.

A curly-haired blonde woman dressed in a regular pair of cut-off jeans and white tank top answers the door.

"Can I help you?" she asks, in what sounds like a Boston accent.

"We came for the crown," Remy tells her.

I roll my eyes. Apparently, subtlety isn't one of Remy's strong suits.

"Could we speak to the owner, please?" I ask.

The girl shrugs and opens the door wider for us to enter. We walk down a dimly- lit hallway and around the corner. She knocks on a door and another woman calls out for us to come in. The blonde sticks her head inside the room.

"There're some people here to see you, Terry."

"Show them in."

The woman opens the door wider and looks at us. "Go on in."

When we walk into the office, my eyes are drawn immediately to the crown sitting on the Madame's desk.

The owner of the whorehouse isn't what I expected. She's a woman in her early forties, sharply dressed in a dark blue suit. She stands when we enter and has her lips stretched into a practiced smile. Her long brown hair is straight and falls evenly on either side of her face. She isn't wearing much makeup, which gives her a clean appearance.

"Can I help you?" she says.

"We came for the crown," Remy replies.

I feel like banging my head against the wall. Remy seemed to be a one-note wonder. Getting the crown was the only thing his scrambled brain seemed to be able to concentrate on.

The woman sits on the edge of her desk and crosses her arms over her chest.

"You're welcome to have it if you can pick it up."

Remy lets go of Leah's hand. "Go ahead, Leah."

"No."

Remy and I both look at Leah.

"What do you mean 'no'?" I ask.

Leah looks at the Madame. "I want you to tell me about my mother first."

The woman stares at Leah for the space of ten seconds and then nods. "I thought you looked familiar when you came in. Your mother was Grace, right?"

"Yes, that was her name."

"She went through the Tear the second year it opened."

"She was pregnant with me at the time."

The woman looks surprised but then she nods. "I guess that explains things. I was wondering why she was crying all the time. She wouldn't speak to me, though."

"I was born on an alternate Earth."

"Ahh, the one we saw the other night?"

"Yes."

"You got really lucky to make it back."

Leah shrugs. "Had some help."

"So what do you want to know about your mom?"

"Everything," Leah begs. "Anything. All I know is her name and that she left me after I was born."

"Your mom wasn't like most of the girls here. Usually they can distance themselves from the Johns, but not your mom. I don't think she was cut out for the business, to be honest. She ended up falling in love with one of her clients, but he didn't want anything to do with her. He even asked to have another girl become his regular when your mom became too possessive of him. Your mom went ape-shit crazy after that. Come to think of it, that happened just before the Tear opened and she disappeared."

"Where was she from?"

"I don't know exactly. All I do know is that she was here illegally from China. A lot of girls end up here if they're trying to live in the States without papers."

"Do you know anything else?"

"Sorry, hon, but that's about all I knew about your mom. I'm not even sure her real name was Grace, to be honest with you."

Leah's shoulders sag in disappointment. She walks up to the desk and grabs the crown. The Madame's eyes look like they're about to bulge out of their sockets.

"How the hell did you do that? We've had almost everyone in Nevada try to move that thing after the box it was in disintegrated."

"It belongs to me," Leah tells her.

Leah walks back to us.

"Ready?" Remy asks.

Leah nods, and Remy phases us back to my house.

When we get back home, Mason is already gone. I grab my phone from its charger in case he needs to get in touch with me while we're separated.

I decide I should I head over to Mama Lynn's house alone before bringing Leah and Remy to meet her. When I fill her in on the situation with Leah, she reacts just like I knew she would.

"You bring her to me," she tells me. "Poor thing has been stuck over there for far too long. I bet she hasn't had a home-cooked meal in ages."

This sets Mama Lynn off into the kitchen to whip up a lunch for Leah while I go back to my house to get her.

On my way home, my phone vibrates. I quickly grab it to see if it's a text from Mason.

Are you back yet?

Yes, we got back thirty minutes ago. Taking Leah to meet Mama Lynn now.

Let me know how that goes. BTW, red or white?

Red or white what?

Roses

A mixture?

Silk or cotton?

Silk or cotton what?

Sheets

Never slept on silk so don't know how comfortable they would be. Let's go with cotton.

In or out?

Definitely in. I think. Unless I'm missing the point of the question.

Indoors or outdoors...

Oh, then definitely in. Isn't it too cold to be doing something like that outdoors?

Not where we're going...We can always do both...

If that is an option then I vote for both.

I like the way you think, Agent Riley...

I like the way you plan, Mr. Collier...

See you at five. Got lots to do before then. Love you, with all that I am.

Love you, with all I will ever be.

Remy holds Leah's hand as we walk over to Mama Lynn's house. My dad and I walk slightly ahead of them.

"She's gonna love you," Remy says to Leah, forcing himself to sound optimistic even in the face of his imminent departure.

"Guess we'll see," Leah replies, uncertainty in her voice.

"You know, my mom picked Mama Lynn to be my mother before she left me," I tell Leah over my shoulder. "Sort of like your mom picked Remy to leave you with. She knew I would be in good hands, and I know you will be too."

"Why does she want me?"

"Why wouldn't she?"

"Because I'm a complete stranger! She doesn't know anything about me."

I come to a stop so I can face Leah.

"Sure she does. She knows you're my friend. She knows you were stranded on a world you didn't belong on your whole life. The rest she can learn while you two get to know each other. That's one advantage to being the new kid. She doesn't know all your secrets just yet."

Before we even get to the door, Mama Lynn and Faison have it open, watching us walk over. Mama Lynn is smiling from ear to ear, and Faison is even trying to grin.

Mama Lynn walks out the door and meets us halfway up her sidewalk.

"Mama Lynn, this is Leah…I'm sorry, do you have a last name?"

Leah shakes her head.

"Well," Mama Lynn says, "how would you like to be a Mills like me and Faison? Jess kept her family name when I adopted her, but since you don't have one already, you're more than welcome to become a Mills."

Leah smiles shyly and nods. "All right. That's really nice of you. Thanks."

Mama Lynn looks at me. "I assume Mason can handle all the legal paperwork for us?"

"I'm sure he can," I tell her. "He knows the President. He should be able to pull a few strings, I would think."

Mama Lynn faces Remy. "I want you to know that I will take very good care of her for you. And you're more than welcome to come and see us anytime you want."

"Thank you," Remy says, truly thankful for Mama Lynn's openness.

"Now, I hope you two like meatloaf, mashed potatoes, black-eyed peas, biscuits, and gravy, because that's what we're having for lunch."

"You eat all that just for lunch?" Leah asks, completely amazed.

"Honey, you're in the South. That's just considered a snack here." Mama Lynn puts an arm around Leah's shoulders and starts asking her how she wants to decorate her room upstairs, even offering some suggestions.

"You're right," Remy says to me, as he watches Leah and Mama Lynn walk into the house. "She's perfect. Just what Leah needs right now."

"You know, God lets my dad come visit me," I tell Remy. "I can even call him to come to me anytime I want. I'm sure you'll get the same privileges, considering how long you've been with Leah."

"You think so?" Remy asks hopefully, looking between me and my dad. "I just figured since Zeruel is your real father that was the reason he got to come see you."

"You *are* Leah's real father," I remind Remy. "And if God doesn't let you, have Him talk to me because I'll certainly have some choice words for Him about it."

"Wow, Zeruel, you were right…"

"Right about what?" I ask, looking at my dad.

"I said you were feisty and fought for what you believed to be right."

I loop an arm through one of my dad's. "Come on, you two. Mama Lynn's food waits for no man."

While we're eating lunch, I ask Remy, "Do you know which archangel Leah carries?"

"Uriel," Remy says, his eyes shift away from mine uncomfortably.

"Why do you say that like it's a bad thing?" I ask.

Remy looks at my dad. "Should I tell her or do you want to?"

My dad sighs. "Uriel tried to kill Lilly when she was younger."

I put my fork down and give my dad my full attention.

"And why would he try to do a boneheaded thing like that?" I ask.

"He thought if he could kill her it would be a fair price to pay to save the universe. He tried to make sure Lucifer couldn't use her to follow through with his plan."

"And this S.O.B is inside Leah?" I ask, not trying to hide the hostility I feel towards Uriel.

"Yes. He was only doing what he felt was right at the time," my dad tells me. "Just because he's an angel doesn't make him infallible, Jessi. We all make mistakes. His intentions were good; he just went about it the wrong way."

I try to let my father's words sink in, but I can't help the way I feel. Anyone who would harm Lilly is no friend of mine. Yet, he's inside the most innocent of us all. I look at Leah and see her concern over learning about her archangel's nefarious past deeds. My feelings are torn, and I wonder if that's why Uriel and Leah chose one another. Perhaps he thought being bound to such an innocent soul would temper his own volatile one. I can only hope that's the case, but I decide to keep an eye on Leah after she connects with Uriel. To my way of thinking, an archangel like that can't be completely trusted.

After lunch, I can tell Remy is procrastinating about going back to Heaven. He stays to help Mama Lynn clean the dishes. Who does that unless they're procrastinating?

Eventually, my dad gently reminds him that they need to be leaving.

Leah walks over to Remy as he stands by my dad.

"Do you need to go back to Heaven now, Remy?" Leah asks, her voice quivering slightly.

"Afraid so, baby girl," Remy puts his arms around Leah's shoulders while hers go around his waist, and she lays her head against his chest.

"Will I ever see you again?" she asks, sniffling.

"Well, I can't say for sure. Jess said she'll talk to God about it, and I'll talk to Him too next time I see Him. She seems to think I can do the same thing her dad can do and see you whenever you need me."

Leah leans away from Remy and looks back at me. "Do you really think God will do that for us?"

"Yes, I do," I say with confidence.

Leah looks back at Remy. "Then I won't say goodbye. If Jess thinks it'll happen, then it will. We'll see each other again. I know it."

Remy kisses Leah on the forehead. "Even if He doesn't, I'll find a way to come back to you. I can't live without you in my life."

Leah hugs Remy tightly one more time before letting him go.

"Let me know how things go with that surprise you're planning," my dad says to me.

"Ok," I smile. "I'll call you when I know how it turns out."

My dad smiles back and puts his hand on Remy.

After they phase, Leah lets the full flood of tears she was holding in fall. I wrap her in my arms, and Mama Lynn stands behind her, rubbing her back with a comforting hand.

"I know what we need to do," Mama Lynn says. "It always helps me when I'm upset. Let's go shopping!"

Leah lifts her head from my shoulder and looks at Mama Lynn.

"I don't have any money," Leah says.

"Yes, you do," I tell her. "I've got plenty to go around."

Leah shakes her head. "I couldn't take your money, Jess."

"Yes, you can. My grandfather gave it to me to use as I see fit. And I'm going to give some of it to you. I'll put it in Mama Lynn's name for now, but when you turn eighteen, it's all yours. You won't want for anything for the rest of your life."

"Well, the first thing I think we need to do is get you some new clothes," Mama Lynn says, looking at Leah's threadbare garments. "What do you think, Faison? Outlet mall time?"

Faison nods. "Yes, most definitely."

I leave Leah in the capable hands of Mama Lynn and Faison.

When I get back to my house, it's empty, and I feel extremely lonely all of a sudden.

I decide to take a short nap. It's been a long couple of days, and I don't want to fall asleep on Mason tonight. Wait, scratch that. I do *literally* want to fall asleep on Mason tonight. I just don't want to yawn at an inappropriate moment and break the mood. When I lay down in my bed, I hug his pillow and sniff. It still smells like him, which makes it easier for me to fall asleep.

CHAPTER 9

I wake up to butterfly kisses across my cheek. When I open my eyes, I see Mason lying on his side of the bed. I smile.

"How long have you been here?" I ask, drinking in his presence.

"I just got here," he murmurs, brushing his lips against mine.

"Do you have everything ready for tonight?"

"Anxious, are we?"

"Very."

Mason smiles. "Yes, everything is ready."

I sit up. "Is it five already? I didn't realize I was that tired."

"No, it's four."

I stare at Mason. "You're *early*? I thought you didn't do early."

"I needed to see you."

I lay back down beside Mason. "Just can't do without me, can you?"

"No," he says, gently rolling me onto my back. He looks down at me and caresses the side of my face with the tips of his fingers. "I will never be able to do without you."

"Jess! Jess, I am here with your dress, *mon ami!*"

Mason kisses me quickly on the lips. "You'd better go see what JoJo has for you."

"Do I have to?" I whine. "I was looking forward to a preview of tonight."

Mason smiles and kisses me one more time. "I'll be back. I promise."

He phases and I groan in frustration.

I roll out of bed to go see what JoJo has brought me.

When I get in there, JoJo has Isaiah helping her lay out some very simple-looking summer dresses on the couch.

"Ah, there you are, *ma chérie.* Come, come, and look to see what I have brought for you."

There are five gowns lined up on the couch, but one in particular catches my eye.

"I thought you might like a few choices for tonight," JoJo tells me.

"If you ladies will excuse me," Isaiah says, "I need to attend to something. JoJo, call me when you are ready to leave."

"*Oui; merci*, Isaiah."

After Isaiah leaves, I go to stand in front of the one red dress JoJo brought.

"Do you happen to know where Mason is taking me tonight?"

"*Non*, he just said it would be warm. I don't believe he intends to share you tonight, *ma chérie*. Even Isaiah doesn't know where you are going."

"Did he pick the dresses out, or did you?"

"I did, but," JoJo smiles at me, "he did make one request."

"What was that?"

"That it be easily removable."

I instantly bury my face in my hands and shake my head.

"*Ma chérie*," JoJo said, coming up to me and taking my hands away from my face, forcing me to look at her. "Do not be embarrassed. It is a beautiful thing that you and Mason will share tonight. I envy that you get to share your first time with someone you love so much. There is nothing like it in the world. Do not hide your face and act ashamed. Making love with the man who holds your heart is not something to be embarrassed about."

"I think everyone I know knows what we're going to be doing tonight," I lament.

"So?" JoJo shrugs as if it's no big deal. "I cannot speak for the others, but I am jealous of you right now. I have waited my whole life to find a love like yours and Mason's. Yet, I have not. Though, I can't say I haven't enjoyed the many lovers I've had over the years, but none of them have been the one for me. Cherish the memory of tonight, because your first time will only happen once in your life."

"So you've had a lot of lovers?" I ask, testing the waters as to how experienced JoJo is.

"*Oui*, some good, some bad," she laughs.

"Do you have any advice for me?" I ask, not wanting for JoJo to give me a play by play of her love affairs, but some pointers couldn't hurt.

"The best advice I can give to you is to relax and let things unfold naturally. You will know what to do when the time is right. Wonderful lovemaking is not something you plan like a pattern for a dress. Trust Mason to lead you where you need to go."

I lean down and pick up the red full-length gown.

The dress is made out of silk with a plunging neckline which vees at a twist in the material just underneath the bodice. The back is crisscrossed in an intricate pattern, and there is a zipper on the side that matches Mason's one request of it being easily removable.

"Could you stay and help me get ready?" I ask JoJo, not wanting to be alone while I prepare for my night with Mason. I need the company of a friend.

JoJo puts an arm around my shoulders and squeezes. "I would like nothing more."

We don't go over the top with my makeup and hair. After I shower, we simply blow my hair dry, and JoJo uses the large-barreled curling iron I have to add in some soft curls. I forgo foundation and just use some translucent powder, mascara, and red lipstick. JoJo says Mason told her I wouldn't need shoes, so I don't put any on. It's almost five when she calls Isaiah to come pick her up and take her home.

I'm looking out the window to my backyard, my fingers fiddling with the crystal star on my necklace, when I feel Mason's presence behind me. I turn and see him standing in the middle of my living room, dressed simply in a collarless white linen shirt and black slacks.

We stare at each other, neither of us saying a word, but both feeling an excited tension filling the space between us.

"You look beautiful," he tells me, smiling shyly.

"You look quite handsome yourself," I reply, placing my hand over my heart to ease its sudden ache as I realize just how much I love the man standing in front of me.

Mason walks over, stretching out his arm for me to take his hand.

"Are you ready?" he asks.

I swallow hard and place my hand into his, never feeling more ready for anything in my life.

Before I know it, we're standing on a terrace overlooking a sandy white beach. The sun is setting, and the ocean air smells clean and salty. To the left of me is a small table set for two people to eat dinner, complete with white china, silverware, and a small arrangement of red and white roses. The sound of the ocean waves crashing against the beach does little to ease my nervousness.

"Are you hungry?" Mason asks me, still holding my hand, rubbing the pad of his thumb up and down in a soothing pattern.

I look over at him and shake my head.

"Would you like something to drink? Some wine?"

I shake my head again.

Mason's brows draw together in concern. "Jess, are you all right? If you're not ready, we don't have to do this tonight. We can wait."

I turn to fully face him and lift my hand to gently caress his cheek. Our eyes lock and everything around us seems to fall away, leaving us in a world where only he and I exist.

"No," I say in a low whisper, "I don't want to wait. I don't need to eat. I don't need to drink. All I want and need right now is you."

Mason smiles, pleased by my words. He tugs on my hand, indicating I should follow him through a pair of French doors off the terrace and into a spacious bedroom. The room is filled with vase after vase of red and white roses infusing the space with their sweet scent. White and red candles of various sizes are lit on every surface of the room. Their flickering flames glint off the crystal vases, causing them to sparkle like diamonds. Standing prominently in the middle of the room is a king-size bed with a dark mahogany headboard, white cotton sheets, comforter, and pillows.

Mason gently pulls me against him. As I look up at his handsome face, my heart begins to race, and I have to remind myself to simply breathe.

"If you decide you aren't ready for this at any time," he tells me, gently sweeping a wayward tress off my shoulder and letting the tips of his fingers glide down the inside curve of my neck, "the same rule applies tonight. All you have to do is tell me to stop and I will." Mason looks into my eyes to make sure I hear his next words. "No questions asked. No feelings hurt. Making love is something I desperately want to share with you, but it's not everything. Just being with you is enough for me, Jess."

"I know it's not everything," I tell him. "But I'm ready to share all of me with you. I don't want there to be any barriers between us, Mason, and I feel like this is the last one we have left. I need to have all of you, and I freely give you all of me."

Mason takes a shuddering breath, and I know my words are ones he's been waiting to hear for a while now. I firmly press my lips to his, leaving absolutely no doubt that I want tonight to happen. I know Mason has wanted this moment just as much as I have, and to finally have the long wait almost over seems like a small miracle. I know now that my soul was simply waiting for Mason to enter my life to make me whole. Without his patience, love, and understanding, I never would have been able to overcome the events in my past or even entertain the idea of a future filled with so many wondrous possibilities. His love healed the shattered remains of my heart and showed me that my life is only limited by my imagination.

Mason's lips leave mine to start a maddening, wet trail

of kisses down the side of my neck. The fingers of his right hand easily find the tab of the dress's zipper, and I hear the distinct sound of it being slowly drawn down. I feel one of his index fingers loop around the strap over my right shoulder and gently pull it to the side as his lips glide down and welcome the newly bared flesh. His other hand performs the same task on the left, and the dress slips past my arms in a whisper of silk to the floor, forming a circle of red around me.

I stand in front of Mason, completely naked except for the black stretch lace panties I'm wearing. Not wanting to be the only one unclad, I reach up and begin to slide the ivory colored buttons of his shirt through their holes. I lean in and kiss his now bared chest. My eyes follow the path of my hands as I slowly glide them over his hard, muscled torso and shoulders. As the shirt falls to the floor behind Mason, I look up to see him watching my every move, his breathing shallow.

Mason takes one small step back from me, and I watch as his eyes caress the contours of my body, which are completely exposed to him for the first time.

He reaches out a hand and cups one side of my face, rubbing the pad of his thumb across my cheekbone lovingly.

"My God," he murmurs, a catch in his voice, "you're so beautiful."

In one swift motion, he cradles me in his arms and walks over to the bed, laying me down on the soft sheets and comforter. I watch as he undoes the button and zipper of his slacks and lets them fall to the floor. The full sight of his manhood pressing against the restraining confines of his underwear doesn't cause me any worry. In fact, I crave to know what it will feel like to have him deep inside me.

Mason eases his weight down beside me on the bed, but doesn't gather me close like I thought he would. Instead, he lies on his side with his head propped in one hand and uses his other hand to gently explore my body. The tips of his fingers leave a tingling trail as they move across my chest and into the valley between my breasts. He languidly circles one nipple with his index finger, making it instantly stand erect, and then slowly makes his way over to the other for the same adoration.

I watch him as he performs this slow torture. He seems lost in his private mapping of my body, completely focused on his intimate exploration. Briefly, his eyes gaze into mine as if checking to make sure I'm ok with what he's doing before they return to watch my body's reaction to his gentle caresses. Having accomplished his mission of arousal on my breasts, his fingers glide past them and splay across the tender flesh of my stomach. He allows the tips of his fingers to run along the lacey edge of my panties, causing me to shiver with need for him to continue his exploration past the thin fabric.

Mason looks up at me, silently asking if he has my permission to delve even deeper.

I give a small nod and whisper the word "Yes", beseeching him to continue.

He traces the outline of my panties, from where it begins just below my bellybutton down to where it cuts off on my thigh. His fingers glide down the inside of my thigh, causing me to sigh from the pleasure of his touch there. They then travel teasingly across my aching core, but don't stop until they reach the inside of my other thigh, where they slide up and travel back to where he started, just below my bellybutton. This very simple act sets the deepest part of my body on fire with an aching need that I know only Mason can satisfy.

"Mason," I beg, wrapping the fingers of one hand around the back of his neck, urging him closer because I can't take much more of his teasing exploration without finding some sort of release.

Mason drags his gaze away from my body and looks into my eyes. I instantly see that his are glazed over with a need of his own. He leans down and brushes his lips lightly against mine in a chaste kiss. Our warm breath mingles as he teases my mouth with the tip of his tongue. I bury my fingers in his hair, forcing his head lower to fully bring our mouths together. I feel as though I'll go insane if I can't gain at least this small release.

Mason groans and brings his body in closer to mine. I feel one of his hands brush the skin of my stomach before his fingers slip past the lace of my panties to find my sensitive flesh. When his finger first touches me in that deliciously sensitive spot, I close my eyes as a wave of pleasure wracks my body. I draw in a quick shallow breath, which causes him to break our kiss. I open my eyes and look at him; a look of concern is on his face.

"Are you all right?" Mason asks, breathing heavily, stopping the rhythmic motion of his finger against me.

"Yes, please, Mason, don't stop," I moan, bringing his mouth back down to mine.

I feel him smile against my lips, and the rhythmic back and forth motion of his finger continues, quickly setting my body on fire. His finger briefly leaves that sensitive spot only to find another as he easily slips it inside me, causing me to take another sharp, shuddering breath. I feel Mason begin to lift his head again, but tighten my hold and don't allow his mouth to leave mine, silently answering what I feel sure would have been another question about how I'm doing.

How do I tell him he makes me feel like I'm burning from the inside out and only his touch can relieve the pain? I ache to feel him inside me and finally connect with him, not only emotionally but physically.

While holding his head to mine with one hand, I let the other brush down the muscles of his chest and abdomen until I reach the elastic band of his underwear. Without stopping, only needing, I plunge my hand down further and find the hardness of him.

This time it's Mason who takes a sharp breath against my mouth, but I don't stop to ask questions. Fueled by my deep desire and need for him, I run my hand up and down the length of him, amazed at how hard he is, but at the same time, how soft his skin is there. My hand continues to play, tease, and explore until Mason lets out a deep, almost guttural moan, and gently lifts his lip from mine.

"Jess," Mason says against my mouth, "I don't think I can take much more."

"Then take me," I beg him.

Mason quickly removes my panties, and I watch as he stands to release the full hardness of his erection from his underwear. He returns to the bed and kneels in between my bent legs. He props himself above me with his hands on either side of my head. I feel his manhood press my tender flesh, as if testing whether or not my body is ready to accept him.

"Mason, please," I beg, "I need you. I need to feel all of you."

Slowly, so my body can adjust to the girth of his manhood, Mason pushes into me. I don't feel any pain, just a fullness, like I've finally found a missing part of myself. Once he's fully inside me, he doesn't move, just lets my body get used to him being there. When he does begin to move his hips, I feel a spark of electricity that emanates from our joining and sets every nerve ending in my body on fire. Mason stokes the fire he's created with every thrust of his hips until I scream out his name, reaching the cliff of bliss and free-falling into oblivion.

CHAPTER 10

Mason pulls the comforter over us afterwards. I lay my head on his chest and listen to the slowing beat of his heart. I snuggle into him, basking in the afterglow of our first time making love. He holds me, and I hear him sigh contentedly.

"Thank you," I tell him.

"For what exactly?"

"For making me wait until we were back home. If I live to be a hundred, I will never forget this moment."

Mason kisses the top of my head. "Neither will I, Jess."

I rest my chin on Mason's chest and look at his face. "Do you age at all?" I ask.

"No, not as a Watcher."

"So you're immortal?"

"For now."

I feel my forehead crease in confusion. "What do you mean by 'for now'?"

"Do you remember what I said in the alternate universe? About Brand being human here in ours?" Mason asks.

"Yes."

"After we seal the Tear," Mason says, hesitating before he finishes his statement, like he's not sure how I'm going to take what he has to say, "I'll ask God to make me human too so we can live a normal life together."

I feel tears of joy sting my eyes and don't try to stop them from falling.

"You would do that for me?" I ask. "You would give up what you are... for me?"

"I would do anything on this Earth for you, Jess. You need to know that. I don't need super strength or instant teleportation. I don't need any of it if I have you."

I lean up and press my lips to Mason's, my tears making the kiss salty.

"I love you," I tell him.

"I love you too."

We lie in each other's arms for a while longer until hunger for food reminds me I need to eat.

Mason gets out of bed, and I watch him as he walks naked over to the entrance of a walk-in closet. He turns the light on in the closet and is out of my sight for a moment. When he returns, he's wearing a pair of silky black pajama bottoms and holding something made of white silk in his left hand.

I sigh in utter and complete disappointment. "And here I thought I would have a naked Mason at my beck and call for the rest of the night."

Mason smiles. "I'm fine with that when we're inside the house, but I thought you might like to eat outside, like I had planned to do before you seduced me."

I sit up in bed and shrug. "I just knew I didn't want food then. Wasn't it you who said a girl with a healthy appetite usually has a healthy appetite for other things as well?"

"I remember saying something like that."

"Well, I guess you were right."

Mason hands me what he has in his hands, and I see it's a nightgown with a lacy plunging neckline.

"I bought it for you to wear around the house. I hope you like it."

I kneel up on the bed and make my way to the edge of it, towards Mason whose eyes are on my body, not my face. I rest my arms across his shoulders and press my breasts against his chest.

"Didn't you say something about having good stamina?" I ask, feeling him stir against my legs through his pants.

"I thought you were hungry," Mason says, his voice husky.

"After," I say, kissing the side of his neck. "I think I need you more than I need food right now."

Mason tosses the nightgown on the floor and neither of us thinks about clothes or food again for a long, long time.

Eventually, our bodies do require food, especially with all the calories we're burning up. I sit out on the terrace at the table while Mason serves me the meal he prepared.

"It's a little cold," he says of the poached salmon and tarragon potatoes.

"I could probably eat it even if it were raw I'm so hungry," I laugh, fork at the ready.

I look around the terrace and ocean view while I nibble on a piece of potato.

"Whose house is this anyway?"

"Mine."

I look at Mason. "Just how many mansions do you own?"

Mason smiles shyly. "A few."

"Are we going to make love in all of them?" I ask coyly.

Mason almost chokes on the potato in his mouth. He clears his throat.

"If you would like to, I'm pretty sure I can arrange that."

"Hmm," I say, mulling the idea over in my mind. "I most definitely think that's what I want. Would that allow us to make love on every continent?"

"All except Antarctica. But I could always arrange something there if you want."

"No, too cold," I say, taking a bite of my salmon.

"I feel confident I could find ways to keep you warm,"

Mason says suggestively, with a roguish grin and the promise of sexual delights in his eyes.

"I'll get back to you on that," I tell him, feeling myself blush under his gaze.

"Are you seriously blushing?" he asks. "After the things we just did in my bed?"

"I'm still a little new to all this, you know," I say in my own defense.

"You're a fast learner," he replies, smiling appreciatively at me.

"You need to stop smiling at me," I say. "I really do need to eat."

Mason turns his smile into a scowl and I laugh.

"You are such a goof," I tell him, turning to my plate so I can concentrate on eating as fast as I can without choking.

When we get through with our meal, Mason takes me down to the kitchen with him. I sit on one of the wooden stools at the large kitchen island while he cleans the dishes.

"So, I have a question," I say.

Mason closes the door on the dishwasher and turns to face me, leaning his back against the counter with his arms folded in front of him.

"Yes?" he asks, looking intrigued to hear what I'm about to ask.

"That text you sent, about the indoors or outdoors, where exactly outdoors did you have in mind?"

A slow smile spreads Mason's lips. "And why do you ask?"

I roll my eyes. "You know why."

"Maybe," he hedges. "But I want you to tell me."

"Why?"

"Because I want to hear you say it."

"Why?"

Mason phases over to me, standing beside me. I turn to face him and he spreads my legs so he can stand in between them.

"Tell me," he murmurs, leaning down and kissing the side of my neck.

I feel my pulse quicken and a now-familiar warmth spreads within the depths of my body.

"Because I want to make love to you in as many different places as we can," I confess as his lips travel up to that secret spot behind my ear that only he knows exists.

"Now, was that so hard to say?" he whispers in my ear, a tease in his voice.

"No," I sigh, "not hard at all."

Mason slides his hands up my thighs, scrunching the length of my nightgown up to my hips. He easily lifts me off the stool, placing his hands under my thighs so my legs naturally wrap around his waist. I place my arms around his neck for balance as he phases us.

The light of the full moon casts a silvery glow against the leaves of the forest we stand in. The sound of flowing water draws my attention, and I turn my head to find a small waterfall behind me. Mason kneels down on the dewy grass beside the small pool of water in the glade. He keeps me perched on his thighs so I don't get wet, but I have another idea.

I scramble off his lap and stand up. When I look back down at him, he looks completely and adorably confused.

"I need to give you something," I tell him, which makes him look even more puzzled. "Wait here."

I walk over to the waterfall and find a small rocky ledge that runs behind it. Once I'm shielded by the wall of water, I take off my nightgown and stand under the spray until my hair is soaking wet, and I feel sure my makeup is washed off. I leave my nightgown where it lay against the rocks and walk out from behind the falls to give Mason his gift.

He's standing now and watches me with parted lips as I emerge from behind the fall of water, completely naked.

As I walk up to him I say, "Is this how you pictured me?"

I hope to remind him about his comment just that afternoon and the night of my fake date with Chandler. He said then that he wanted to see me completely naked, without makeup, and my hair freshly washed.

"No," he says huskily, with a small shake of his head, "I never could have imagined you looking this beautiful."

He gathers me against him and lays claim to my lips in a searing kiss. Mason lies on the ground, bringing me with him in the circle of his arms, positioning me to lie on top of him. I drink in the sweetness of his lips, unable to get enough, and desperately wanting more. I feel his arousal stir between my legs. I reach down with one hand to push the top of his silk pajama bottoms down far enough to release him. Mason groans his pleasure as I wrap my fingers around him and guide him into me. I soon realize I'm in complete control of how quickly my body envelops him. I slowly ease myself down his shaft and feel Mason tremble underneath me as I instinctively begin to move my hips, gliding my body in a steady, smooth dance against him.

Unable to take it anymore, Mason rolls me onto my back and pushes into me so hard and fast I feel as though I might split in two, but I welcome the pleasurable pain. I arch my back, pushing him even deeper into me until my world explodes into a million glittering pieces.

I feel Mason slow his movement inside me as I fall back to Earth and begin the slow process of coming back my senses.

I open my eyes and see Mason gazing down at me with so much love and tenderness my heart immediately begins to ache. My heart, my mind, my soul knows there will never be anyone who can make me feel as loved as he does.

He leans down and gently kisses my lips.

"I like watching you lose yourself with me," he murmurs. "I like knowing I can shatter your world and help you pick up the pieces afterwards, just to shatter them all over again."

Mason begins to move faster within me.

"I hope you like your world in pieces, Jess, because I promise to break it quite often tonight," he groans, gathering me in his arms.

And Mason always keeps his promises…

When Mason phases us back to his home, we clean off together in his large shower. He treats me like a fragile doll as he insists on washing my body and shampooing my hair for me. It's an intimate act that only lovers share. Afterwards, he dries me off, dressing me in one of his white V-neck T-shirts because I left the nightgown behind, and tucks me into bed with him. As I lay in the warm fold of Mason's arms, I feel my body completely relax against him. No one has ever made me feel so cherished and completely loved. It's a feeling I know the love of my life will always make me feel.

When I wake up the next morning, the back of me spooned against Mason, I feel one of his hands rub up and down the curve of my hip. I can feel a certain part of Mason is also fully awake and pressing firmly against me.

I turn to face him and instantly feel my heart ache at the sight of him, tousled hair and hooded blue eyes.

"Good morning," I say.

He smiles. "Good morning."

I lift the sheet we're under and look down between us.

"Good morning to you too."

When I look back up at Mason, his eyes are wide open in shock.

"What?" I say innocently. "He worked hard last night. He deserves a good morning too."

Mason buries his face in his pillow and shakes his head, but I feel him begin to chuckle. When he returns his gaze to meet mine, he looks adorably amused. He pulls me firmly against him.

"Well, in that case, he would like to say good morning to you personally."

"I have no problem with that," I say unequivocally. "But, would you mind if I brush my teeth first?"

Mason throws the cover off both of us and takes my hand as he leads me to the bathroom. Of course, Mason prepared for all my needs, and already has a brush and toothpaste for me. There is a double sink so we can brush our teeth at the same time. After we brush our teeth, I sit up on top of the marble counter in between the sinks and look over at Mason.

I pop my bare buttocks up and down on the counter.

"Seems sturdy enough," I tell him. "Is it the right height?"

Mason smiles and walks over to stand in between my legs. I soon learn it is exactly the right height.

Afterwards, Mason dresses simply in a pair of faded jeans and a black T-shirt. I realize it's the first time I've seen him dressed so casually. Since I only have the red dress I wore, albeit briefly, to Mason's beach home, he phases me back to my house to put on some of my own clothes.

Fortunately, he phases us directly into my bedroom.

I pull him to me. "We really should make love in my bed too. I mean, it's only fair to christen her as well. I wouldn't want her to feel left out."

Mason shakes his head at me. "If I'm incorrigible, *you* are insatiable."

"Weren't you the one who bragged about having great stamina?" I ask. "Put your money where your mouth is, buster."

"Hmm," Mason begins to nuzzle the side of my neck, "I have a few places I would like to put my mouth on you."

"Oh really, Mr. Collier? Would you like to perform a little demonstration?"

"Yes, I would, Agent Riley." He lightly pushes me down on the bed and kneels on the floor between my legs. "I most certainly would."

After we christen my bed, Mason goes into the kitchen to make us breakfast, and I get dressed. I know we have things we need to do today, but all I honestly want to do is play with Mason. I giggle at the thought. It makes me sound like Mason's my favorite new toy... not a bad analogy, actually.

My happy mood is soon tarnished by the sound of a rocking chair moving on my front porch. I grab my coat and slip on some tennis shoes to talk to my visitor.

"Going to go talk to Lucifer on the porch," I yell to Mason on my way towards the front door.

I hear a pan drop, and Mason phases to stand in front of the door, blocking my way.

"You say that like it's the most natural thing in the world to be doing," Mason says, a confused look on his face.

I shrug. "I guess it is… for me." I lean up and kiss him. "Don't worry. He won't hurt me."

Reluctantly, Mason steps away from the door.

I walk out onto the porch and shiver slightly from the cold. I turn up the hood on my coat.

Lucifer sits in his favorite rocking chair, dressed in only a blue jersey tee with a Gucci crest on the front, and a pair of jeans and tennis shoes.

"Casual day?" I ask.

Lucifer shrugs.

"Aren't you cold?" I ask him. I know it can only be about thirty degrees outside.

"You *do* know where I live, right?" Lucifer asks.

"Oh," I say, indeed remembering, "I didn't know if it was actually hot there. I thought it might just be a metaphor."

"The torturing of souls produces a lot of heat," Lucifer explains. "Exothermic reactions and all. Speaking of which," Lucifer eyes me curiously, "the last time I was there, I noticed one soul in particular was missing."

"I had God put Uncle Dan in the Void for me," I tell Lucifer. "I didn't want to owe you any favors."

"Strange that He should do such a thing for you so easily. He's never interfered with any of the souls once they reached my domain."

Stunned doesn't exactly describe the way I feel hearing Lucifer's words.

"In the whole history of time," I say slowly, making sure

Lucifer understands my question, "He's never once moved a soul out of Hell?"

"No."

I pause to gather my thoughts before asking, "Why did He do it for me?"

"You seem to have that effect on people," Lucifer grumbles. "Doing things for you that goes against our grain seems like a natural occurrence."

"Then stop what you're trying to do," I tell him, knowing it's pointless but needing to beg for it anyway. "Whatever it is can't be good for your soul."

"Do you think I have a soul left to care about?" he scoffs.

"Everyone does. You were one of your father's favorite sons. Don't you yearn to go back to Heaven one day?"

Lucifer averts his gaze from me and looks out at the neighborhood I live in, but I know he isn't really seeing anything. He's lost in his own thoughts.

"He would never allow me back there," Lucifer whispers. "I've done too many horrible things here. He could never forgive me."

"I think you're wrong," I tell him. "I think He wants to forgive you more than anything, but you have to ask for it and truly mean it. If He can forgive humans for any sin when they are truly repentant, why wouldn't He do the same thing for you?"

"You see things too simply."

"And you make things too complicated."

Lucifer looks back over at me.

"Speaking of complicated. I've been sitting out here for half an hour," he reveals, "but you seemed otherwise occupied at the time of my arrival."

I feel my cheeks flush hotly. "And how exactly would you know that?"

"The walls aren't that thick," Lucifer tells me, grinning wickedly. "You are rather vocal during sex, Jessica. If I were you, I might think about investing in more insulation."

I tug the hood of my coat a little lower to hide from Lucifer's laughing eyes.

"I'll take it under advisement," I mumble.

Lucifer laughs and stands up.

"I should be going now. Mischievous plans to devise and all. I'll see you soon, Jessica."

He phases and I feel like I want to melt into the Earth.

CHAPTER 11

I decide not to tell Mason about Lucifer's voyeurism. They have a tenuous relationship as it is. I didn't want to cause even more tension.

While we eat our breakfast at my kitchen table, I ask Mason, "Do you know what Leah's talisman is?"

"I have an idea about what it is," he tells me. "Though, it might be tricky to get."

"Why?"

"I believe it's in the hands of a djinn."

"A what?" I ask, completely confused.

"Like a genie from a bottle. A creature that can make your wishes come true."

"They really exist?" I ask.

"In a way. They don't actually live in a bottle, though. The djinn fell to Earth during the fall, with Lucifer, because they fought on his side. They trick people into making wishes."

"Why would they have to trick someone? Don't most people just naturally like to wish for free stuff?"

"A djinn's wish never comes free. There's always a price."

"Why do you think a djinn has Leah's talisman?"

"Because of Leah's power. It's the power a great sorceress would have, and I only know of one item still around that used to belong to a sorcerer."

"Who was the sorcerer?"

"Balaam."

"Never heard of him."

"A king by the name of Balak went to Balaam when Moses was leading the Israelites into Canaan. He wanted Balaam to curse them, but after a visit from God, Balaam refused the King's request. Still, Balaam lusted after money and did lead some of the Israelites astray by showing them how to worship idols. The Israelites eventually killed him."

"So what object did he have that you think Leah will need?"

"Balaam's staff."

"Do you know the djinn who has it?"

"Yes. His name is Faust."

"Why does he have it?"

"Where do you think Balaam's power came from? He made a deal with Faust to become a great sorcerer. If the staff still exists, Faust will have it."

"Do you know where this Faust is?"

"Yes. He's been with the same patron for over fifteen years now. You've probably heard of him, Heath Knowles. I think he writes books."

"Yeah, Faison and I used to sneak-read them when we were kids."

"Oh, did you now?" Mason says with a lop-sided grin. "Doesn't he write erotic romance novels?"

"We were teenagers," I defend. "We were curious. Though, nothing in those books prepared me for the real thing."

"And do you prefer the real thing to fantasy?"

I lift an eyebrow at Mason. "What do you think?"

Mason chuckles. "I think you enjoy the real thing very much."

"And you would be right," I admit freely, seeing no reason to pussyfoot around the issue.

Mason stands and walks over to me, pulling me from my chair and into his arms.

"I wish we could just spend the rest of the day in bed," he tells me, resting his forehead against mine.

I close my eyes and breathe him in. "Me too. Why can't we again?"

"Oh, you know, the world needs saving," Mason shrugs nonchalantly.

I sigh. "Once the world is safe, I don't intend to let you out of whatever bed we're in for at least a week."

Mason smiles and lifts his head from mine to look down at me.

"I was thinking more like a month," he confides.

I smile. "I can live with that."

I ask Mason to bring Chandler and JoJo to my house while I go get Leah from Mama Lynn's. With four of us together now, and me without any emotional baggage, I have high hopes we can locate the fifth vessel in record time.

But before I go to Mama Lynn's, I grab a piece of notebook paper and make a quick sketch on it. I walk over to George's house and knock on his door.

When he opens it, I find him dressed in khakis and a red flannel shirt.

"Jess!" he says, giving me a bear hug. "What brings you to my door this early in the morning?"

I hand George my drawing. "You still have that jigsaw, right?"

"Yes," George says, looking down at the paper in his hands. "You want me to make this for you?"

I nod. "Yes."

"Looks simple enough. Just the four pieces?"

"Yeah. When do you think you can have it done for me?"

"I can knock this out for you this afternoon."

"Great," I smile, unable to contain my excitement.

"Mind me asking you what it's for?"

I tell George because I feel sure I will need his help in my surprise for Mason.

"You're the first person I've told, so don't say anything to Faison or Mama Lynn until I get a chance to tell them."

"Ok, Jess," George says. "My lips are sealed. You just let me know when you need my help with things."

I leave George's house and go over to Mama Lynn's. Faison opens the door, and I feel like I'm looking at the old Faison again. Her hair is fixed, makeup on, and there's even a real smile on her face.

She grabs my arm and pulls me inside the house.

"I can't believe you had sex last night and didn't tell me it was going to happen," she laments.

I quickly scan the area to make sure Leah is nowhere around.

"I really couldn't find the right time to tell you, Fai."

"Well?" Faison asks looking at me expectantly. "How was it?"

I feel my eyes begin to tear up.

"Oh God," she says, "was he that bad? I thought for sure since he was so old he would have had enough practice by now to be good at it."

"No, Fai," I say, wiping at my tears. "It was that good. It was everything I could have hoped for and more."

A slow grin stretches Faison's lips. "Good. I'm glad he made it so special for you."

"You look really good," I tell her.

Faison sighs. "I just realized John Austin wouldn't want me to mourn him, especially if his death was destined to be. His life wasn't for nothing because we'll always remember him. Besides, Leah needs me. I can't be a big sister to her if all I do is mope around the house and cry my eyes out all the time. I need to set a better example for her. She's been through so much in her short life. She doesn't need more baggage, and that's what I would be. So, I'm pulling myself together, and that's that."

I hug Faison, glad to have my sister back.

I see Leah bound down the steps from the second floor, and almost don't recognize her. She has a new haircut that feathers the hair around her face, accentuating its exotic beauty. Her clothes are brand new and more in line with someone her age. She has a little bit of makeup on but not enough to be overpowering.

"Hey, Jess," she says, coming to stand with me and Faison.

"Leah, you look beautiful. I love the hair!"

Leah looks bashful. "Thanks. Faison suggested it."

"It looks great," I reassure her.

Faison puts an arm around Leah's shoulders. "Yep, we'll have those boys at school eating out of the palm of your hand in no time at all."

"School?" Leah asks.

"Uh, yeah," Faison says. "You know, where you learn things."

Leah looks at me with panic in her eyes. "I've never been to school."

"Oh," Faison looks at me. "What do you think we should do?"

"Did Remy teach you things when you were moving around?"

"I know how to read and basic math," Leah says. "But other than that…"

"I'll talk to Mason. We might just get you a tutor or something. Don't worry. We'll figure it out."

"I would like to go to school one day," Leah says. "I've never been around a lot of other kids my age."

"Well, let's take it one step at a time," I tell her. "We need to get you up to speed first, especially on the history of *this* Earth. It's a lot different from the one you know."

Leah nods. "Ok, Jess."

"I came over to get you," I tell Leah. "I think we should try to connect with the fifth vessel. Since there are four of us now, I'm hoping it won't take very long to find the person."

"When do you think you'll be done?" Faison asks. "I thought I would take Leah to the mall so we can get some stuff to decorate her room with."

"I'm not sure how long we'll be, but I wouldn't think more than an hour or two."

Faison's face brightens. "Cool! We can get some lunch while we're out then."

As Leah and I walk to my house, I decide to see how she feels about being Faison's new pet project.

"She needs me," Leah says, mirroring Faison's words. "We talked a lot last night about our lives. Her heart's still broken over John Austin, but helping me seems to help her push through the pain."

"So you don't mind all the attention?"

"No, because I need her too," Leah admits. "I think together we can get through our sadness and come out ok."

I take Leah's hand in mine and squeeze it, wanting her to know Faison isn't the only one she can rely on.

When we get to my house, I encounter a strange scene. Both Chandler and JoJo seem to be having conversations with themselves in my living room. It doesn't take me long to realize what they're actually doing: speaking with their archangels. It instantly makes me feel guilty. I haven't spoken with Michael since my flying lesson.

"What are they doing?" Leah asks in a low voice out the side of her mouth, apparently thinking Chandler and JoJo have completely lost their minds.

"Talking to their archangels. Don't worry. They're not crazy."

When Chandler and JoJo see us, they walk over and give us hugs.

"And how was your evening?" Chandler asks me with a sly grin.

I see Mason step out from the kitchen and lean against the opening, obviously interested in the answer as well.

"It was great," I tell him and JoJo, not really wanting to go into any details in front of Leah. "But enough about me; let's get to work."

When I pass Mason, he's smiling at me.

"Be right with you guys," I say, taking a detour and

grabbing Mason by the arm, pushing him up against the other side of the wall in the kitchen.

"Am I in trouble again?" he asks, happiness setting his eyes on fire.

"What am I going to do with you," I say, shaking my head at him. "You just seem determined to keep smiling at me."

His smile grows wider as he gathers me up in his arms.

"I can think of a few things you can do with me," he murmurs for my ears only.

I feel a hunger build deep within my body and spread like wildfire.

I push away from Mason, my heart beating so fast I'm having trouble catching my breath.

"I need you to build me a fire," I tell him.

He roughly pulls me back to him. "I thought I was doing that already."

I push away again. "That particular fire is lit and burning fiercely," I tell him, taking a deep breath to get my mind back on track. "We need to locate the fifth vessel, and I need my fire."

Mason pouts, which is like throwing gas on the inferno already burning every inch of my body.

I lean out and tell the group, "Mason and I need to go get some matches to make the fire. We'll be right back."

I look back to Mason. "Beach house. Now."

He doesn't argue. Time is of the essence.

When we get there, we fall on the bed and into each

other. I'm not sure you can call what we did making love. But it was fierce, fast, and extremely satisfying.

Mason lies on top of me afterwards, attempting to catch his breath. He doesn't withdraw from me immediately, and I revel in the feel of him still inside me, connecting us.

He takes a deep breath, and I feel his body shudder against mine.

"Please, don't ever leave me," he says. The sadness I hear in his voice literally breaks my heart.

I tighten my arms around him. "Where did that come from? Why would you even think about that right now?"

Mason lifts up and looks down at me. I see his eyes are wet with unshed tears.

"Because I can't live without you. Just the thought of a life without you in it scares me."

"I'm never leaving you," I promise him, putting every ounce of conviction I can in my words. "I think I've told you this before."

He's quiet for a moment, and I can tell he's debating whether or not to say what's really on his mind.

Finally he asks, "Then, why don't you want to marry me?"

I feel caught off guard by the question.

"It's not because I want to leave the door open so I can leave you sometime down the road. Is that what you think?"

Mason doesn't answer me, and I know that's exactly what he's thinking.

"I'm never leaving you," I say to him again. "*Never.*"

Mason nods, but not convincingly. I can still see the hurt in his eyes, and want nothing more than to wipe it away.

I pull his face down to mine and kiss his lips, wanting him to feel through my touch just how much he means to me. How much I need him, too.

Mason soon becomes more fervent and demanding of the kiss, as if wanting to leave his brand on me, proving to the world that I'm his, even if I don't have a ring on my finger symbolizing a formal commitment. I feel him grow large inside me again, filling me, making me feel whole as he takes possession of me once more.

CHAPTER 12

As we're readjusting our clothes before phasing back to my house, I ask, "Could you give me Malcolm's number?"

Mason zips up his pants. "Why would you need to contact him?"

"I need to ask him to do something for me."

Mason looks curious now. I feel like banging my head against something. I should have just called Isaiah and gotten Malcolm's number from him.

"Can I ask what this something is?" Mason says.

"No, you may not," I say matter-of-factly. "It's a surprise. If I told you, then it wouldn't be a surprise anymore."

"What on Earth could Malcolm help you with?"

"You keep asking the same question, just in a different

way," I tell him, becoming exasperated. "Are you going to give me his number or not?"

"I'll text it to you."

It's almost like I can see the gears of Mason's mind going into overdrive, trying to figure out what I'm up to. I feel confident he won't guess but the less I say, the better.

"I'll be right back," Mason says, phasing somewhere and phasing back a few seconds later. He's holding a box of kitchen matches in his hands.

I laugh. "Good memory. I completely forget."

Mason grins. "I'm not sure they will believe it took thirty minutes to get a box of matches, but it would definitely look suspicious if we didn't return with them at all."

"I'm pretty sure Chandler and JoJo know what we've been doing. It's Leah's impressionable young mind I'm more concerned about."

Mason brings me into his arms. "She'll see how much we love each other. That's the most important thing. It's the best example we could set for her, to wait until you find someone you love to share yourself with."

Mason phases us back to the kitchen in my house. When I walk into the living room, there's already a fire blazing in the hearth. Chandler is playing a happy tune on his pipe, and JoJo is teaching Leah how to dance, something I feel sure is a foreign concept to her. Laughter fills my home, and I feel truly blessed to have the people in it be my friends.

When Chandler sees us, he grins.

"You know, we have our own little fire-starter," he reminds me, tilting his head towards Leah.

"Oh, yeah, I totally forgot about that," I say, clearing my throat nervously.

Leah giggles. I'm pretty positive she didn't buy the matches story either.

"Ok, then," I say, ignoring JoJo's questioning eyes. "Let's see if we can find the fifth vessel together."

We sit in a circle in front of the fire. I instruct Leah as to what to do, and we all close our eyes and try to connect with our next archangel.

It's almost instantaneous. The picture of the fifth vessel appears in my mind like I'm watching a movie in my head. It's even clearer than when we saw Leah. I feel like I can touch him if I just stretch out my hand.

He looks to be in his mid-forties and of Middle Eastern origin, with his dark olive skin and short black hair. He's dressed in a white lab coat with a white T-shirt underneath emblazoned with a symbol of a running man marked out in red horizontal lines. Underneath the symbol are the words 'Doctors Without Borders'. He's bent over a small examination table, ministering to a black child who looks severely malnourished. I hear the sound of gunshots being fired. The man looks up and stands straight, holding his hands in the air like he's being robbed. The vision ends.

We all open our eyes and stare at one another.

"Crap," I say, standing up and running to the kitchen.

I tell Mason what we saw, and he immediately gets on the phone with Nick.

"Nick says he'll call us back after he speaks with his contacts."

I instantly feel guilty. If Mason and I hadn't wasted 30 minutes having sex, maybe I could have gotten to the fifth vessel before those gunshots were fired.

"Don't," Mason says to me.

I look up at him and can see in his eyes that he knows exactly what I'm thinking.

"It's true," I say. "If we hadn't...."

"There's no guarantee we would have located him in time," Mason says. "What if you had seen him 30 minutes ago? You wouldn't have seen that he and the other people he's with are in danger. Do you think he would have appreciated us taking him away before the trouble started, or do you think he would rather have been there so we know to send help?"

I hadn't thought about it like that. A person who dedicated his life to such an organization was someone who wanted to help as many people as he could. Mason was right. If we hadn't delayed our vision by 30 minutes, we wouldn't have known the clinic the fifth vessel worked at was in trouble. There were probably a lot of sick people there and other doctors there who needed help too.

For almost two hours, we wait for word of what's happening. Faison comes to get Leah, even though she says she wants to remain with us. I tell her it's useless and that she should go out and have some fun like a normal teenager. Faison tempts her by saying she'll take her to the latest number one movie about a vampire love affair. Having never seen a movie, Leah jumps at the chance.

In the middle of the third hour, Mason finally gets a call back from Nick.

"And you're sure he's all right?" I hear Mason say. He looks at me and nods.

I breathe a sigh of relief. Our fifth vessel is still alive.

"Really?" Mason grins at me. "So they were able to save everyone there? Good to know, Nick. I'll pass the information along." Mason pauses as he listens to Nick. "Ok, sounds good. I'll let them know."

Mason ends the call and looks at the three of us as we anxiously wait to hear what happened.

"The local militia was able to take out the gang that tried to steal the medicine from the clinic. Your vision gave them a heads up of what was going on, and saved a lot of lives, from what Nick told me."

Mason winks at me as a little 'I told you so'. Honestly, I'm just relieved our fifth vessel is alive.

"When will we be able to meet him?" Chandler asks.

"Nick said Isaiah was there speaking with him now. He'll let me know when Rafe is ready to come meet you."

"That's his name?" I ask.

"Yes, Rafe Anany."

"Where is he?" JoJo asks. "Where was that place that we saw him?"

"His clinic is in Sierra Leone. There are gangs there all the time, stealing from the free clinics and selling the medicine on the black market. So your vision not only saved the lives of the people there, it also saved the lives of all the people the medicine will eventually help."

JoJo and Chandler ask Mason to take them back to their homes since we have to wait anyway. They *do* have lives outside of our archangel duties, after all. JoJo says she is in the midst of preparing to show her line of clothing during New York Fashion Week, which is in a couple of weeks. Chandler is preparing for a few concert dates, including his Valentine's Day concert in Denver.

"You've gotta be there," he tells me. "I can't have all my teenage fans think I would ditch my girlfriend on Valentine's Day."

I look over at Mason, because I have no idea if he has anything planned for our first Valentine's Day together.

Mason shrugs. "I'm ok with that as long as I can be there with you."

"I've got no problem with you coming," Chandler says. "As long as you guys don't, uh, you know get caught doing something you shouldn't be doing. You know, no going for 'matches'." Chandler says, making air quotes.

"Well, sometimes you just need 'matches'," I say in our defense.

"Could you at least wait until after the concert to get your 'matches'?" Chandler asks. "Otherwise, it'll look suspicious."

"Just how much longer does Jess have to play this game with you?" Mason asks, not even attempting to hide his irritation. "Isn't it about time for a guy like you to have some sort of break-up by now?"

Chandler shrugs, not in the least bit offended by Mason's words. "It's a good cover with everyone. If someone in my usual entourage wants to know where I am, I just tell them I'm spending time with Jess. Maybe after everything is over, we can have a public break-up."

Mason sighs, and I know he isn't pleased.

I take advantage of Mason dropping JoJo and Chandler off, and call the number he gave me for Malcolm.

"Hello?" Malcolm answers his phone. I feel sure he's wondering who's calling him from an unlisted number.

"Malcolm, it's Jess."

"Ahh," Malcolm is silent for a moment. "I heard you met my alter ego in the alternate Earth you traveled to."

"Who told you?"

"Mason and I discussed it yesterday while I was helping him prepare his beach house for your…date. Have fun last night?" Malcolm asks, a teasing smile in his voice.

Who *didn't* know Mason and I had sex last night?

"It was fine," I answer, seeing no reason to expound on my private time with Mason. "Listen, aren't you like an architect or something?"

"Yes," Malcolm answers cautiously.

"Then I need your help."

I proceed to tell Malcolm exactly what I need built.

"Do you think you can do that in my backyard?"

"What's the time frame?"

"ASAP."

"Hmm, let me speak with a few of my fellow Watchers. If they have time to help, we can have it built by tomorrow afternoon."

"So, it would be ready for tomorrow night?" I ask, becoming excited that all the pieces were falling into place so easily.

"Yes, I can promise you it will be ready by then. Leave the details to me. Do you have people lined up to help you?"

"Yes, I think so. I just have to ask, but I know they'll help."

"Then I suggest you find a way to keep Mason away from your home tomorrow. We'll be there bright and early."

"Ok, thank you, Malcolm. I owe you one."

"Really?" Malcolm says, sounding intrigued by the possibility of me owing him a favor. "I will keep that in mind, Jess."

Just as I get off the phone with Malcolm, Mason phases into my living room.

"I just got a call from Jonathan," Mason tells me as he walks towards me, causing my heart to flutter by such a simple action. "He and Angela want to know if we can come over and have dinner with them. It would be lunch for us, but dinner time in London."

"Sure. Will I get a chance to meet your grandchildren this time?"

Mason smiles and I can tell he takes a lot of pride in them. "They should be there. The little ones at least. I'm not sure about the twins."

"Twins?"

"Yes, Brianna and Bale. They were Angela and Jonathan's first-born. They're fourteen. Then there's Kyle, who is nine, and Emma, who just turned five right before I met you."

"You have four grandchildren?" I ask, completely flabbergasted.

"Yes," Mason says. "You did say I was an old man, didn't you?"

I wrap my arms around Mason's waist. "Not so old, but I did just realize we'll be the quintessential backwards family when we have our children."

Mason smiles at my mention of having children with him.

"How so?" he asks.

"Our children will be the aunts and uncles of your grandchildren, but the ages will be completely reversed from normal."

Mason caresses the side of my face. "How many children do you see us having?"

"Three sounds like a good number," I say. "What do you think?"

"Three sounds perfect," he says with a smile that isn't all the way happy.

"What's wrong?"

"Nothing."

I know what's wrong but can't exactly fix the problem just yet.

"Should we get going?" I ask. "I don't want them to think we're getting 'matches'."

Mason chuckles. "Is that what we're going to be calling it from now on?"

"It'll be our secret code word," I say. "If I'm in desperate need of matches when we're around other people, I'll let you know."

Mason leans down and leaves a lingering kiss on my lips.

"Please do," he murmurs.

Mason phases us into a cacophony of sound.

"I swear to God, Bale," a feisty little brunette shouts to a handsome blond boy her age, "if you don't give me that phone I'm going to kill you!"

Bale is jogging backwards in the living room to avoid his sister's clutches.

"I'm just texting him what you would, Bree. That you love him and can't wait to see him at school tomorrow."

"Bale," Mason says sharply, causing the boy to come to a complete stop and immediately wipe the smile off his face.

Brianna sees her chance and snatches the phone out of her brother's hands.

"Thanks, Grandpa," Brianna says, stuffing the phone in the back pocket of her jeans.

Brianna walks over to Mason and gives him a big hug.

Bale comes over to stand by his sister. They both end up staring at me.

Yeah… a little awkward. I begin to wonder if they know we had sex last night, too, from the way they're both looking at me.

"Bree, Bale, I would like you both to meet Jess."

Bale holds out his hand to me, and I shake it. Bree does the same.

"It's nice to finally meet you," Bree tells me with a genuinely happy smile.

"Yeah," Bale says, a slow appreciative grin appearing on his face as he looks me up and down. "Now I see why Grandpa's been acting so distracted when he comes over lately."

Bree hits her brother on the arm. "Stop leering at her, you git. She's Grandpa's girlfriend."

Bale looks over at Mason, and the smile quickly vanishes from his face.

Bale shrugs. "Well, she *is* beautiful, Grandpa. Surely you can't fault me for appreciating that."

Mason sighs. "No, I suppose I can't. But keep your eyes on her face."

Bale blushes.

Bree laughs. "Ha!"

Angela and Jonathan walk into the room, with their other two children in tow.

Jonathan comes up to me and gives me a peck on the cheek. "It's so good to see you again, Jess. We've been meaning to have the two of you over for ages, but there never seemed to be a good time until now."

I feel a tug on my shirt and look down to find little Emma standing there, holding a small, pink, slightly-wilted flower in her hand. I'm not sure what it is, but she holds it up for me to take.

"I picked this for you," Emma says shyly.

I kneel down and take the flower from her little outstretched hand.

"It's beautiful," I tell her, holding the flower to my nose and taking a whiff. "And it smells nice too."

Emma giggles and runs over to stand by her mother's legs.

"She's been waiting all day to give you that," Angela tells me.

I stand back up.

Kyle comes up to me with no shyness at all and holds out his hand to me.

"I'm Kyle," he says.

I shake his hand. "I'm Jess. It's a pleasure to meet you, Kyle."

Kyle goes to stand by his father and Jonathan puts a hand on his shoulder, smiling down with pride.

"Supper is prepared. Father is just setting the table to meet his requirements," Angela says, reminding me of Allan's odd OCD.

Everyone starts to leave the room.

"Jonathan," I call out, gaining not only Mason's son's

attention but everyone else's as well. "Could I speak with you alone for a moment?"

Out of the corner of my eye, I see Mason look confused, but I don't acknowledge it.

"Of course," Jonathan says, just as confused as his father.

I look over at Mason and wave my hand at him. "Go on," I tell him. "I need to ask your son something without you around."

Mason lifts an inquiring eyebrow at me.

"You'll know soon enough," I tell him. "But that's all you're going to get out of me. Now shoo!"

Once Jonathan and I are alone, I ask him a question that he immediately says yes to, and tell him about my surprise for Mason planned for the next night. Jonathan offers to help in any way he can, and we arrange for him to call Malcolm after Mason and I leave to fine tune the details.

"I thought my dad was happy now," Jonathan tells me as we walk out of the living room. "After tomorrow, he'll be over the moon."

"What's happening tomorrow?" I hear Mason say, as he walks towards us from the dining room.

"You'll see tomorrow," I tell Mason. I see him start to open his mouth, and immediately hold up my hand. "Don't even ask," I warn him. "You're not going to get another word out of me about it. Except," I say, realizing I do need to say a few more words, "you can't come over to my house tomorrow. Not until I tell you to, anyway."

"And I don't get any explanation for this exile?" he asks.

"Not until tomorrow night," I tell him, looping an arm around one of his and walking down the hallway to the dining room.

Halfway through the meal, Mason gets a call from Isaiah letting us know that Rafe is refusing to leave his clinic.

"It looks like we'll have to go to him," Mason tells me. "He doesn't want to leave his patients."

"Admirable," I say, respecting the wishes of the next member of our small club of archangels.

Mason and I finish eating quickly and say our goodbyes.

"See you soon," Jonathan tells me, giving me a kiss on the cheek.

Mason and I phase back to my house to wait for Isaiah to take us to where Rafe is.

"So what is your devious little mind cooking up for me for tomorrow night?" Mason asks, unable to hide his curiosity.

"Like I said, you'll have to wait until then to find out. Now, stop asking me questions."

"Hmm," I see a glint of mischief in Mason's eyes. "I bet I could get the answer out of you."

"Oh really?" I ask skeptically. "And just how do you intend to work that small miracle? Or haven't you noticed my stubborn streak?"

"Oh, I've noticed," Mason says. "I've noticed a lot of

things about you lately, especially where your sensitive spots are."

"The promise of sexual pleasures will not get you an answer," I tell him imperiously.

"That's not the sort of sensitive I was talking about."

I feel Mason's hands creep up my sides, and he begins to tickle me unmercifully over my ribs.

"Stop!" I beg, squirming against his hands, laughing.

But he doesn't stop; he continues his torturous tickling, and I do something unexpected. I fly up to the ceiling.

"Ha!" I say to him below me. "Didn't see that coming did you?"

I fold my arms across my chest and openly mock him.

"Hmm, do you really think that will work?"

Mason phases right in front of me in the air, and grabs me. Then he looks completely confused because we're both floating in the air now.

"Why aren't we sinking?" he asks.

"What do you mean?"

"I can phase vertically, but I don't usually float."

"Let go of me," I suggest.

Mason does, and he falls back to the floor, landing on his feet.

"Phase back up here and grab me again," I tell him.

He does as instructed, and again he's able to float while holding me.

"Ok, I'm going to completely rip off a Chandlerism, but this is wicked cool!" I say.

"I have to agree," Mason says. "Do you feel my weight at all?"

"No," I admit. "I mean I feel you, of course, but it doesn't feel like I'm carrying you. It just feels like you're doing what you're doing, holding me."

Isaiah phases in below us.

"Jess?" he calls. "Mason?"

I start to giggle.

Isaiah looks up. His eyes grow wide as he sees us floating in the air. "How are you both doing that?"

I fly us back to the floor, and we explain it to Isaiah.

"I've always wanted to fly," Isaiah says, sounding slightly jealous of my ability. "But that's not why I'm here. Rafe is waiting for us at his clinic. Are you ready to go?"

I nod. "Yes. Just let me get my sword."

I go to my bedroom and grab my sword, quickly placing it over my shoulders, onto my back, and buckling the belt around my waist.

When I get back into the living room, Isaiah phases us to Sierra Leone.

CHAPTER 13

I find myself standing in a room that contains twelve beds, six against each side wall. Each bed is canopied with a white mesh material that I assume to be mosquito netting. The room itself is plain; nothing like what you would find in a modern hospital.

Rafe is speaking to a woman sitting up in one of the beds, using his stethoscope to listen to her breathing. Sensing my presence, his eyes are drawn away from his patient to find me. I see a smile play across his lips, which he instantly tries to quell but can't. He says something to the woman and stands from her bed.

As he walks over to me, he starts to shake his head.

"Isaiah said I would feel connected to you when you arrived, but," he pauses, trying to contain his emotions, "I never expected to feel this."

I hold my hand out to Rafe, and he takes it, no questions asked.

"Is there somewhere we can talk privately?" I ask. "I'll explain everything to you."

Rafe nods and leads me through the clinic, past the beds with the sick and dying, and into a room that looks to be his office at one end of the building. Mason and Isaiah stay back in the infirmary while I speak with Rafe.

I explain to him why he feels connected to me and what our mission is.

"So you don't know what we're supposed to be doing exactly? What we're meant to stop Lucifer from doing?" he asks.

"No. Not yet. We're still working on that. Lucifer keeps things well hidden. I'm not even sure we'll know what he's doing until he actually does it."

Rafe holds a fisted hand to his mouth, and his eyes glaze over as he stares off into space, presumably thinking through everything that I've just told him.

"What exactly do you need from me?" Rafe asks. "I have a lot of people who require my help here. I can't just leave."

"You can stay here at your clinic, but we will need you to help us find the next vessel. Plus, I think you could benefit from meeting with all of us. The connection we share with one another magnifies exponentially the more of us there are in a room."

"More?" Rafe asked amazed. "When can I meet with the others?"

I smile at Rafe's anxiousness.

I go speak with Isaiah and Mason, and we agree we shouldn't waste any time. We decide to bring the five of us together as soon as possible and attempt to locate the sixth member of our group. Rafe agrees to leave the clinic for an hour while another doctor there looks after his patients while he's gone.

We decide to take everyone to Mason's villa since neither Leah nor Rafe have been there yet. It will be the place they can go to when it's time for them to fully connect with their archangels. I figure it's a good idea they spend some time there beforehand.

Mason phases to go get Leah and JoJo. Isaiah takes Rafe and me to Mason's villa then he leaves to pick up Chandler. In no time at all, we're all together in Mason's living room. The feeling in the room is electric and almost overwhelming. We don't immediately try to find the sixth vessel, but instead just sit around and talk with one another.

I learn that Rafe has been with Doctors Without Borders for five years. Oddly enough, Chandler, JoJo, and I all give to that charity each year. Leah opens up a bit more to all of us. She tells us stories about how she and Remy used to move from sector to sector in the alternate Earth reality. The hardships she faced were many: never knowing if they would have a safe place to sleep at night, not having food some nights and having to go to sleep hungry, and running from Watcher agents who tried to capture her and make her play in the vicious game of Bait.

It makes me feel like my life has been a fairytale compared to hers. I have no more pity left in me for the things I've gone through, especially now that I have Mason in my life. There isn't a moment I would change now. If I did, I might not have ever met Mason, and that is not a possibility I even want to think about. No, my life went the way it was supposed to, and now I have almost everything I could ever want. There was only one thing missing. The last emotional tie that needed to be resolved was finding my mother.

I wasn't sure I wanted to find her when my father first told me about her willingness to abandon me the night the Tear first opened. Now I realize I need to know her side of the story. If there is one thing I have learned in my life, it's that there are always two sides to every story. I don't know what made her choose to leave me, but in my gut I feel as though it wasn't an easy decision for her to make. I can still remember the woman who home-schooled me, bathed me, took me out for ice cream every Friday afternoon, and read me bedtime stories each and every night. That woman deserved to be heard out, and I was determined to finally learn the truth.

We spend almost two hours with each other before we even realize how much time has passed. I finally tell everyone we should gather around and try to connect with our sixth member. I know Rafe needs to get back to his clinic, even though he seems content to just stay with us. It's different now that there are five us. The bond feels stronger for some reason. It's similar to the old adage that there is strength in numbers. All I know is that these people, even though we've only just met, are a part of my family now. What God told Chandler and JoJo is right: we are permanently connected. When we finally do stop Lucifer from doing whatever it is he is planning, I feel confident we will always want to spend time together. We are lifelong friends now, and I know that friendship will carry over even into Heaven.

Before we start, Mason comes up to me and gives me a kiss.

"Good luck," he tells me. "Let me know if you need anything."

I needed a lot of things from Mason, none of which I could possibly get in front of our present company.

I shake off the effect his kiss has on me and try to concentrate on what needs to be done.

We stand in a circle together around the coffee table in Mason's living room and hold hands. Again, the vision is almost instantaneous. Yet it doesn't make a lot of sense. We don't actually see anything, only blackness. I hear the sound of machines running in the background. One sounds like a heart monitor but the other one is foreign to my ears. There is someone crying softly in the background of it all. As quickly as the vision comes, it goes.

We all open our eyes.

"Ok, what was that?" Chandler asks, voicing the question I feel sure we're all thinking.

"There was a heart monitor, right?" I ask Rafe, thinking he would know better than any of us what the sounds we just heard are.

"Yes," he answers. "There was also an oxygen machine running."

"Why couldn't we see a face?" Leah asks.

I shake my head. "I'm not sure. But odds are they're in a hospital somewhere. Let's try again and see if we can pick up anything else that might be helpful."

We connect with the sixth vessel again, but nothing is different. The only clues we have are the heart monitor, oxygen machine, and crying. Not a lot to go on.

I tell Mason what we've 'seen'. He calls Nick and sets him to work on trying to figure something out.

"My friends," Rafe says to us, "I must leave now and return to my patients. I've been gone longer than I told my fellow doctor I would be."

"We should try to connect with the sixth vessel again soon," I tell everyone. "Maybe something will happen, and we'll hear or see something else to add to the clues we already have. Either way, let's try again at my house tomorrow."

"Have you figured out what I'm supposed to do about school?" Leah asks me.

I turn to Mason. "I really don't want to put her in public school if we don't have to just yet. Maybe after everything is over, but her schedule might be too erratic for it now. Should we hire a tutor?"

"No, I think I have a better idea," Mason says. "I think we can teach her what she needs to know in-house. I'll teach her about history. Allen can handle the sciences. Nick is a wizard at math. Angela can teach her English and literature, and Joshua can teach her about computers. I would rather not hire a regular tutor. They might ask too many questions."

"Do you mean Josh is here too?" Leah asks excitedly.

"It's Joshua here," I tell her. "He'll be similar to the Josh you used to know, but not exact."

"Do you think I could go see him?" Leah asks.

I turn to Mason. "Why don't you take her to headquarters and introduce her to everyone? Isaiah can take me home."

Mason steps up to Leah and holds his arm out to her. "Shall we?"

Leah looks shyly up at Mason and loops her arm through his.

Mason looks over at me and winks. "See you at home?"

I nod, feeling that flutter in my stomach again.

Once Mason phases away, I turn to my friends.

"Ok, here's the deal. I need your help tomorrow night."

After I explain what's going on, everyone is eager to help out. I arrange their pickups with Isaiah, who is more than willing to lend a phasing hand.

Once Isaiah phases the others home, I ask him to phase

me to a store in New York City. After making my purchase, I have him phase me home. Mason isn't there yet, so I go over to George's house to see if he's finished with the little project I asked him to make. True to his word, he has it completed. I let him know his services will be needed tomorrow night too, and he tells me he'll be there with bells on.

I then walk over to Mama Lynn's to face the last two people I need to tell my plan to. I know Mama Lynn will be happy, but I have no idea how Faison will react. I hope she will be happy for me, but I have no way of knowing until I tell her.

When I walk into Mama Lynn's house, Faison is sitting on the couch in the living room, flipping through the channels on the TV.

I sit down next to her.

"Anything good on?" I ask.

Faison turns off the TV. "No, not really. Where is Leah?"

"She's with Mason. We're going to have the people I work with be her tutors. We thought it might be a good idea if she met them. Plus, she wanted to meet our version of Josh."

"Ahh, she told me about him," Faison says with a smile. "Apparently, she had a bit of a crush on the Josh in her reality."

"Well, I hope that doesn't transfer over to here. Our Joshua is pretty smitten with someone else."

I sit there, trying to think of how to tell Faison what I need to without hurting her feelings.

"What's wrong?" Faison asks. "I can always tell when you're procrastinating about telling me something."

"Ok, well, there's no good way for me to tell you this, so I'm just going to blurt it out."

I tell Faison what I plan to do. At first, she doesn't react. Then a slow, almost happy smile appears.

"I'm happy for you," she tells me. "How can I help?"

Mama Lynn walks into the living room, and I tell her my plans and show them both what I bought in New York and what I had George make for me.

"Do you have any paint?" I ask Mama Lynn.

Mama Lynn used to be an arts and crafts addict. She would have George make her all types of things made out of wood and paint them up to decorate the house with. She brings out her five-gallon box of paints and lets me pick out what I want. I choose a red acrylic paint and thin paint-brush, and set to work on finishing Mason's surprise.

I get a text on my phone just as I'm finishing the inscription.

Leah is spending some time with our Joshua. Isaiah will take her back to Lynn's when she is ready. I'm home. Where are you?

I'm at Mama Lynn's house. Be home in a minute.

Do you want me to come over there?

NO

No need to shout...

Sorry, no. Please stay at home. I will be right there.

Good. I'm dying for some matches.

And you call me insatiable?

I will never get tired of getting matches with you. NEVER

Who's shouting now?

I was making a point...

I'm almost through with what I'm doing. I promise I won't be long.

I want to kiss your lips...and not just the ones on your beautiful face...

Incorrigible...coming home now...

I'll be waiting...naked...in your bed...

"Isaiah will be bringing Leah home after she gets through talking with Joshua. I've gotta go now, though. Mason is waiting for me," I tell Faison and Mama Lynn. "I'm going to leave this here to dry."

"I have some little white boxes I could put the separate pieces in," Mama Lynn offers.

"That sounds great," I reply, quickly making my way to the door. "Call you guys tomorrow!"

I run back to my house.

"I'm home!" I yell, quickly locking the front door behind

me as I start to undo the buttons of my blouse and walk to the bedroom.

"I'm waiting!" Mason calls back.

When I step into the bedroom, Mason is just as promised: in my bed, completely and gloriously naked.

I can only think of two words as I hurriedly take the rest of my clothes off to join him: all mine.

The next morning I make sure to have Mason out of the house before Malcolm and his crew of Watchers is expected to arrive.

"What's the rush?" he asks me, stretching in bed, looking completely irresistible.

"I don't want you to see your surprise. Now get dressed and go!" I order.

"You know, your bossiness just turns me on," he says smiling, rubbing his hand up and down one of my thighs, making my body ache for him.

I quickly get out of bed.

"No seducing me this morning," I say resolutely. "I have things to do before tonight. Now go!"

Mason lies on his side with his head propped on a bent arm. His eyes rake my body with undisguised lust.

"If you want me to go, you really shouldn't stand there looking so delectable. Now I've truly lost the will to leave."

I snatch the comforter off the bed and wrap myself in it.

"There. Is that better?"

"Not really," he sighs. "Now all I can think about is unwrapping you from that thing."

"Mason, please. I love you more than life itself, but please go. I'm begging you."

Mason groans in frustration and rolls out of bed to grab his clothes.

"I won't have you begging me for anything," he tells me as he puts his clothes on. "What time do you want me back here?"

"I'll text you. Do you have something to keep you busy today?"

"Yes. We're supposed to move everything into our new headquarters."

"Where is it?"

"Still in Denver," Mason says, standing to zip and button his pants. "Joshua would kill me if I moved us. Then he wouldn't be close enough to Caylin when Brand and Lilly stay there with the kids. Plus, he's big into snowboarding and skiing."

"I'm surprised he finds time to do anything like that."

"He's young. He doesn't need a lot of sleep."

Mason walks over to me and wraps his arms around me.

"You know you're driving me crazy with this surprise thing, right?"

"It'll be worth it," I tell him. "Trust me."

He kisses me quickly on the lips and lets me go.

"Text me," he tells me.

"I will."

After Mason leaves, I go take a shower and dress for the day. Just as I'm putting my sweater on, I hear my visitor rocking on the porch. I grab a coat and go out to see Lucifer.

"Two mornings in a row," I say to him. "To what do I owe this pleasure?"

"Do you find my company pleasurable, Jessica?" Lucifer teases.

The expression on his face is almost playful. It's not something I'm used to seeing.

"It's not disagreeable," I admit, realizing it's the truth. In a way, I've almost come to enjoy my little conversations with Lucifer.

What's wrong with me?

"I guess even you aren't immune to my charms," he says with a genuine smile.

"Are you playing with me?" I ask him. "Is this all an act, you being something like a friend to me?"

Lucifer's smile falters. I can tell he doesn't want to answer my question.

"Would it matter?" he asks.

"Yes," I say. "It matters to me."

Lucifer lowers his eyes and seems to be lost in thought.

"I'm not sure what this is, Jessica," he admits. "I'm still trying to figure it out myself."

"I think you need friends," I tell him. "True friends who won't stab you in the back the first chance they get."

"Can you say you would be such a friend?" Lucifer asks. "It seems to me you're recruiting people to do just that to me."

"If you would stop whatever it is you're planning, I could be that sort of friend to you."

"I can't do that."

"Why?"

"Because He deserves what I'm about to do!"

"God?"

"Who else?" Lucifer says with a roll of his eyes.

"Why can't you let go of your hate for Him?"

"I don't hate Him."

"Then why do you keep trying to do things you think will hurt Him?"

"Because He hurt me!" Lucifer roars. "He had Michael just leave me here! My best friend left me and never looked back. He treated me like I was a piece of garbage that needed to be gotten rid of."

"I don't think Michael thought of it like that at all," I say, knowing I'm treading on thin ice. "Maybe he thought it would be good for you to come here and live with humans for a while."

"My father built this universe to stroke His own ego," Lucifer says scathingly. "Do you really think He cares about you? Don't you think if He did, He would do more to help you? You're nothing but a science experiment to Him. He just lets you go unchecked to see how far you'll make it. He knows as well as I do that one day you'll do something stupid and end this world. All I'm doing is speeding things along their merry little way."

"What do you mean?"

Lucifer leans back in his chair. "I'm going to help the monkeys destroy themselves."

"How?"

"By scaring them so badly, they'll want to decimate this world instead of live in it. Your species is prone to self-annihilation. You act before you completely think things through. And God forbid you come face to face with something you know nothing about. You scurry around like mice in a flood, not knowing which way to go, so you end up drowning."

It's the most he's told me about his plans, but I still have no idea what he's going to do.

Before I get a chance to dig for more information, Malcolm phases onto my front porch. He's dressed in a pair of tight-fitting faded blue jeans with rips across the thighs, and a blue and black flannel shirt tucked into the jeans but open at the front, down to the waistband. A leather tool belt hangs from his hips, and his long wavy black hair is tied back in a ponytail.

Malcolm looks at Lucifer and sneers. "Well, look what the hounds of Hell dragged up this morning."

"Hello, Malcolm," Lucifer says, looking Malcolm up and down in disgust. "I see you still haven't learned how to dress yourself properly."

Malcolm grins but there's no friendliness in his smile, only contempt. "The ladies don't seem to mind it."

"Does it really matter what the ladies think?" Lucifer

says. "From what I hear you're still pining for that bitch, Lilly."

I see Malcolm's fists clench and his jaw muscles tighten. I don't want to be the cause of Malcolm's death.

"You need to leave now," I tell Lucifer. "If you want to come back to see me again, you should go before you do something that ends this between us."

Lucifer shrugs. "As you wish."

He gives Malcolm one more scathing look before phasing.

"I'm sorry about that," I tell Malcolm. "He can be a real ass sometimes."

"Most of the time," Malcolm amends.

"Thank you for doing this for me. I know it's asking a lot. I could probably do something simpler, but I want to make it special for Mason. Something he won't ever forget, because I know that's what he would do for me."

Malcolm's shoulders lose their tension as Lucifer's words slowly leave his mind.

"It's not a problem, Jess. Mason deserves to be pampered for once in his life. I don't think anyone has ever arranged so much just for his benefit. It will show him how much you truly care."

"I hope so."

Just then, ten Watchers phase onto my front lawn.

Gotta love Watcher punctuality.

Malcolm and his crew work in my backyard for most of

the day. Mama Lynn, Faison, and Leah all come over to enjoy the show.

"My God they're gorgeous," Faison says, openly leering at my backyard full of Watchers.

I have to agree. They are nice to look at.

At one point, Malcolm must notice us all staring at him because he stops hammering on one of the buildings, and proceeds to take his shirt off and stretch his arms over his head so we're sure to get the whole picture.

"Oh...my...God..."

These words from Faison would be natural, but they aren't from Faison. They're uttered by Mama Lynn.

"You know he's just showing off," I tell her. It's not hot enough outside for Malcolm to be shirtless, so I know he only did it for our benefit.

"Baby, I can honestly say I don't have a problem with that. He can show off as much as he wants."

I cover Leah's eyes with one of my hands. "I think that's enough of your male anatomy education for today," I tell her as I lead her into the kitchen to start another pot of coffee.

"I've been meaning to ask you," Leah says, leaning against the counter as I pour water into the coffee pot, "if you've heard from your dad about Remy. When will I be able to see him again?"

"No, I haven't seen my dad since he came and got Remy. I'll tell you what. I'll call to my father tomorrow and ask him what God decided. I want to tell him how tonight goes anyway."

"Thanks," Leah says gratefully. "I know I can't see Remy everyday like I used to, but it would just be nice to know I can call him to me whenever I want."

"I completely understand. That's the way I feel about my dad. Just knowing for sure that I can see him when I need to is all I need."

"Jess!" Mama Lynn calls from the living room. "You've got to see what they just brought over!"

Leah and I walk back to the window Faison and Mama Lynn seem to be permanently glued to. When I look outside, I feel sure I'm hallucinating.

"I didn't even know they could phase things that big," Mama Lynn says, completely dumbfounded by what she's seeing.

"I guess I knew," I say. "It just never even occurred to me that they would."

"Wow, I've never been on one of those," Leah says as they phase in another large object to sit by the first one.

"Oh sweetie," Mama Lynn says. "They must really care about you and Mason to go through so much trouble."

I tear up at the Watchers' sentiment, and know in my heart that the night will be one neither Mason nor I will ever forget.

CHAPTER 14

The Watchers continue to amaze me by putting up what seems like a million twinkling white lights in the tall standing oaks and newly-built buildings in my backyard. They even bring in a plethora of accessories to fill the small buildings and make them look authentic. Everything is so wonderful, I feel a bit guilty that only a few of us will be able to enjoy all of their effort. It makes me form a new plan.

Mama Lynn, Faison, and I get on the phone and call everyone we know in Cypress Hollow and invite them over to share in my special evening with Mason. I'm in such a happy place emotionally that I figure the more the merrier, which is odd for me. I realize I've never felt so content in my life.

Around three that afternoon, I text Mason.

. . .

Be at my house at exactly 5.

Should I already be naked when I come over? Please say yes...

Dear Mr. Incorrigible,

Please do not show up naked. There will be impressionable young minds present and I would hate for them to be scarred for life by seeing little Mason in all his glory.

Scarred for life?? That seems a bit extreme.

The girls will go through life thinking all men are so well-endowed, and the boys will feel inferior to you for the rest of their lives. So yes, scarred for life. I do not want to be the cause of years of therapy for them. So please, arrive with clothes on, and dress warmly because we will be outside quite a bit this evening.

Can you at least promise me there will come a time this evening when I have you to myself to satisfy my incorrigible, insatiable appetite for your Heaven-sent body?

Yes, that is a promise I can make. In fact, I have something new I would like to try with you.

Oh really?? Would you like to expound upon this brilliant new idea of yours?

No, it's a surprise.

How many surprises do you have planned for me this evening?

Just the two that I can think of...

I wish it were already 5. At least then I would have you in my arms...

We will be together soon, and I promise you it will all be worth it. I love you.

I love you too

As planned, Isaiah brings Chandler, JoJo, and Rafe over to my house so we can try to connect with the sixth vessel again, and so they can help me with my surprise for Mason. All three of them stand at my back window and stare in awe at what the Watchers did to my backyard.

"It is *magnifique*," JoJo almost purrs. "I never could have imagined they could do such a thing in so short a time."

"I know," I say. "In my mind it was much smaller, and frankly not nearly as elaborate. But Malcolm certainly outdid himself."

"He is such a sweetie," JoJo says, and it reminds me that she and Malcolm were friends even before we knew she was one of the archangel vessels.

"How well do you know Malcolm?" I ask JoJo.

"Oh, we were lovers years ago when I was in my youth."

"Really?"

"*Oui*," JoJo smiles at the memory of her love affair with Malcolm. "I knew nothing would come of it, but it was wonderful while it lasted."

"How did you know it wouldn't lead to something like marriage?"

"Oh, he was never in love with me. I knew that. He

never made promises he could not keep. And I was fine with our arrangement because he was such a good lover."

JoJo hugs herself as she allows herself to remember her days, and presumably nights, with Malcolm.

Leah instantly conjures up a fire in my hearth, and we all gather around, holding hands to connect with our missing archangel.

As we connect with the sixth vessel, we're met with the same thing as before: total darkness, and the sound of a heart monitor and oxygen machine. No new clues present themselves. We don't even hear the weeping in the background this time. Just as our connection begins to fade, we hear the sound of footsteps. There's a rattling, like the person is doing something near the sixth vessel, and then the footsteps fade away.

After the connection fades completely, we open our eyes, none of us any closer to understanding what's happening to our sixth member.

"The only thing we can assume is that they are in a hospital somewhere," I say.

"It could be anywhere in the world," Chandler laments. "We need something, anything else, to point us in the right direction."

With no new clues to go on to find the sixth vessel, I show them what their duties are for the evening. Rafe is the only one who can't stay.

"I really wish I could help out," he tells me. "But I'm

needed at the clinic. It's hard enough for me to come here just for the short time I'm able to."

I place a hand on his shoulder. "It's ok. We have things handled. You're doing important work over there. Don't ever apologize for caring about your patients."

Rafe grins, pleased with my praise. "I would wish you luck with your endeavor tonight, but you don't need it. I know everything will turn out just as you've planned."

"Thanks," I tell him.

After Rafe leaves and everything is set up outside, I wait impatiently in the living room for Mason to arrive.

At exactly five, Mason phases into my living room. He sees me sitting on the couch waiting for him, but his eyes are immediately drawn by the spectacle of lights shining through my window, showcasing what's waiting for him outside.

"Uh, Jess," he says, looking and sounding completely confused. "Why is there a carnival in your backyard?"

I stand from the couch and take one his hand in mine.

"It's part of your surprise," I tell him. "Come on."

As soon as we walk outside, the sounds of laughter and talking from almost everyone who lives in Cypress Hollow surround us. When I look at Mason, his expression is one of complete shock, which makes me giggle. His eyes soon find the Ferris wheel and elaborate carousel the Watchers phased in to perfect the scene.

Malcolm and his crew built far more than I had originally designed. Ten small buildings, five on each side of the small corridor leading to the rides, house games for people to play. I tug on Mason's hand and lead him to the first one.

As we walk over to the first game booth, which Mama Lynn and George are in charge of, various people from the town greet us and wish us the best. Mason seems even more confused, because he has no idea why they are bestowing their well wishes on us.

The booth Mama Lynn and George are in is set up with the milk bottle game where you try to knock down the three milk bottles standing in a pyramid formation with a baseball. The booth itself is loaded with various stuffed animals like all the booths are, as prizes, a gift from the Watchers.

"Step on up here, Mason," George calls. "Let's see how good your aim is. Maybe you can win the special prize we have just for you."

Mason takes the ball from George and looks at me, holding the ball with the tips of his fingers.

"Are these challenges to win your favor?" Mason asks me.

"No, you have that, but you just might win something else."

Mason rears back his arm and throws the ball, easily shattering the milk bottles.

"And we have a winner!" George says.

Mama Lynn hands Mason a small white cardboard box, like one you would place a piece of jewelry in, tied up with a red ribbon.

Mason looks at the box and raises an eyebrow. He looks at the small tag attached to the bow.

"One of four?" he asks me.

"You have to win four games to get all four boxes," I tell him. "And you can't open the boxes until you've collected them all."

Mason grins. "Ok, I'll play along just to see where this is leading."

The next booth we go to is manned by Jonathan and Angela. Bree and Bale stand on either side of it and give Mason a hug when he reaches them.

The corkboard wall within the booth is decorated with a multitude of different colored balloons pinned to it. Jonathan hands Mason five darts.

"If you can pop five balloons in a row," Jonathan tells his dad, "you win your prize."

Mason hefts the arrows in his hand and proceeds to throw them one after the other in quick succession to pop the required five balloons.

Angela hands Mason his next white box.

Chandler and JoJo are in charge of the third booth, which simply has a black tire hanging from the ceiling. Chandler hands Mason a football.

"Dude, this is so simple a baby could do it. Throw the ball through the hole and you get this," Chandler says, holding up the third white box.

Mason throws the ball through the hole in the tire and wins the third box.

The last game is a test of strength. Malcolm stands at the ready, with the ten Watchers who helped him construct my backyard carnival standing behind him. Malcolm is holding a large black mallet.

"What are all of you doing here?" Mason asks, pleasantly surprised to see so many of his friends.

"Jess asked us to help her," Malcolm tells Mason. "And just to make it a bit more of a challenge, we wanted to see if you could win one of our games."

Challenging? I never said anything about challenging. I made the games easy for a reason!

We soon have almost everyone in Cypress Hollow standing around us to see what sort of challenge the Watchers have set up for their fearless leader.

Malcolm hands Mason the large mallet in his hands.

Mason looks at the metal tower with a silver bell at the top. All he has to do is hit the metal see-saw platform at the bottom of the tower to propel the two-foot-high cylinder up the wire to hit the bell. Seems simple enough to me.

Mason swings the mallet behind his back and strikes the see-saw on his side. The metal cylinder only rises a foot.

Mason narrows his eyes as he examines the cylinder more closely.

"Not made out of lead or steel, I presume?" he asks Malcolm.

Malcolm folds his arms in front of him, and the other Watchers look on quite amused.

"Now where would the challenge be in something so

light?" Malcolm questions. "You're going to have to put in a little more effort if you want this."

Malcolm holds up the last of the white boxes, like he's taunting Mason with it.

I'm pretty sure I have a 'what the hell are you doing?' look on my face because Malcolm just winks at me and smiles.

"Osmium?" Mason questions.

Malcolm nods.

"I'm sure you don't want to disappoint Jess," Malcolm tells Mason. "Just put a little bit more effort into it if you want the fair maiden's prize for you."

Mason sets the head of the mallet on the ground and leans the handle against his legs as he takes his coat off and hands it to me. He doesn't look upset, just amused by Malcolm and the other Watchers' challenge.

Mason turns to the crowd of onlookers behind us.

"You all might want to stand back," he warns. "I have no way of knowing where it will land."

Everyone ends up walking completely to the other side where the first set of booths is located. I stay by Mason because I feel it's the safest place for me.

Mason firmly grips the handle of the mallet and seems to put every bit of strength he has into his next swing. I feel the ground beneath my feet tremble from his effort and watch as the osmium cylinder flies into the silver bell at the top of the metal tower, crushing it before it even gets a chance to ring. The cylinder flies high into the air and ends up landing behind the High Striker with a loud thud as it comes back to earth.

The Watchers smile at Mason.

"Now," Malcolm says, "doesn't that feel more like you earned what you're about to get?" Malcolm tosses the last of the white boxes to Mason who snatches it out of the air easily.

"Do you know what I'm getting?" Mason questions, putting his coat back on.

"We all do," Malcolm answers. "Now go claim your real prize."

Mason takes the other three white boxes I was holding for him from me and looks at me questioningly.

"What now?" he asks me.

I take his free hand and lead him to the carousel.

A few of the children from Cypress Hollow are riding it, and we have to wait for it to stop so we can have our turn on it. Faison and Leah are in charge of operating the carousel. After they bring it to a stop, they ask everyone to get off so Mason and I can have a private ride.

I lead Mason over to one of the stationary carriages. After we take our seats, the carousel begins to move.

"Open the boxes," I tell Mason.

Mason sets the four boxes between us on the seat and opens the first one. He pulls out a wooden puzzle piece with part of a picture on it. After he opens all four boxes, he lays the pieces on his thigh and assembles them. The picture on the front is that of two red hearts joined together.

"Did you make this?" he asks me.

"I had George cut it out for me, and I painted it."

"Thank you, Jess. It's lovely."

"Turn it over," I tell him, holding my breath.

Mason picks it up and flips it over to read the words on the back.

Will you marry me?

Mason stares at the inscription I wrote in red paint, for what seems like forever. I have an irrational fear that he's going to say no.

Finally, he looks over at me.

"Are you going to give me an answer?" I ask, laughing nervously.

Mason continues to stare at me. His eyes look beyond my attempt at a joke and seem to be searching my face for something else.

"You did all this," Mason says, "just to ask me this question?"

"I wanted it to be another special memory for us," I tell him, becoming worried by his reaction. "I wanted you to know how much you mean to me, and that I would do anything for you."

"Do you really want to marry me, Jess, or are you just doing it because of what I said yesterday?"

Now I understand.

"No, it's not because of what you said yesterday. I had already set these plans into motion before we went to your beach home to get 'matches' together. And yes, I want to marry you. My father helped me figure out why I'm so nervous about marriage in the first place. It's not the commitment to you. It's the wedding. And before you give me your answer, I have to tell you that I cannot do a big wedding like the one Faison was planning to have. I don't want the frou-frou dress, or hundreds of people staring at me. It makes me sick to my stomach just thinking about it, to be honest. If we get married, I just want something simple, not over the top."

"If?" Mason asks.

I shrug. "You still haven't given me an answer," I tell him.

Mason grabs the front of my coat with both hands, sliding me to him as his mouth claims possession of mine. I feel his hands gather me closer to him by sliding inside my coat, around my waist to my back, pressing me against his warmth.

Eventually, he pulls back and looks down at me with happy eyes.

"Is that enough of an answer for you?"

"Hmm, better answer me just one more time. I'm not sure I quite got it all," I tease.

Mason obliges without any hesitation.

When he ends the kiss the second time, I pull my next gift for him out of my coat pocket.

"I bought you this," I tell him, holding it up so he can see it.

It's a platinum wedding band with eight small diamonds embedded in the top, in two rows of four. I have it looped through a slim silver box chain necklace.

"I didn't think you would want to wear it on your finger," I tell him, leaning in towards him to put it around his neck. "Not until the wedding anyway."

The carousel begins to slow down because my putting the necklace on Mason's neck was Faison's cue to bring it to a halt.

I take one of Mason's hands. "Come on. Everyone is waiting to know what your answer is."

"I feel confident they already knew what my answer would be," Mason teases.

I smile. "True. But we'd disappoint them if we didn't say anything."

Mason follows me, and we stand on the edge of the platform. Everyone in attendance is waiting expectantly to be told Mason's answer.

"He said yes!" I tell them.

Everyone claps, and you can hear well wishes all around.

Mason leaps off the platform and helps me down. We're immediately swallowed up by people telling us how happy they are for us and asking when the wedding will be. I try to tell as many people as I can that we will just have a small wedding. They seem disappointed. After dragging them all into the arrangement for the proposal, I begin to feel bad.

Finally, I stand back up on the carousel platform and tell everyone gathered, "Like I told most of you, we just plan to have an intimate wedding, but you're all invited to the reception afterwards. We haven't set a date yet, but I will let you know when it will be held. It's not like we don't all know what goes on in this town anyway."

This seems to placate everyone, and I don't feel as bad.

Eventually, Mason pulls me back into the house for a private moment.

Holding me in his arms he asks, "Considering what the first of your surprises was, will I be able to survive the second one?"

I realize that's a good question.

"Pretty sure," I say, really having to think about it.

Mason lifts his eyebrows at me. "Pretty sure? You don't sound too confident."

"Worst case scenario, you'll have to phase," I say.

"Curiouser and curiouser," Mason says. "And when will I be able to have my second surprise?"

"Well, we have to be naked first."

A slow grin spreads Mason's lips. "I'm completely fine with that condition."

I look out at the people milling about my backyard. "I don't think they'll miss us while we go get matches, do you?"

"No," Mason says, "I don't think they will. Do we have to go somewhere in particular for this surprise?"

"On the island where the beach house is. It's warm there."

"Would you mind if we stopped by my villa on the way. I need to pick something up."

"Sure."

We phase into Mason's living room at the villa. He walks over to a decorative cabinet on the sidewall and opens one of its doors. He pulls something out and walks back over to me.

"I bought this a while back because I thought it looked like something you would like," he tells me. "When you said you weren't sure if you wanted to get married or not, I put it here for safekeeping, and hoped I would be able to give it to you one day."

Mason bends down on one knee before me and opens the small brown velvet box in his hands. Inside is a beautifully simple pear-shaped diamond solitaire ring. I say simple. The diamond was the size of a quarter, and if I had to guess, I would say it was at least 10 carats.

"You've already beat me to the punch, but I thought maybe we should confirm things on both sides anyway. Jessica Michelle Riley, would you do me the honor of becoming my wife, to have and to hold, on Earth and in Heaven?"

I smile. "Yes I will, Mr. Collier. I most definitely will."

Mason places the ring on my finger, and I instantly feel its weight.

I look at the sparkling diamond. "You couldn't find something bigger?"

Mason looks confused by my question until I start to giggle.

"If it's too big, I could always get you something smaller."

"No. I'm just teasing. Now, as for your second surprise, can you think of somewhere on the island where we can be completely naked and alone, and preferably high?"

"High?"

"Like on a mountain high."

"Yes, I can think of a spot," Mason says uncertainly.

"Then let's go."

Mason phases up to the top of a grassy knoll over-looking the ocean. The warm sea breeze blows through the strings of my heart, lifting my love for Mason like notes of a love song.

We take our coats off and toss them on the ground. Mason pulls me to him and slips his hands underneath my sweater, sweeping it off in one quick motion over my head. He pulls me to him for a smothering kiss while using his wonderfully dexterous fingers to release the hooks on the back of my bra. He slips the straps down my arms and tosses the unneeded undergarment to the grass at our feet.

I push back from Mason.

"Get naked," I order, making quick work of the rest of my clothing.

Mason smiles and does what I tell him without asking any questions.

Once we're completely devoid of clothing, I wrap my arms around Mason's shoulders.

"Hold onto me," I tell him. "Don't let go."

I roll from the back of my heels to the tips of my toes and fly us into the air. Mason quickly wraps his arms around my waist. When we come to a stop, the bright full moon seems so close I feel like I can touch it. Mason chances a look down to where we started and smiles.

"This certainly brings new meaning to the Mile High Club," he says.

"And have you made it into that club already?" I ask.

"No," he looks back at me. "This will be a first for me."

"Well, I'm glad I can find things which are a surprise even to someone of your elderly age."

"Elderly, uh?" Mason says as he moves one of his hands from my back to in between my legs. He groans when he finds how ready I am for him.

I wrap one of my legs around his hips to give him ample room as he slowly guides himself into me, always the gentleman, and giving my body time to adjust. I then wrap my other leg behind his as the breeze from the ocean twirls us in the air as we ride the ever-rising waves of our passion.

CHAPTER 15

The next day Mason and I decide to go see Lilly and Brand at their home in Lakewood. Mason tells me Lilly has a ring that will let us control the djinn Faust and force him to give us Balaam's staff.

Lilly and Brand's home is a large grey cypress house with a dark green tin roof and matching shutters on the windows. There is a wraparound porch with white rocking chairs and hanging potted plants filled with a variety of winter greenery. The yard is immaculately maintained with tall crepe myrtles, hawthorn bushes, and a blacktop circle driveway out front.

Mason knocks on the door, and Brand answers it dressed in a pair of jeans and short sleeve dark blue polo shirt.

He smiles at us, and, as always, I'm instantly put at ease.

Brand holds his hand out to Mason. "Good to see you, Mason. You too, Jess. Come on in."

Just as I would expect from anywhere Lilly and Brand lived, the inside of their home is warm and cozy. The first floor is an open floor plan with lightly stained cypress walls and an exposed beam ceiling. There is a staircase to the right of the entryway leading to a second floor and loft area, visible from the first floor. To the left is a living room with a wall of glass looking out onto a picturesque lake. In the center of the glass wall is a beautiful river rock fireplace. Three light brown leather couches are situated across from each other in front of the fireplace. There is a large chandelier made of deer antlers hanging from the cathedral ceiling.

From the entryway, I can see that they have a full house. Malik and Tara are sitting at the dining room table that is situated on the opposite wall from the front door. Tara is holding a baby in her arms and cooing to it. She looks over at us and waves. I wave back.

Malik is thumbing through something on his computer tablet. Sitting on stools at the kitchen island are Caylin, Tara and Malik's son, Will, and a blond-haired boy around the same age as Will that I don't know. Malcolm is in the kitchen, pulling out a tray of what looks like chocolate chip cookies from the oven.

Malcolm lifts a dubious eyebrow as he sniffs the cookies and looks at the kids.

"I'm not sure any of you are worthy of my cookies. What have any of you little heathens done for me lately?"

"Oh, Papa," the blond boy I didn't recognize says, "please give us a cookie. We've been waiting forever."

"Patience isn't always a virtue, my dear grandson. Sometimes it has to be learned. Think of it as a life lesson."

"Stop teasing them," I hear Lilly say.

I look up the staircase and see her walking down, shaking her head at Malcolm as if she's having to discipline him like one of her own children.

"But it gives me so much pleasure, dearest," Malcolm complains.

Lilly lifts a delicate eyebrow at Malcolm. And that's all it takes, apparently. The next thing I know, Malcolm is stacking the cookies on a plate and setting it on the counter in front of the kids.

When Lilly reaches us, she hugs me, and I feel a happy warmth infuse my heart, telling me how much joy Michael gains from seeing his daughter again.

"It's so good to see you," she tells me. She pulls away and looks at both Mason and me. "I'm so sorry we couldn't make it to your house last night. Mae was colicky, and we just couldn't come. But I heard everything went as planned."

I nod. "It was perfect."

"No small thanks to me," I hear Malcolm say from the kitchen area.

"I couldn't have done it without you," I agree.

"Malik!" I hear Malcolm bark. "Dishes!"

Malik groans and puts his tablet down on the table.

"I never should have made that bet with you," Malik complains as he walks into the kitchen area.

"No," Malcolm agrees, "you really shouldn't have."

Tara giggles from her seat at the table. "Maybe you should have come up with the perfect name yourself. Then you wouldn't be his kitchen boy."

I see Malcolm grin as Malik begins to wash dishes in the sink.

"What's the baby's name?" I ask, curious to know.

"Ella," Tara says. "It means 'beautiful fairy'."

It was perfect.

"Lilly," Mason says, bringing our attention back to the task at hand, "we came to see if we could borrow King Solomon's ring from you. Do you still have it?"

"No," Lilly says, looking troubled. "Why would you need it?"

"We need to get something from Faust. I thought it would be the easiest way to gain his cooperation. Do you mind me asking where it is?"

"I was going to return it to King Solomon's tomb, but before I could, God asked me for it."

Mason looks troubled by this information. "Do you know what He wanted to do with it?"

Lilly shakes her head. "No, He didn't say. All He told me was that He needed it to complete something. That's all I know."

"Well, we'll find another way to get what we need from Faust," Mason says, but I hear the uncertainty in his voice.

He was counting on the ring to make it easy for us. Now he'll have to think of something else.

"Do you have time to stay for a little while?" Lilly asks me.

"I really wish I did," I tell her, truly wanting nothing more than to stay and just be with her, not only for Michael's sake but for mine as well. There's a peace which emanates from Lilly that I've never encountered before with anyone else. She simply makes you feel good when you're around her. There's really no other way to put it.

"I just have too much to do today. Maybe when everything is over, we can spend more time together. I really would like that if it's possible."

"I would like that too, Jess."

I ask Mason to take me home so I can contact my father. I want to tell him that Mason and I are official engaged, and I need to ask about Remy for Leah. Since I'll be busy for a while, Mason decides to go to headquarters and help Joshua locate Faust's exact location.

When I call to my dad, he instantly phases into my living room.

"What's up, Buttercup?" my dad says, coming to sit with me on the couch.

"So I did it," I tell him. "I asked Mason to marry me last night."

"And he said yes of course," my dad says, full of confidence.

"Of course he did," I say, like I hadn't been worried about the outcome at all. "He'd be crazy not to, right?"

"Right," my dad agrees, smiling. "Have you set a date yet?"

"No, we haven't had a chance to talk about it, but I'm not one to procrastinate about the important stuff. I'm thinking the sooner the better."

"And you're going to have a wedding I can actually give you away at?"

"Yes," I tell him, having already decided not to deny him something he seems so determined to experience. "I'll let you know when and where. In fact, I think I might ask my grandfather if we can do it at his house."

"Have you had much time to spend with your grandfather?"

"No," I say, instantly feeling guilty. "In fact, I need to call him today. I've just been so busy with things that I haven't had much free time to spend with him, which brings me to another thing I wanted to discuss with you. Have you seen God? Do you know if He plans to let Remy come see Leah any time soon? She asked me about him yesterday. She really wants to see her father."

"About that…" my dad says hesitantly.

"I swear if He said Remy can't come back, He and I are going to have fighting words," I say, feeling my temper begin to flare.

"No, no," my dad is quick to say, "He just told me that you would have to make the request in person."

"In person?"

"You'll need to pray to Him," my dad says. "And He'll come speak with you about it face to face. Apparently, my father has something else He would like to talk to you about. He wouldn't tell me what it is; only that it was a favor."

"He wants to ask me for a favor?" I ask. "I didn't know God asked for favors. Doesn't He usually just tell people what to do instead of asking?"

"I feel sure He knows that wouldn't work with you," my dad says, an amused smirk on his face.

"Well, I can't say you're wrong about that. I'm not much for being told what to do. When does He want to meet with me?"

"Whenever you're ready to see Him again and talk."

After my dad leaves, I decide there's no time like the present. Plus, I needed to get God to let Leah see Remy again. She deserved a little peace of mind.

I still wasn't much on praying, but it didn't seem like you needed to be eloquent about it to have Him answer you.

God, Jess here. Heard you wanted to ask me for a favor. Come on over when you can.

"Hello, Jess."

I open my eyes and see God standing in front of me.

215

"Does everyone get their prayers answered this quickly?" I ask.

"You are a special case," God says, grinning down at me. "I feel as though I should take advantage of the times you want to speak with Me. They are so few and far between."

"Yeah, been a little busy."

"So I've noticed."

I swallow hard. "Just how much of what we do down here do you see?"

God smiles. "Everything."

I feel myself begin to blush profusely. "Could You close Your eyes the next time I'm with Mason? Otherwise, I'm going to be a paranoid mess."

God chuckles. Well, at least He has a sense of humor.

"I will try," He promises. "Now, what favor did you want to ask Me for?"

"Let Leah call on Remy when she needs to. You know how much she's been through. She needs her dad just like I do."

"I will grant what you ask, if you do Me the same courtesy."

And here it comes….

"What kind of favor can I do for God?" I ask.

God lifts his right hand in the air, and a silver crown, much like the archangel crown I have, appears in his grasp. The only difference is that this crown looks tarnished, not shiny silver like the one I have in my possession. There are minute cracks along its surface, as if it was shattered once but now pieced back together.

"What is that?" I ask.

"Lucifer's crown."

"And what do you want me to do with it?"

"I want you to offer it back to him."

"Why?"

"I want My son back. I want to give him a chance to redeem himself."

"Then why don't *You* give it back to him?" I ask. "Why do You want *me* to give it to him?"

"You can't give it to Lucifer. You can only offer it to him. I want you to do it because he feels a kinship with you. You are the closest thing he has to a friend."

"But that's just because of Michael's presence."

"No. It's not."

"What else could it be?"

"Lucifer is drawn to you, Jess. Michael's presence is what made him come to you at first, but now he enjoys being with you, Jess the human; not Jess the vessel."

"But I still don't understand why You don't give it to him Yourself."

"I feel sure he wouldn't take it from Me directly. He's far too prideful. He would feel like he was admitting that he has been in the wrong all these years."

"Well he has, hasn't he?"

"For the most part, but I need him to know there isn't

anything I couldn't forgive him for if he would only ask Me to."

God hands me the crown. I debate whether or not to take it.

"You *do* realize if I offer this to him, it might set him off. I have a feeling he'll go ballistic."

"Are you refusing?"

I take in a deep breath and let it out. I take hold of the crown, and God lets it go, giving me complete control over it.

"So what do you want me to say to him exactly?" I ask, not sure how I should broach the subject with Lucifer without him going downright psychotic on me.

"Tell him that if he takes the crown, all will be forgiven."

"And if he doesn't take the crown?"

"Then I will know he isn't ready for forgiveness yet, and I'll take it back until another opportunity presents itself."

"But if he does take it, does that mean all the evil in the world will disappear?"

God smiles indulgently at me. "Lucifer is not responsible for evil."

"I thought he was," I say hesitantly. "You know people say the devil makes them do stuff all the time."

At least that's what Pastor Cary always preached in his sermons. According to him, the devil was to blame for leading us poor humans astray from God's righteous path for our lives.

"Evil is present in everyone. It can be fostered by the actions a person commits or through their thoughts. Lucifer can gain power over someone through their evil deeds, but he doesn't have the power to make them perform evil acts. The choice between being good or bad is always left up to the individual. Everyone makes their own decisions, Jess."

"You should really tell that to some Southern Baptist preachers I know," I say, being completely serious.

"People are smart enough to decide things for themselves. Look at you. You didn't even believe I existed until you had proof."

"Can I ask You something else?"

"Yes. You can ask Me anything."

"Did You kill John Austin to make sure I went through the Tear?"

"No, I did not cause his death."

"Could You have stopped it from happening?"

"Would you have stopped it from happening knowing what you do now?"

It wasn't a question I was prepared to be met with. He deftly turned the tables back on me to make me consider the effects of saving John Austin's life. If John Austin had survived the wreck, Faison would have never gone through the Tear, just like she said. We would have never found Leah any other way. One life in exchange for a chance to save billions. What would I have done if I had been able to control the outcome?

"Sometimes a person's destiny can't be changed without

having dire consequences," God tells me. "People often ask for miracles because that's what they want, but sometimes bad things have to occur for good things to happen."

I look down at Lucifer's crown in my hand. "Why does it look this way?"

"After Lucifer's fall, he forged rings from the crown for his princes. It was his way of being able to call them to his side whenever he needed them. After he made the Tear, I took the rings from the princes. I knew he would find a way to bring them back to him after I scattered them to the far reaches of the universe, but I also knew it would take him time to do it, enough time for a little seven-year-old girl to grow up into a strong woman, someone who could face Lucifer on her own terms and not bat an eye while doing it."

"Thank You, by the way."

God tilts His head at me. "For what?"

"For letting Mason go to that alternate Earth with me. He was finally able to let go of some of his guilt."

"That was My hope."

God looks down at the floor in front of Him. I get the distinct feeling he wants to say something to me, but he isn't sure how to put it.

"I'm aware you've been looking for your mother," He finally says.

I remain quiet and just stare at him.

Finally I find my voice and ask, "Do You know where she is?"

"Yes."

I remain silent, waiting for Him to say more but He doesn't.

"Are You going to tell me where she is?"

"I can do better than that," He tells me. "I can bring her to you if you're ready to see her again."

I stand up. "I'm ready."

"Then you need to lie down on the couch, Jess."

I feel my forehead furrow in confusion.

"Why?" I ask, thinking this an odd request.

"Because I need to put you to sleep before you can see her. Trust me."

I sit back down on the couch and lay out flat on it, trusting God knows what He's doing.

God comes over to me and lays His hand on my forehead. I instantly fall to sleep.

I find myself standing in my mother's garden behind our old home. Michael is standing beside me, and I see the back of a blonde-haired woman sitting in the white gazebo.

I turn to Michael.

"I don't understand. Why are we inside my mind?"

I look at the woman in the gazebo and know it has to be my mother.

Michael sighs. "Go talk to her, Jess. She's waited a long time to see you again."

I feel my eyes water with warm tears as realization sets in.

"She's dead, isn't she," I say, not really asking but

needing to say it aloud for my own benefit. "That's why she's here like this."

Michael puts one of his hands on my back. It's the first time since we connected that we've had physical contact. His touch is warm and comforting.

"Let her tell you her story," he gently urges.

I walk over to the gazebo and see my mother stand from the bench she was sitting on. She looks just like I remember her. She's wearing a nude-colored summer dress with black lace appliqués on the front. Her long blonde hair flows freely down her back in soft curls, and her bright blue eyes light up when she sees me walk into the gazebo.

I stand at the entrance, not sure what to do, not sure what to say.

She folds her hands in front of her, twisting them nervously. An anxious smile plays at the corners of her lips.

"Hi, Jessi," she says, taking a tentative step towards me.

My vision blurs and I hold a hand to my mouth to prevent a sob.

My mom walks over to me and takes me in her arms. Arms I haven't felt in fifteen long years. I hold her tightly to me and let myself cry on her shoulder. She rubs my back, telling me everything will be all right. It brings back memories of her doing the same thing when I was a child, soothing the hurt from a scraped knee or comforting me after a nightmare. This is the mother I remember. This is the mother I've been searching for since I was seven.

I let myself enjoy feeling her love for me, but finally lift my head from her shoulders and ask, "What happened to you?"

My mother cups my face with both her hands and wipes the tears from my cheeks with her thumbs.

"Come sit with me," she says.

We sit down side by side on one of the benches, holding hands.

"I'm not sure where to begin," my mom says, shaking her head, at a loss for words. "I want you to know leaving you was the hardest thing I've ever done. But it was the right thing to do."

"Why?" I ask, the seven-year-old girl in me needing to know why her mother chose to abandon her.

"I was so screwed up, Jessi," she says. "I tried to hide it from you when you were growing up, but I knew if I stayed I would just end up ruining your life."

"How can you say that? You're my mom. I needed you."

My mom shakes her head. "No, I wasn't someone you needed in your life. That's why I chose Mama Lynn to be your mother. I knew she was someone who could raise you the way you needed to be raised."

"I still don't understand. Why couldn't you do it?"

"I just wasn't strong enough. I was still an addict, Jessi. I never stopped. I knew if I stayed with you I would end up hurting you in some way."

"How did you die?"

"Overdosed on some meth at a drug dealer's house.

They probably buried me in some unmarked grave some-where. I doubt the police were ever notified."

That had to be why Joshua and Nick couldn't find any trace of her.

"So you chose drugs over me?" I ask.

"It's not that black and white, Jessi. Addictions are hard to break. Unless you've ever gone through it, you just can't understand what it does to you physically and mentally. It's like having a constant itch you can't scratch, and when you do scratch it, it's never enough to take the itch away completely. I wasn't strong enough to fight it. And I knew if I stayed with you, I would make your life a living hell. You deserved better. You deserved to have the love of a good mother who would raise you to be a strong woman, and that's exactly what Mama Lynn did. She helped shape you into someone who is able to stand in front of Lucifer and not back down from him, even when he's angry. I never could have made you into that woman."

"But you didn't even try."

"I did, baby. During those seven years with you, I tried to fight against my addictions, but I just couldn't. I might not have been using, but I sure did want to. I knew I couldn't be the person you needed me to be. That's why I decided to leave. I wish I could have been stronger for you. I wish I could have been the mother you deserved, but I couldn't. So I did the next best thing and found you a mother who could be all those things for you. I loved you enough to let you go."

My mother brings me into her arms. "Never doubt that I love you, Jessi. Of anyone in this world, you hold my heart like no one else ever will. I hope you can forgive me for being so weak."

I hug her back tightly. "There's nothing to forgive. You did the best you could. I love you, Mom."

"And I will always love you."

After a while and after more than a few tears, we pull away from each other.

"I can't tell you how proud I am of you and everything you've been able to overcome in your life. I was so happy when you finally let yourself fall in love with a good man."

"I asked him to marry me," I tell her.

"I know. I saw it," she smiles.

"Uh, how much of what happens on Earth do the souls in Heaven see?" I ask, wondering if everyone up there is a voyeur.

"We don't see everything," she assures me. "God lets us see the happiest times of our loved ones' lives so we can share in their joy."

I sigh in relief.

"Do you get to see Dad in Heaven?" I ask, wondering why he told me he didn't know where my mom was.

"No, I don't think he even knows I'm there, to tell you the truth."

"Why not?"

"We're not in the same part of Heaven."

"It has different parts?"

"Yes. And before you ask me to name them all, I can't," she laughs. "I only know about the part that I'm in."

"Will this be the only time I get to see you?" I ask.

"I'm sure if you really needed me, He would bring me to you again."

What daughter doesn't need her mother?

"Then I won't say goodbye," I tell her as I give her one last hug.

When I wake up, God is standing beside the couch looking down at me.

"Thank You," I tell Him.

"You're welcome," he replies with a pleased grin before walking far enough away to allow me room to sit up.

I feel like a heavy weight has been lifted from my heart. Seeing my mother again helped fill in a part of my past, finally allowing me to close that chapter of my life. My mother loves me. That's all I ever wanted to know.

When I look over at God standing a few feet away from me, I see that a troubled frown has replaced the grin on His face.

"What's wrong?" I ask Him.

"I feel I should help prepare you for something." He pauses, and I'm not sure He's going to finish His thought until He says, "In your final confrontation with Lucifer, a sacrifice will have to be made."

"What kind of sacrifice?"

"That will be revealed to you soon."

"Are you seriously just going to leave me with that answer?" I ask in disbelief.

"I have to be careful with My words," God replies. "I hope I haven't said too much as it is."

"Will I at least get a warning about this sacrifice before it's supposed to happen, or is it just going to be a surprise?"

"There will be a warning. One of the archangels you have yet to find will be able to show you more."

I sit there stunned and, I'll admit, slightly pissed off. He drops a sacrifice bombshell on me and doesn't say anything else? Ugh...

"Also," God says, "tell Mason I would be happy to do what he asked."

"What did he ask?"

"I believe he wants to tell you that himself."

"Ok," I say, not having a clue what Mason would have asked God to do for him, but apparently I was involved in it in some way.

"I should go now," God says to me. "Lucifer is coming."

"Do I offer him the crown now?"

"You will know when the time is right."

God phases just as I hear the rhythmic movement of the rocking chair on the porch.

CHAPTER 16

I have no idea when I'm supposed to offer Lucifer the crown, but I feel certain it isn't today. I run to my bathroom and grab a white towel to wrap it in. I go back to the living room and hide it inside one of the cabinets in my entertainment center. I then grab my coat and walk out to the front porch.

"So what was all the commotion in your backyard about last night?" Lucifer asks me when I come to stand in front of him.

"Were you here?" I ask, certain I would have noticed the devil in my backyard.

"Yes, but I didn't see you; just your neighbors."

"Mason and I must have left by then."

Lucifer looks at me expectantly, waiting for an answer to his original question.

"I asked Mason to marry me last night."

Lucifer grunts.

"Guess I should have seen that coming," he says derisively. "Did he not have enough gumption to ask you himself? Needed a woman to do the job for him, did he?"

"Don't talk about him like that in front of me. If you can't speak civilly about the man I plan to share my life with, don't say anything at all. Better yet, leave."

"At least he's not human," Lucifer shivers, ignoring my ultimatum to him completely. "I would have to seriously reconsider your intelligence if you had chosen a monkey to mate with."

"But in your eyes *I'm* a monkey," I remind him.

"Only partially. You have the soul of a Guardian. That puts you above a normal human in my estimation."

I suppose that's how he's rationalizing his feelings for me now. If I have part of the soul of an angel, I'm not completely human, so he's not degrading himself by being friends with one.

"Tomato, tamato," I say to him.

Lucifer looks confused. "What?"

"A tomato is a tomato even if you try to make it sound fancier. It's what you're trying to do by saying I'm above a regular human because part of my soul comes from a Guardian. You need to face the fact that I'm just a human, Lucifer. You're friends with a regular, ordinary human."

Lucifer grunts again but doesn't say anything.

"I suppose he said yes," Lucifer says, deftly changing the subject. "Is that the biggest ring he could find?"

I look at my diamond. It sparkles even in the shade of the porch, trapping the ambient light within its multitude of facets, and causing a dazzling shimmer.

"Big enough for me," I say.

"Well, I would hope so. A 10-carat diamond doesn't come cheap in your world."

I hadn't even thought about its expense.

"How much does a ring like this usually cost?" I ask.

"At least a million, I would say, if not more."

I feel my mouth gape open and Lucifer chuckles. Wow, I feel really bad now. I only spent a couple thousand on Mason's ring and thought *that* was expensive. He bought me something that could finance a small country!

"I wish you hadn't told me that. Now I'm going to be paranoid I might lose it."

"I wouldn't worry about it too much," Lucifer tells me. "A million to Mason is like a hundred dollars to a regular person."

Lucifer sits silently. I get the feeling he's run out of things to say but doesn't seem to want to leave just yet.

"Would you like some coffee?" I ask.

He grins wickedly. "Are you inviting me inside your home?"

"Uh, no. I'm not stupid."

Lucifer laughs. "No, I suppose you're not. Thank you for

the offer, but I should be leaving. I have plans for this evening."

"Dastardly plans?"

"Do I have any other type?"

"No," I say, resigned to the fact that Lucifer may never want to be saved from his own egomania, "I suppose not."

"I'll see you later, Jessica. Congratulations on your engagement."

After Lucifer leaves, I go over to Mama Lynn's to give Leah the good news about Remy. She's ecstatic when I tell her.

"Do you think if I called to him now he would come?" she asks me.

"I don't see why not. My dad comes almost immediately each time I've called for him."

"What exactly do I need to do?"

"Just close your eyes, picture his face, and call out his angelic name."

Leah closes her eyes and says her dad's name.

Remy appears instantly beside her.

It looks like Heaven has been good for Remy. I barely recognize him. His hair is cut, his beard and mustache are gone, the glasses are off, and he actually looks rather handsome dressed in his grey slacks and white V-neck sweater.

Remy taps Leah on the shoulder. She opens her eyes and throws herself into his arms.

"Hey, baby girl," Remy says, hugging Leah tightly to him. "I sure did miss you."

I see Leah's shoulders begin to shake, and I know she's crying. Mama Lynn, Faison, and I walk into the kitchen to give them some time alone together.

I tell Mama Lynn and Faison about my reunion with my mother.

"My goodness," Mama Lynn says, holding a hand to her heart. "I can't imagine having to make a choice like that. Only a true mother would do what's best for her child no matter the cost to themselves."

Faison smiles at me. "At least you know now that she really does love you."

I nod but don't say anything, because if I do I know I'll start to cry.

"So what happened to you and Mason last night? Where did you go?" Faison asks to lighten the mood. She may look like innocence itself with her question, but I have a sneaking suspicion she knows darn well what Mason and I were doing.

"Getting matches," I tell her.

The confused look on her face makes me want to laugh. I cover my mouth to prevent it.

"Oh my God!"

Faison grabs my left hand and stares dazed and amazed at the giant rock sitting on my ring finger.

"Is it real?" Mama Lynn asks, her eyes as large as saucers.

"As far as I know, it is," I answer.

Both Faison and Mama Lynn seem to be at a loss for words, an unusual state for either of them to be in.

"So have the two of you set a date?" Mama Lynn asks.

"No, we haven't talked about the wedding yet. But I was thinking about asking my grandfather if we could have it at his house. I think it would make him feel more like a part of the family."

"I think that's a wonderful idea," Mama Lynn says. "We really should have him over for supper soon."

"Why don't I call him now and give him your number so you guys can set up a time for that?"

I call my grandfather and let him know about the engagement. He offers his home for the wedding without me even having to ask. I give him Mama Lynn's phone number so they can arrange a time for him to come over and have supper with us. It's one less thing for me to have to worry about.

A little after I get off the phone with my grandfather, Mason sends me a text.

Found Faust. He wants to ask you for a favor before he'll hand over Balaam's staff...

Why me? He doesn't even know me. What's the favor? And why didn't you come get me before going to see him?

I'm not sure why he wants to speak to you. I don't know what the favor is. And I thought I might

be able to get the staff without disturbing your time with your dad.

I appreciate your thoughtfulness, but next time, take me with you. We're a team. Please remember that.

Am I in trouble? A bad kind of trouble...not the good kind?

No, you're not in trouble. I've spoken to my dad, God, Lucifer, and my grandfather while you've been gone. And someone else I would like to tell you about….

You've been rather busy, Agent Riley. Anything happen that I need to know about?

Yes. But I would rather tell you in person. On my way home from Mama Lynn's. Meet you there.

When I get home, Mason is sitting on the steps to the porch. He watches me walk over to him, and a slow, happy smile spreads over his lips. My heart aches at the sight of him, and I feel proud that I'm the one who can make him feel such joy.

I sit down next to him, grab him, and kiss the dog out of him. When I'm done, I let him breathe again.

"Not that I'm complaining, but what was that for? I thought I was in a bad kind of trouble, not the good kind."

I loop an arm around one of his and snuggle in closer to his side. "I love you. Isn't that reason enough?"

Mason smiles. "It's all the reason I'll ever need."

He kisses me tenderly on the temple. "Now, tell me what happened during all these conversations you had today."

"You can tell Joshua and Nick they can stop looking for my mother," I tell him.

"Why?"

I tell Mason about my visit with my mother. I cry a little, but they're happy tears for the most part.

When I tell Mason about Lucifer's crown, he looks troubled.

"God shouldn't have placed that burden on you," Mason says. It's the first time I've heard him say anything against something his father did.

"He must think I can handle it. From what He said, He thinks Lucifer will listen to me. But why would he pay attention to anything I said to him? From what I can tell, Lucifer doesn't take advice from anyone if it contradicts his own beliefs."

"Which is exactly the reason why my father shouldn't have placed you in such an awkward and possibly dangerous position!"

"Listen," I say, trying to soothe Mason's ire, "He wouldn't have asked me to do it if He thought I would get hurt. I got the feeling He thinks I might have a good chance of persuading Lucifer to accept it."

"I still don't like it," Mason grumbles. "I don't like anything that places you in danger."

"Lucifer won't hurt me."

"You keep saying that, but how do you know he won't? The Lucifer on alternate Earth tried to kill you when he learned what you are. What makes you think our Lucifer won't react the same way?"

It was a good question. One I actually had an answer for.

"Because our Lucifer cares about *me*, Jess the human. The other one didn't know me at all."

Mason sighs deeply and shakes his head, looking down at the ground. "Only you would make friends with the devil and think you're safe. Jess, Lucifer was best friends with Michael. He loved Michael. But that didn't stop Lucifer from trying to kill him during the war. I fear you're deluding yourself if you think he cares for you enough to never harm you."

"I know there's a chance he could hurt me," I admit. "I just choose to put a little faith in him."

Mason shakes his head at me, and I know he thinks I'm just not thinking straight where Lucifer is concerned. But, deep in my heart I know there is still a part of Lucifer that wants to ask for forgiveness. He wants to retake his place by his father's side in Heaven. He just doesn't believe it could ever truly happen. Maybe if one person just showed a little faith, a little trust in him, he would at least try to be more than he is. Isn't that all any of us really needs?

"God told me to tell you something," I say, hoping to take Mason's mind off my dangerous friendship with Lucifer.

"What?"

"He said to tell you he would be happy to do what you

asked. He wouldn't tell me what it was you asked for, though."

Mason grins. "I asked him to marry us."

"He does that sort of thing?"

"I guess he does now."

"I don't remember you telling me He came to speak with you."

"He didn't. I just asked in a prayer. It's normally how I talk to Him."

"Oh."

I sit there quietly thinking.

"What?" Mason asks. "What's wrong?"

"How come the only two times I've prayed He's come for a personal visit?"

"I think He wants you to know He'll always come if you need Him. You just started believing in Him, Jess. He probably wants to strengthen that bond with you as much as you'll let Him."

"It's not like I'm playing hard to get."

"Just enjoy His visits. Not many people get them."

"Speaking of the wedding, my grandfather offered us his house to get married in. What do you think?"

"Anywhere is fine with me."

"Do you have any special requests? Anything in particular you want at the wedding?"

"No, as long as you're there, I'm fine with whatever you want."

"I think I'll let Mama Lynn, Faison, and my grandfather

deal with the specifics. I'm not really a wedding-planner. They're more suited for that. Did you have a particular date in mind? I was thinking we'd do it as soon as possible so I can make an honest man out of you. I don't want people to think I'm just using you for great sex."

Mason laughs. "Well, then I guess we'd better do it quickly."

I lean up and kiss Mason's cheek, and he grins shyly.

"So tell me, what do you think Faust is going to ask me to do for him? I don't even understand how he knows I exist."

Mason changes from happy to concerned in a heartbeat with my question. "I don't know, but a djinn asking for a favor is never a good thing. They're notoriously spiteful creatures. We'll need to tread lightly where he's concerned."

"When do I meet with him?"

"I told him I would bring you to him as soon as you were ready."

"Ok, let me get my sword, and we can go."

I wasn't about to go meet a genie without some kind of protection. I decide to leave the plasma pistol at home. I seriously doubt it would make a dent in Faust even if he tried something.

Mason phases us to a condo in New York City where Faust lives with his patron, Heath Knowles. As soon as we arrive, I'm met with white: white walls, white furniture, white kitchen, white-washed hardwood floors. The only things that bring any sort of color into the living space are the black and white pictures hanging on the walls, and the wall of windows letting the colorful view from outside peek in like an urban mosaic.

A man walks around the corner from the kitchen area. He's tall and rather debonair-looking in a classic Fred Astaire kind of way. His brown hair is slicked back and he's wearing, of course, a white shirt, pants, and flip-flops.

"Ahh, Ms. Riley, I presume?" he asks, coming to stand in front of us.

"Faust, I presume?" I answer back.

"Where are my manners," Faust says, holding out his hand to me.

I look at Mason, not quite sure if I should shake hands with the djinn. Mason nods once, letting me know it's safe.

I shake Faust's hand and marvel at how smooth and delicate it feels. I instantly know Faust hasn't done much with his life except feed off the wishes of others.

"Mason said you wanted me to do you a favor before you'll give us Balaam's staff. I'm not sure what I can do for you. You're not going to ask for my first-born child are you?"

Faust laughs. "No nothing as dramatic as that. Aren't you Chandler Cain's girlfriend?"

No one's asked me that directly before. I side-step answering it.

"What does your favor have to do with Chandler?"

"I need you to get something for me."

"Does Chandler have it?"

"No, but his agent does."

"Are you serious?" Mason says unexpectedly, making me jump slightly with the strident way he asked his question. "I thought the two of you buried that hatchet years ago, Faust."

"I would like to bury a hatchet in that nitwit's skull," Faust says, fuming.

"He'll never give it to Jess."

I hold up my hands to make them both stop, because I'm completely lost in the conversation they're having with one another.

"What the hell are you guys talking about?" I ask. "What does this have to do with Chandler's agent?"

"Do you want to tell her," Faust asks Mason, "or shall I?"

Mason faces me. "Chandler's agent is a djinn."

"And you didn't think that was important enough to tell me before now?" I ask in exasperation.

"Horace seemed harmless enough, and I didn't want you to think badly of Chandler for using a djinn to get where he is in the music business. Plus, Horace seemed keen to stay out of the way whenever you and I were around. I didn't see him as a threat to you."

"So Chandler cheated to get where he is?" I ask. "He made a wish with this Horace?"

"It looks that way."

"No."

"No?"

"No. Chandler wouldn't do that," I say with confidence. "Chandler may have led a charmed life, but I don't think he would cheat to get what he wants."

"Well, I don't care about the boy," Faust says dismissively. "I want you to get me Horace's ring."

"Why do you want his ring?" I ask.

"Because if I have his ring, he can't make any more deals with people," Faust tells me, a cruel smile stretching his lips.

"Ok," I say, still not quite understanding, "and why is that so important to you?"

"Because he's a sniveling little bastard who doesn't deserve to be a djinn! He gives us a bad name. If that bitch hadn't used King Solomon's ring on me to take it back, Horace would be where he belongs, in that nasty little pawnshop of his downtown."

"I take it by 'bitch' you're referring to Lilly?" I ask, feeling my temper make my palm itch to slap the crap out of Faust.

"Who else?"

I give in to the itch. I slap Faust so hard across his left cheek he staggers back from the impact. He holds a hand to his cheek and stares at me in surprise.

"Don't ever call her a bitch again to my face or anyone else's. Do we understand each other?" I ask him, not even attempting to temper my anger.

I see Faust's eyes leave my face and travel to the sword

on my back. I get the feeling he knows what it is without me having to take it out and demonstrate its power.

"Fine," he says, rubbing his cheek and lowering his hand. "Just get me Horace's ring and you can have the staff."

"How do we even know you actually have the staff we need?" I ask.

Faust snaps his fingers, and a long wooden staff that doesn't really look like more than some piece of driftwood to me is clutched firmly in his hands.

"Is that it?" I ask Mason, since I have no way of knowing for sure.

"Yes. That's it."

"Ok then. I guess we need to go talk to Horace."

CHAPTER 17

Mason phases us to a hallway in a nice-looking hotel, but it isn't the one I'm used to phasing to when visiting Chandler.

"Did he move?" I ask.

"We're in Los Angeles," Mason tells me. "He's here to attend the Grammys this coming Sunday. I thought he would have mentioned it to you."

"No, we haven't had a lot of time to talk about what he's been up to when he's not with me and the others."

Mason knocks on the black lacquered door we're standing in front of.

Deon answers it, and smiles when she sees me.

"Just the girl I wanted to talk to," she says, grabbing my left hand and dragging me inside the room. "Come on in here so I can get your input."

I have no idea what Deon would want my input on.

I see her look down at the hand she's holding and notice the ring, but she doesn't comment on it.

Deon's helpers are buried in racks of clothing in the middle of the living room. Chandler is in the midst of them, looking at outfits. When Chandler sees me, his face lights up with unabashed happiness. Deon lets go of my hand, and Chandler walks over to give me a hug.

"Remember," he whispers in my ear, "we're boyfriend and girlfriend to these people."

I nod, understanding the ruse we're still involved in.

Chandler takes one of my hands into his and drags me over to the racks of clothes. Mason stands off to the side, letting me take the lead and trying to look as inconspicuous as possible.

"Now," Deon says, "we're trying to decide if we want to go retro cool or current rock star cool."

Deon pulls out some outfits Chandler is supposed to choose from to wear to the Grammys. I've always been a sucker for simple and classic. So I tell them I think he should wear the white suit and black shirt combo that's presented. Chandler agrees.

"Ok, those colors will work with whatever Jess is going to wear," Deon says.

"What do you mean it'll go with what I'm wearing?" I ask, looking from Deon to Chandler.

Chandler laughs nervously.

"You remember," he says, like I should know what he's talking about. "You're coming to the ceremony with me. We talked about this the other day. JoJo Armand is designing your outfit."

I suddenly feel like strangling Chandler. I love him like a brother, but at the moment I want to kill him.

"Oh, yeah," I say, having no choice but to play along, "I forgot."

"Ok, I guess we'll get out of your hair for a little while," Deon tells us, waving to her entourage to get ready to leave. "We'll just leave these clothes here for now and pick them up later. I'm sure you two could use some alone time together."

Chandler drapes one of his arms across my shoulders.

"Thanks, Deon. You know I don't get to spend much time with my sweetie."

I instantly wonder if anyone would notice me slamming my fist in Chandler's smiling face. I could make it quick. Very little blood would be spilt...

Once Deon and crew are gone, Chandler drops his arm back to his side.

"Don't hit me," he says, holding up his hands in front of him to ward off my attack.

"The Grammys?" I almost yell, but don't because I'm not sure how thick the walls are in the penthouse suite Chandler is in. "You didn't think it was important to ask me if I wanted to go before you told everyone I would be there with you?"

"It slipped my mind," he confesses. "With everything else that's been going on, I just forgot until my agent had us on a plane to fly here yesterday. Deon asked me if you were coming with me, and I just blurted out that you were, without even thinking about it."

I sigh, letting my anger fade. "Well, there's nothing to be done about it now. Everyone thinks I'm going. Is JoJo really making me a dress to wear?"

"She will be right after I call her," Chandler says sheepishly. "I just figured you would rather have her make you something than have Deon arrange something for you to wear."

I couldn't fault that logic.

"Why are you guys here anyway?" Chandler asks, looking from me to Mason.

"We came to see Horace," Mason says. "Where is he?"

"Probably down in his room." Chandler looks confused. "Why on earth would you want to see my agent?"

"We know what he is," Mason says.

"My…agent?" Chandler asks, clearly still confused.

And it's then I know I was right about what I said before.

"Do you know what a djinn is?" I ask Chandler.

"I'm not even sure what you just said," Chandler admits, his face a complete blank.

I look to Mason and know my expression says, 'I told you so.'

"How long have you known Horace?" Mason asks.

"Horace has been in my life forever," Chandler tells us. "He was good friends with my dad. When I was younger, I used to call him Uncle Horace. Then when I made it in the music business, he offered to manage me because he knew people who could help me out."

"Horace is like a genie," I tell Chandler. "He can make people's wishes come true, but apparently those people have to take care of their djinn for the rest of their lives."

"Usually such a bargain requires that the patron lose the love of their family and friends though," Mason says. "You still have family you keep in contact with?"

"Yes," Chandler says. "I didn't lose anyone, but I don't remember ever making a wish either."

"Could you call Horace and ask him to come up here?" Mason says. "Don't tell him we're here. I have a feeling he's been avoiding us for a reason."

Chandler gets on the phone, and Horace is at his front door within minutes.

"What's up CC?" Horace asks as he walks through the door.

Horace is about my height, slightly overweight, with balding light brown hair. He has a neatly trimmed mustache and goatee. He's wearing stylish black-framed glasses and a tailor-made blue suit.

When Horace sees us standing in the room, he comes to a complete stop. He does an about-face, but Mason quickly phases to him, grabs the back of his blue blazer, and yanks him back into the room.

"Ok, ok, ok," Horace says, holding up his hands in surrender. "No need to get violent."

Mason closes the front door, and Horace comes to stand with me and Chandler.

"Uncle Horace, Jess and Mason just told me you're a djinn," Chandler tells him.

"So what of it?" Horace asks us defensively. "I've done nothing but help the boy and his family out."

"Who made the wish?" Mason asks. Since we know Chandler didn't make a deal with Horace, we need to know who did.

"The boy's father," Horace tells us.

"What exactly did he wish for?" Chandler asks, obviously hearing this for the first time.

"He wanted a charmed life for himself and his family. That's all."

"And you granted it?" I ask.

Horace looks at us nervously. "No."

"What do you mean no?" Mason asks, like he's pretty sure Horace is lying to us.

"They already had a charmed life! The fool just couldn't see it!" Horace places a hand on Chandler's shoulder. "I knew that if I did what your father wanted it would ruin your family. So, I just let him think I granted his wish. He didn't know any different. He invited me into your home because he thought I had given him what he wanted. After a while, I became comfortable being your uncle, your father's best friend, and your mother's confidant. I was part of a family, something I'd never had before. I liked the way it felt so I let your father keep thinking we had to stay together, or it would all go away."

"But what made you not grant the wish in the first place?" I ask.

"It was something Lilly said to me once," Horace tells me. "She said I ruined lives with my wishes, and I guess I finally realized she was right. We do ruin lives more than we help. I didn't want to be that person anymore. I didn't know I wanted better for myself until after I met Chandler's father and saw what he had. I couldn't believe he actually wanted to make a wish when I offered it to him. Some people think they need more when what they have is already great."

"So, my career," Chandler says. "It's not because of a wish? I did it on my own?"

"Well," Horace says, smiling, "I did help a little bit; I just didn't use my magic to do it. I used yours, my boy. Your gift goes beyond anything I've ever seen. That's why you're a star."

I see Chandler's body sag in relief.

"I need your ring," I tell Horace, not seeing any reason to mince words. "Faust has something we need, but he won't give it to us unless we give him your ring."

Horace looks at the battered gold ring around his finger.

"Guess I really don't have any use for it anymore," Horace says. "I finally got something Faust doesn't have."

"What's that?" Mason asks.

"I have people who truly care about me for who I am; not because they're scared I'll leave them and break the spell." Horace pulls the ring off his finger and hands it to me. "Here, take it. I don't need it anymore."

"Thank you," I tell him.

Mason phases us back to Faust's condo. He's cooking something in the kitchen that smells god-awful.

"Ahh," he says, seeing us phase in. He grabs a white kitchen towel and wipes his hands off. "I assume you were successful, since you've come back."

I hold up the ring.

Faust walks over to me and holds out his hand.

"Staff first," I tell him.

"What? You don't trust me?" he asks in mock shock.

"No, I don't. Staff. Now."

Faust snaps his finger and the staff appears. I'm not sure why he didn't just keep it out from the first visit.

He hands the staff to Mason. Then I hand Faust the ring.

"What do you need that old relic for anyway?" Faust asks. "It's not like it will stop Lucifer from doing what he's planning."

I'm completely speechless for all of two seconds.

"Do you know what he's going to do?" I ask.

"We all do," Faust says. "All of us under his command anyway. We needed to know so we could prepare."

"Prepare for what?" Mason asks, just as anxious as I am to gain more information.

Faust shakes his head. "Sorry, can't say. He would have my head if I did."

Faust looks at me. "Why don't you ask him? I've heard he has something of a soft spot for you."

"I have asked. He just won't tell me."

"Just as well, I suppose," Faust says with a shrug. "It's not like a human could stop it from happening anyway." Faust looks over at Mason. "Not even you Watchers can stop it or that b--," Faust looks over at me and amends what he was about to say. "Not even Lilly can prevent *this* from happening. She can't go against all seven of them at one time."

"Could you give us a hint?" I ask, almost ready to beg for more information.

"No. I've said too much as it is. You should leave now. You got what you came for."

"Hey, you dirty old bastard!" I hear an agitated male voice say. A door slams shut somewhere in the condo, and a man I recognize walks into the living room.

I can remember when Faison and I were teenagers thinking Heath Knowles was quite handsome. I'm not sure what the hell happened to him. Standing in front of me is a mess of a man who weighs about two hundred pounds more than he should. His blond hair is matted to his head like he hasn't taken a bath in ages, and his sweat suit is stained all over from I don't even want to know what.

"Why don't you go back into your bedroom, little piggy," Faust taunts.

Heath barely acknowledges our presence. He glances our way but soon turns his full attention back to Faust.

"Why don't you get the hell out of my life, old bastard? And take that crap in the oven with you. You know I hate the smell."

I have to agree. It smells like someone threw up and Faust made it into a soufflé.

"And if I left, where would that leave you?" Faust asks.

"Happy."

"Exactly," Faust smiles tauntingly at Heath, "which is exactly why I stay."

I feel like I'm in the middle of a lovers' quarrel. And who knows, maybe they were at one time. But the years they've spent together seems to have turned them into bitter enemies.

"Let's go," I say to Mason.

I don't have to say it twice.

Mason phases us to Mama Lynn's house.

When we tell Leah we have her talisman, she looks apprehensive.

"What if this Uriel is mean?" she asks. "If he tried to kill Lilly for all those years, I'm not sure I want to meet him."

I couldn't say I blamed her. I could feel Michael's unease and knew he had no love or trust for Uriel either.

"I'm sure God wouldn't have let him come back if he wasn't going to be helpful. After this, you don't have to talk to him unless you want to anyway. He's mostly inside you to lend his powers."

"Yeah but Michael can take control of your body," Leah

reminds me. "How do I know Uriel won't do that to me without my permission?"

I sigh because I'm not sure what to tell her to ease her worry. Michael did that to me once, and I knew he was a good guy.

"Why don't I stay with you while you make first contact with Uriel?" Remy suggests to Leah before looking up at us. "That's ok, isn't it?"

"Of course, Remiel," Mason tells him. "I think Leah would rather see your face when she wakes up than any of ours."

Leah silently lets us know this is true by wrapping an arm around one of Remy's and laying her head against his shoulder as they stand in front of us.

I reach out and cup the side of her face with one of my hands.

"Everything will be all right," I tell her.

Leah leans her face into my palm and finds comfort in our connection.

"But," I say dropping my hand back to my side, "I think the five of us should gather together one more time before you meet Uriel. You'll be asleep for at least a couple of days, and we shouldn't wait that long before trying to find the sixth archangel again."

Mason and Isaiah gather everyone at my house for our third attempt to connect with the sixth member of our party. This time when we connect with number six, we hear someone talking in the background.

"I can't just leave him," a female voice says then pauses. "What if he wakes up?"

She pauses again, but we don't hear anyone replying. It has to be assumed she is speaking to someone on the phone.

"Ok, ok," the woman says in irritation. "I'll look over the papers. Just send them to the hospital." Another pause. "Yes, I'm at the Ronald Reagan Medical Center."

The vision ends but our spirits are lifted. We know where he is now.

Mason contacts Nick, who in turn contacts the head of the hospital our sixth member is in. Even with the small amount of information we have, Nick is able to narrow down which of the patients we're looking for. Instead of having all of us go, it's decided that Rafe, Mason, and I will go to the hospital. Since Rafe is a doctor, it seems logical for him to come along. He would understand our sixth member's condition better than any of us.

Isaiah takes Chandler and JoJo back to where they need to be. Then he takes Remy and Leah to the villa so she can connect with Uriel.

Nick meets us outside the hospital and escorts us inside to where we need to go.

"What's his name?" I ask Nick as we walk down a white, sterile-smelling hallway within the hospital.

"Zack Hall," Nick tells me. "He was involved in a car accident about a week ago, and has been in a coma ever since."

"Who was the woman we heard in the vision?"

"Maggie, his sister."

"Did they tell you his prognosis?" Rafe asks.

"They told me he had some brain swelling caused by trauma from the accident. The swelling has gone down now, but he still hasn't awoken from his coma. They're not sure what's wrong."

We step into an elevator, and Nick takes us up to the second floor. Once there, we are met by a female nurse dressed in green scrubs who takes us directly to Zack's room.

Zack lies on the hospital bed, hooked up to machines that seem to be keeping him alive. His head is wrapped in a white bandage, and there is a tube in his mouth providing oxygen to his lungs.

When we enter the room, Zack's heart monitor begins to beat erratically. The nurse runs over to check on Zack, and the heart monitor eventually goes back to a normal, steady beat.

The nurse seems apprehensive about leaving us alone with Zack, but Nick works his charms and deftly gets her out of the room.

Rafe looks over Zack's chart.

"They are doing everything they can for him. Comas are rather mysterious sometimes. Even in this day and age, we still don't completely understand how the brain works, which means we don't always know how to fix it."

I walk over to the side of Zack's bed and take one of his hands into mine. I feel connected to him, but the bond wavers like a wave on the ocean. One minute it's strong, and the next it's weak. I feel sure he knows we're here with him, but I have no idea what to do to help him.

"Sometimes, physical stimulants have been known to help coma patients," Rafe says, sitting on the side of the bed and taking Zack's other hand in between his two large ones.

"I wish I could help you, my friend," Rafe says to Zack. "I wish I could heal you."

Then it happens. Rafe's hands begin to glow a light, iridescent blue. The light from his hands travels up Zack's arm and into his skull. Before I can ask what's happening, Zack's eyes open, and he appears to be choking. Rafe acts quickly.

"Calm down," Rafe tells him. "I'm going to remove your intubation tube so you can breathe on your own. Do you understand?"

Zack nods. Rafe works his doctor magic and removes the tube so Zack can take a deep breath all on his own.

After Zack catches his breath, he says in a raspy voice, "Water."

Mason pours him some water from a pitcher on a side cabinet and brings it to him.

Zack drinks it down quickly, like it's nectar from the gods, and asks for more.

Once he's had his fill, he lays back and looks at Rafe and me.

"Do I know you guys?" he asks. "I feel like I know you."

Rafe and I explain who and what we are. Zack seems to

take it all in stride and doesn't seem surprised to hear any of it, even if it all sounds completely farfetched.

"So you're Michael's vessel," Zack says looking at me, "and you're which angel?" he asks Rafe.

"I'm not sure yet," Rafe admits. "But from what Jess has told me, I should be able to find my crown now, right?" Rafe asks, looking to me for confirmation.

"Yes, you've woken some of your power, which means it should be giving off a radiation signature we can track. We'll have Joshua do a search for it as soon as possible."

"I think I already know who Rafe's archangel is," Mason says. "Yours too, Zack."

This is news to me.

"How?" I ask.

"All of you have variations on the names of your archangels. I had my suspicions when JoJo's angel ended up being Jophiel, but now I feel more confident in my assumption."

"Who do you think we are?" Rafe asks.

"I believe you are Raphael," Mason tells him before looking at Zack. "And you would have to be Zadkiel. That only leaves one archangel left to find: Gabriel."

Mason's phone buzzes. He answers it and looks over at me, his eyes wide.

"We'll be right there," Mason tells the person on the other end of the line.

"What's wrong?" I ask.

"The Tear is open," he tells me.

CHAPTER 18

We decide Rafe should stay with Zack. Mason takes me and Nick to our new headquarters. As far as I can tell, it's pretty much identical to the old one.

Joshua, Angela, and Allen are standing in front of a holographic display of the Tear. Through the Tear, I see a green planet. The Tear closes but immediately opens again, revealing a red planet surrounded by a series of white moons. The Tear closes and opens a third time, revealing a constellation.

"What's going on?" I ask Mason. "I've never seen it do that before."

"Show me the Antarctica site," Mason tells Joshua urgently.

Joshua works his magic on the control panel.

"Do you know what he's doing?" Angela asks Mason.

"I have an idea." Mason replies, and I don't like the foreboding way he makes this statement.

"He's searching, isn't he?" Allen asks.

"That's my guess," Mason says.

"Searching for the one prince he has left to find?" I ask.

"Yes. He must have enough of them to open and close the Tear at will now."

An image of Lucifer standing in the middle of a circle of five of the Princes of Hell with his arms raised to the sky appears on the holographic display. Lucifer spreads his hands wide and then brings them together, matching the opening and closing of the Tear.

As I look at the five Princes of Hell, I breathe a sigh of relief. He doesn't have all of them yet. He needs one more just like us. However, I notice something oddly different about two of the princes.

"Why do Mammon and Asmodeus look like they just crawled out of a grave?" I ask.

The once cruelly-handsome face of Asmodeus and the craggy face of Mammon are ashen white with small red pock-looking marks dotting both their faces.

"Lucifer didn't tell you how he punished them for trying to kill you?" Mason asks.

"No," I say, realizing Lucifer and I never talked about them after I informed him of their failed attempt to assassinate me. "What did he do?"

"He trapped their souls in the bodies they inhabit, and then killed them."

"So they're dead?"

"Just the bodies they're in. They can't jump to a new body until he releases their souls."

"What's the point of making them stay in dead bodies?"

"They have to feel the pain of a decaying corpse. I'm sure the smell isn't very pleasant either."

I shiver at the thought. It's the first physical evidence I've seen of Lucifer's cruelty toward those who cross him. I suppose I knew he wouldn't let them off the hook easily, but to make them live in rotting corpses seemed beyond any punishment I could have imagined.

"Is it dangerous to do what Lucifer is doing?" I ask. "To open and close a wormhole so many times in a row must be damaging something, right?"

It makes me wonder if doing such a thing with a wormhole is analogous to phasing a human too many times. The night Asmodeous phased me multiple times in a row almost killed me, and made my body feel like a bowl of jelly afterwards. Could Lucifer be doing the same thing to the universe?

"I'm not completely sure what the effects will be," Mason admits. "I would have to consult with some of the Watchers who are more adept in the field of astrophysics to give you an answer. But it's not good; I know that much."

I watch as Lucifer opens and closes the Tear two more times, and decide something needs to be done.

"Take me there," I tell Mason.

Mason looks at me, his eyebrows lowered. "I don't think there's anything you can do."

"Take me there," I say more stridently, "unless you have a better idea on how to stop him."

"There are six of them there, Jess. I'm not going to take you to a place where everyone present wants to kill you!"

"Lucifer won't let them hurt me," I say, filled with confidence in my security. "Plus, all of our lives might be in danger. We should at least try to do something to stop him! It's what we were sent here to do, Mason. Put your feelings for me aside for now and let's do our job."

Mason's eyes tell me he knows I'm right, but that he still doesn't want me in harm's way.

"I can go by myself," Mason says. "I'll try to stop them."

"You know that won't work," I tell him, trying to be patient because I know his love for me is clouding his judgment. "He won't listen to you. Hell, he probably won't listen to me, but I have a better chance with him than you do."

Mason's mouth tenses, and I can tell he's frustrated because he knows I'm right.

I hold out my hand to him. "Take me there."

"Wait here for a moment," he grumbles at me before he phases. He reappears a minute later, with a dark blue parka and my baldric and sword in his hands.

"You're not going anywhere near those things without your sword," he stridently informs me.

Mason helps me into the coat he brought, which seems to be one of his since it's so big. He then helps me readjust the baldric to fit around the added bulk of the coat. He flips the fur-lined hood over my head and tightens the snap closure.

"Be careful," he tells me, leaning down and kissing me firmly on the lips. "I'm getting us out of there if even one of them takes a step towards you. Do you understand?"

I nod. "Ok."

I'm not going to argue with him. If I do, I know he won't take me. Besides, I trust his judgment. He may be worried about my safety, but he knows me going to talk with Lucifer is the only real option we have left.

Mason takes one of my hands, and we phase to Antarctica.

The wind is so cold and biting I feel as if it might blister the skin off my face. I look up at the sky and see that the sun is out again, making me wonder if it's ever nighttime here in Antarctica.

I look to where Lucifer is standing in the middle of his five princes. The vortex of power emanating from their combined energies seems to be physically swirling the air around them, something I wasn't expecting to encounter.

"Lucifer!" I yell over the howling of the wind between us.

"Go away, Jessica," Lucifer yells back, like he's scolding a child for being somewhere she shouldn't be. Lucifer brings his hands together, and immediately separates them again as he continues to open and close the Tear. "I'm a little busy right now. I can't stop to have one of our conversations."

"You need to stop what you're doing!" I plead.

"Your pet human seems to think she can boss you around, Lucifer," the newest member of the group says as he leers at me. He's slim with short brown hair, a high fore-head, and sharp, angular bone structure, which lends his face a sinister look. His hooded eyes stare at me with unadulterated disgust.

"You might want to think about shutting your mouth, Levi," Asmodeus advises, gazing at me with so much hatred I feel like I might melt through the ice from the heat of it, "unless you want to end up like me and Mammon, that is."

"Not really," Levi says with open revulsion for his two brothers' current condition. He scrunches up his nose at his fellow princes, as if their stench is overwhelming. "Though, I still can't believe you took a human's side against two of your own, Lucifer."

Levi's statement does what I could not.

Lucifer lowers his arms and the Tear closes. Without even looking in Levi's direction, Lucifer holds a hand out towards the outspoken prince. Levi's body lifts into the air a few inches off the icy artic floor and floats to Lucifer's outstretched hand. As Lucifer's fingers wrap perfectly around Levi's throat, I hear the prince desperately gasp for air. Finally, Lucifer looks over at his minion, and a cruel smile plays at the corners of his mouth.

"Would you like to say that to my face this time, Levi?" Lucifer asks, the promise of uncompromising pain in the question.

"You shouldn't care for her more than you do us," Levi squeaks out, clawing at Lucifer's hand, trying to pry it loose from his neck.

Lucifer simply tightens his grip. "I realize your gift is envy but, really, shouldn't you be above such a petty emotion by now?"

"She's nothing," Levi gasps. "She's an ant that should be put out of her misery just like any other human."

Throughout Levi's threats, my attention remains focused on Lucifer, but out of the corner of my eye, I see the other princes shaking their heads. I don't know if it's because they agree that Lucifer cares more for me than them, or if they are thinking what I'm thinking: Levi should really shut the hell up. But I fear it's too late.

"You shouldn't talk about things you know nothing about!" Lucifer roars, squeezing Levi's throat even more firmly, getting ready to break the other man's neck.

I walk closer to the edge of the circle with Mason by my side.

"Lucifer," I call to him, "don't do it. Don't do to him what you did to Asmodeus and Mammon."

Lucifer looks directly at me for the first time since Mason phased us here.

"What do you care what I do to him?" he asks.

"I don't care about him," I say, staring straight into Lucifer's eyes. "I care about what doing something to him will do to you."

"Do to me?" Lucifer questions, obviously not understanding my true meaning. "I can tell you what it will do to me: bring me satisfaction that I can put him in his place so easily."

"But your soul will suffer the consequences," I try to reason. I take another step forward, inside the circle. I know I'm taking a chance, but Mason is right behind me, refusing to let me go in alone.

"And what would you know about my soul?" Lucifer scoffs, eyeing me warily.

"I know you have one. You just don't use it very often."

Lucifer stares at me coldly. I can't tell what he's thinking.

"You need to leave," he says to me in a controlled voice. "I'm about to do something you won't like."

"Don't," I beg. "Don't give up on yourself. If you do this…if you punish him, you're only letting yourself sink deeper into the black abyss you seem to think is the only place you belong. You can do better, Lucifer! You don't have to be what everyone expects you to be. There's still good in you!"

Lucifer's eyes widen in surprise at my statement, and I see a look of confusion pass fleetingly across his features. Then he stares at me as if I've completely lost my mind.

"Good and bad is a concept you humans seem fixated on," he says scathingly. "I'm beyond either of them. I do what needs to be done, and right now Levi needs to understand his place in the order of things." Lucifer looks over my shoulder at Mason. "You need to take her away now."

I feel Mason put his hand on my shoulder, but I quickly

shrug it off and walk directly up to Lucifer, not caring that he's scowling at me now.

"Please," I beg. "Don't do this. Don't be this person. You can be more than what you are. You've shown that with me. You *are* that person when you're with me."

A moment of uncertainty enters Lucifer's eyes, and I see the arm which is holding Levi lower a small degree. I feel his want to be the person I can see him becoming. Then, a new determination clouds his features like a mask, and he hides his true self behind it.

"Get her the hell out of here, Mason!" Lucifer screams.

Almost instantly, Mason and I are standing in my living room.

Mason whirls me around to face him.

"What were you thinking, Jess?" he asks, his voice simmering with controlled anger. "He could have killed you!"

"No, he won't kill me," I answer, my voice sounding small.

Mason pulls me into his arms. "Please, for my sanity's sake, don't do that again. I can't lose you."

I wrap my arms around Mason's waist.

"You won't lose me," I reassure him.

Mason pulls his head back and I do the same. When our eyes meet, I can see the worry and love he holds for me in the depths of his eyes.

"If I ever lost you," he says, his voice low, "I think I

would lose myself. I don't think I would want to go on living."

"Don't say that," I tell him, cupping his face in my hands. "Don't ever say that. We don't know what will happen in the future, and if something does happen to me, I need to know you would be able to go on. Promise me you would find a way to live a full life."

"I can't make that promise to you," Mason says, a shimmer of tears in his eyes, "because I truly believe my heart would stop beating if yours did."

I feel tears of my own spill down my cheeks, and I bring Mason's face down to mine in a desperate kiss, one filled with a need to let him know how much I love him. Mason deepens the kiss, ravaging my mouth with his.

We quickly shed our clothes, needing to feel the other without any obstructions in our way. Our lovemaking is filled with a quiet desperation to prove we're still alive. The world might be on the brink of destruction, but one thing will remain steadfast in the face of everything: our love.

Afterwards as we lay on the couch, spent of our energy, Mason cradles me in his arms and plants small, tender kisses filled with love all over my face, making me smile.

He kisses my lips just as tenderly before bringing my naked body even more firmly against his.

"Can we just stay like this forever?" I ask, nuzzling the inside of his neck, planting small kisses of my own against his tender flesh, loving the taste of him.

"I wish we could," he sighs, rubbing my back with one

hand and letting it slide down to my hip to rest possessively there.

We're both silent for a moment, basking in each other's warmth, reveling in the feel of being utterly and completely loved by someone else. I can tell Mason wants to ask me something. He opens and closes his mouth twice before finally spitting it out.

"Did you mean what you said to Lucifer?" he finally asks.

I lift my head off his arm to meet his eyes. "Which part?"

Mason's forehead creases as he says, "About there still being good left in him. Did you mean that?"

"Yes."

Mason shakes his head and closes his eyes, but he doesn't say anything else. There's no need to really.

I know he doesn't understand how I can believe such a thing is possible. I feel sure he thinks I'm deluding myself by even entertaining such a possibility. I rest my head on his arm and against his chest. Knowing the history between Mason and Lucifer, I know the love of my life would never be able to completely understand what I see in my strange friend. I no longer feel that it's Michael's influence which makes me have a little faith in Lucifer. I know it's I who desires to see Lucifer rise above what he's allowed himself to become.

And I'm willing to risk my life to prove I'm right.

CHAPTER 19

Mason ends up having to leave early the next morning, but not after giving me a completely satisfying goodbye.

"I need to help Joshua and Nick finish moving everything to the new house," he tells me while I watch him stuff the bottom of his button-down shirt into his slacks before fastening them.

I can't help but sigh. I much prefer Mason naked and in bed, any bed.

"When will you be back?"

He shrugs. "I can't say for sure."

"Well, can you at least come back and take me to Zack after I get dressed? He and I didn't get to talk much yesterday. I feel bad for just leaving him the way we did."

"I'm sure he understood. Rafe probably told him what was going on."

"I know, but I feel like I should be there for all of them. I need to see him this morning."

Mason walks over to me and gives me a kiss.

"Call me when you're ready," he says. "I'll take you to him."

It doesn't take me long to get ready, less than an hour.

Just before I call Mason to come and get me, I get a call from Faison.

"Have you seen the news?" she asks me.

"No," I say, not understanding why she's asking me such a question.

"So," she says, taking a deep breath, "the world seems to think you're engaged to Chandler Cain."

"What?" I say quietly, positive I misunderstood her. "Why would they think that?"

"There's a picture being splashed on every gossip site on the Internet of you and him standing together in his suite in Los Angeles. They have a close-up of that 10-carat diamond on your ring finger."

"Crap," I say, remembering Deon looking at it suspiciously but not saying anything at the time. "Mason's going to go ballistic when he finds out."

"Who do you think told the news media?"

"I think I know," I say. "I'll handle it. Chandler and I might just have to have a break-up sooner than we thought. I'm not putting Mason through this unnecessarily. We'll just have to find Chandler another cover story besides me."

When I get off the phone with Faison, I decide to text Mason instead of calling.

I have some bad news…

Your texting…not calling… it must be bad…

I sigh. He knows me too well.

Apparently, one of Chandler's entourage took a picture of me while we were in his suite the other day. With the biggest diamond in the world on my ring finger, that same world is now under the impression he and I are getting married…

I wait…and wait…and wait for a response. Since I don't get one, I text him again.

How mad are you?

Still no response.

That mad, huh?

Give me a minute please…

Listen, I've already decided that Chandler and I need to end this charade. I will not have people thinking I'm about to marry him when I'm desperately, wholeheartedly in love with you. It's wrong, Mason. I can't go on like this.

One second…I need to think clearly before I answer…

I wait. Five minutes later Mason appears in my living room.

The first thing I notice is a lot of what looks like white powder all over his shirt and black slacks.

"Why do you look like you were just hit by a large powder puff?" I ask him.

Mason clears his throat, like he's embarrassed to answer my question.

"Because I put a few holes in a certain wall in the new house. It'll have to be replaced now, of course."

I bite my bottom lip as I watch Mason try to dust himself off, but the dry wall material doesn't look like it's going to come off that easily.

"I guess I should change," Mason says, giving up his futile efforts.

"I love you," I say, bringing his eyes to me instead of his ruined clothes.

"I know," he replies, trying to smile. "And I don't like the charade either, but it works. It shouldn't be for much longer. I can deal with it."

"But the world thinks Chandler and I are getting married."

"Let the world think it," Mason tells me. "We all know the truth. You know, I've been meaning to ask you why your neighbors have never said anything to the news outlets about you and me. They all saw us get engaged the other night, yet I've never heard any of them ask about your relationship with Chandler."

"These people have been in my life forever, Mason. They know me. They know I love you. They're not the type of people who would pry into my private life or gossip behind my back."

"But they could make a lot of money telling the real story."

"They're my friends, Mason. They wouldn't betray me like that. We don't have to worry about them telling any nosey-body reporters the truth."

My phone buzzes. It's Chandler.

"Hello hubby," I answer sarcastically.

"Oh God, Jess, I'm so sorry," Chandler moans. "How mad is Mason? Is he going to throw me through a wall the next time he sees me?"

"Well, if it's any consolation, the wall already has a lot of fist-size holes in it."

"That mad, huh?"

"No, he's ok. He thinks we should just let the world continue to think what they want. But, Chandler, after this is all over, you and I need to have the mother of all fights in front of a large group of paparazzi."

"Agreed." Chandler pauses and I can tell he wants to say more, because he doesn't say goodbye or hang up.

"What's up, Chandler?" I ask.

"It's my folks. They want to meet you."

I close my eyes and pinch the bridge of my nose with my index finger and thumb.

"Are you seriously going to make me meet your parents and pretend that we *are* getting married? Do you realize how uncomfortable I will be just flat-out lying to them?"

"I know," Chandler groans, "but I can't hold them off forever. They've been hounding me for a while now to bring you over to their house. Please, Jess. Just once to get them off my back, and I promise you won't have to meet them again while we're pretending to be a couple."

I sigh heavily. "All right," I grumble. "When?"

"I'm not sure yet. I'll get back to you when I set it up with my mom. Thanks, Jess. You're the best."

When I get off the phone, I tell Mason what Chandler needs me to do for him.

"Do I need to remind him to keep his hands to himself during this little visit with the folks?" Mason asks tersely.

"No. Chandler knows what's allowed and what's not. He won't do anything he shouldn't. You don't have anything to worry about as far as that's concerned."

Mason runs his fingers through his hair, and I can tell he's still frustrated by the whole situation. I go to him.

"I don't think it'll be for much longer," I tell him, placing a comforting hand on his chest.

Mason places one of his hands over mine and squeezes gently. "I know. And I'm glad about that and scared by it all at the same time."

"Why scared?" I ask, tilting my head as I see the worry in his eyes. "Don't you think we'll win?"

"I'm scared about the cost of that win," he tells me, and I can hear the dread in his voice.

I smile reassuringly at him. "Everything will be fine. Don't worry."

He squeezes my hand even tighter. "If anything happened to you…"

I see him swallow hard, not able to continue his thought. For some reason, he seems fixated on the idea that something will happen to me.

Dusty or not, I move in closer to him and touch the side of his face, which still holds the mark of what remains of his scar. He closes his eyes, enjoying my caress.

"Please, stop thinking that I'm going to get hurt. Nothing will happen to me."

"You keep saying that, but you don't know that for sure. You can't promise me nothing will happen to you," he says, opening his eyes to look at me. "You're going up against seven archangels, Jess. You can't say anything for certain."

"Then it's an even match, Mason."

"But Lucifer is strong. He was always one of the strongest."

"So was Michael, right?"

"He was the only one as strong as Lucifer."

"Then don't worry," I say. "Michael won't let me fail. Or is it me you don't have enough faith in?"

"Of course I have faith in you, but Lucifer plays dirty and you don't. How do we know this friendship he's been trying to forge with you is even real? Maybe he's using it to make you pity him and lower your guard, so he can strike when you least expect it."

"No, I don't believe he's playing that sort of game with me. He sees me as a friend; as close as he can get to one anyway."

"You're playing a dangerous game with him, Jess."

"I know. I'm not that naïve, Mason. I realize he's like a rabid dog that could turn on me at any moment and try to bite my hand off. I'm fully aware of that possibility. But, I also think he just needs someone to have a little faith in him, a little trust. It's just like Malcolm on alternate Earth. All he needed was for someone to believe he could be a better person. I think that's all Lucifer needs. I don't have any delusions that he'll change his ways overnight, but all I need right now is for him to believe that he can become more than he is. If I can help give him the courage to try, maybe he will."

Mason cups my face with both his hands.

"Be careful," he tells me. "He won't just bite your hand off if he turns on you, Jess. He'll kill you because you'll be a reminder to him that he can never change."

"But I believe he can."

"And I don't believe he will."

"Then on this one point we'll just have to disagree."

Mason sighs and leans into me, kissing me softly on the lips, making me feel cherished and loved by the simple action.

"Please be careful," he begs, resting his forehead against mine.

"I will. I have too much to live for."

Mason smiles.

Mason changes into some clothes I didn't even realize he'd placed in my closet.

"You don't mind, do you?" he asks. "I thought it would be easier to just have clothes here when I need them."

"Of course I don't mind," I tell him, watching him from the doorway of my bedroom. "I like knowing that you think of my home as yours too now."

Mason smiles. "You know, I have six homes around the world, but your house has always felt more like my home than any of them."

"Then you have seven homes," I tell him, which makes him smile even wider.

I raise an eyebrow at him as he stands in just his underwear.

"Stop smiling or I may not let you put those clothes on," I tell him.

Mason promptly pulls his underwear down and throws them on the floor. When he turns to face me again, he smiles and winks.

"Oh," I say reaching for the bottom of my shirt and swiftly removing it as I walk towards him, "you're asking for it now."

"Why, I believe I am," he says innocently.

I punish Mason for a good hour, and feel sure afterwards that he'll always smile and wink at me for as long as we both shall live.

When we arrive at the Ronald Reagan Medical Center, an older female nurse in pink scrubs is in Zack's room, checking his vitals.

"You're like the poster child for coma patient recovery, sweetie" the nurse tells Zack, taking his temperature.

"Just got lucky," Zack tells her with an easy grin.

When we walk further into the room, Zack's eyes immediately settle on me, and he smiles.

"I was wondering when you would come back," he says, sitting up straighter in his hospital bed.

"Sorry I had to leave so suddenly yesterday. Things got a little crazy," I tell him, coming to stand by his bed.

The nurse looks up at me.

"I know you, don't I?" she questions.

"I don't think we've ever met," I say, trying to remember if I met her the day before when we came to find Zack.

"Oh, now I remember. You're Chandler Cain's fiancée! Congratulations on the engagement. I can't tell you how many people around here are completely heartbroken that he's off the market. Not like any of them ever had a chance, mind you," she laughs.

I smile brightly at the woman, but cringe for all I'm worth on the inside. Out of the corner of my eye, I see Mason's scowling face.

"Thank you for your well wishes," I say. "I'll be sure to pass them on to Chandler."

"Well, I'll leave you two to visit," the nurse says. "I'll be back in a little while to check on you, Zack."

"When do you think the doctor will let me go?" Zack asks.

"Well, I don't know for sure, sweetie. Like I said, you're

a miracle. But, if you remain stable, I don't see why he wouldn't let you out in a couple of days."

Zack nods. "Ok, thanks."

After the nurse leaves the room, Zack pats the side of his bed, indicating I should have a seat.

When I do, he tentatively reaches for one of my hands.

I hear him sigh contentedly as our skin touches.

"Your hands are a lot nicer to hold than Rafe's," Zack says with a small laugh.

I smile because I enjoy the contact too. "Did he explain everything to you yesterday after we left?" I ask.

Zack nods. "Yes. Honestly, I can't believe someone like me is involved in something so monumental."

"What do you do for a living?" I ask him.

"I run a charity organization for abused children," he tells me. "We're small but we do good work for the kids who come through. I'm a child psychologist, so I help them cope with their feelings and attempt to get them past what's been done to them."

"That sounds like a worthwhile endeavor," I tell him, wishing someone like Zack had been around when I was a child, going through my own abuse.

"Rafe said I would need to find my crown and talisman," Zack says.

"As soon as you awaken whatever power it is you possess, your crown will send out a beacon of sorts to help us find it."

"Isaiah took Rafe to get his crown this morning," Mason

tells me. "I meant to tell you earlier, but we got preoccupied with getting those matches."

I look over at him because he's standing on the other side of Zack's bed now, and find myself unable to prevent a huge smile from appearing on my face.

"The never-ending quest for matches," I tell him with a sigh. "I don't think we'll ever get enough."

Zack looks confused by our conversation, and I decide he needs to stay that way.

Mason's phone buzzes and he walks away from the bed to answer it.

"So," Zack says, "tell me what the deal is with Chandler Cain. Are you really engaged to him? I know Rafe said he was one of the seven."

I begin to tell Zack everything he needs to know about Mason and me, and how my relationship with Chandler is simply a cover story to prevent anyone from asking too many questions when he needs to disappear for a while.

"I need to leave," Mason tells me, coming to stand in front of me.

"What's wrong?" I ask, standing from my seat on Zack's bed.

"I have to go coddle the President again. Apparently, he got upset about what happened with the Tear last night, and he wants me to explain to him what exactly happened."

"Ok, well, will you be able to take me home when I'm ready to leave?"

Mason sighs. "I have a feeling he's going to keep me

there longer than usual. I'll let Isaiah know to expect a call from you. He can take you home when you're ready to leave."

Mason leans in and kisses me lightly. "I'll come home as soon as I can."

I smile. "Ok. I'll keep the home fires burning for you."

"Should we plan on getting matches later then?"

"Yes. Definitely plan on getting matches later."

Mason winks and then phases, taking a large part of my heart with him.

"Matches equals sex, right?"

I turn to look at Zack and feel myself blush.

"Were we that obvious?" I ask him.

"Yeah," Zack says with a smile, "you kind of were."

"Sorry," I tell him, sitting back down beside him.

He reaches for my hand again. "Don't be. It was cute."

Zack and I talk for a good two hours as we share things about our past, our present, and our future plans. I learn that he has lived in California all his life with his mom and dad. He has a sister named Maggie.

"I think she's the one we heard when we were searching for you," I tell him.

"Yeah, she's great. She came to spend time with me every day after the accident. She never gave up hope I would wake up. Rafe met her when he was here. Hopefully, I can introduce the two of you sometime."

"I'm sure I'll get to meet her."

My phone buzzes. I look at it but don't recognize the number that's calling.

"Hello?" I answer.

"Is this Jess?"

I sort of recognize the male voice on the other end of the line, but it takes me a moment to place it.

"Horace?"

"Yeah. Hey, you happen to know where Chandler's at?" he asks in a rush.

"No. Why?"

"None of us can find him. I thought he might be with you."

I can hear the worry in Horace's voice, which makes me start to worry too.

"Are you sure he didn't just step out for lunch?" I ask.

"No, we had lunch together," Horace tells me. "The last thing he said to me was that he wanted to work on a new song. Usually, he does that in the bathroom."

"The bathroom?" I ask, sure I heard Horace wrong.

"Yeah, whatever city we're in, he always goes into the bathroom to write. He says the acoustics are better in there."

"I assume you've tried calling his cell phone."

"I'm looking at it right now. It's sitting on the coffee table in the living room. That's weird too, because he almost always carries it with him wherever he goes."

"You keep looking for him, Horace. I'll see what I can do on my end. Tell him to call me if you find him."

"Ok." Horace doesn't hang up, so I wait for him to say something else. "I have a bad feeling about this, Jess. I think something's happened to him."

"We'll find Chandler," I promise.

I tell Zack what's going on, and immediately call Isaiah. I tell him the situation.

"Let me come get you and bring you to headquarters. I'll have Joshua pull up any security footage he can find at the hotel."

"Ok."

Isaiah appears in Zack's room five minutes later.

"Let me know what happens," Zack tells me.

I nod. "I will."

When we arrive at headquarters, Joshua has a mosaic of surveillance video up on the large holographic display.

"Have you been able to find anything yet?" I ask.

Nick, who is standing by Joshua's chair, is studying the different videos intently.

"Not yet," Nick tells me. "But we just started. It took a bit to break through the hotel's firewall."

I'm not sure how either of them can tell what's going on. It looks like a jumbled mess to me. There have to be at least a hundred different cameras stationed around the hotel.

"There," Nick says, pointing to one particular camera angle and pulling the video forward with the motion of his hand.

"Wow," I say, "I didn't know you could do that."

Nick smiles, a first for him I think.

"We upgraded during the move," he tells me.

I look at the video Nick's pulled forward to separate it out from the others, and feel my breath catch in my throat. It's not hard to recognize Baal. He would stand out in any crowd with his boy-next-door good looks.

"Do you think he'll kill Chandler?" Nick asks me.

"No," I say, my heart sinking into my stomach. "He'll use Chandler to make me tell him what I am."

"If he plans to use Chandler against you," Isaiah says, "then he should be trying to contact you somehow."

I call Horace to ask if he found a note or something in Chandler's apartment that would tell us where Baal has taken my friend.

"No, nothing," Horace tells me. "Jess, you have to save him."

"I'll get him back," I tell Horace. "Don't worry."

There's only one other place a message might be.

"Take me home," I tell Isaiah.

Isaiah phases us to my living room, but I know where the message will be.

I walk out onto the porch and see the note sitting in Lucifer's rocking chair.

Go to the cemetery and come alone

B

"What does it say?" Isaiah asks.

"Just says Baal has him and to wait for further instructions," I tell Isaiah.

Isaiah narrows his eyes at me, and I realize he knows I'm lying.

Stupid Watcher lie-detector. I decide to change tactics.

"Can you go get Mason for me?" I ask, hoping this will diffuse Isaiah's suspicions. "I know he's with the President. I'm not sure how hard it will be to get him away from there."

"Yes, I can go get him," Isaiah says. "But Jess, don't do anything stupid while I'm gone. I won't be long."

I nod. "Ok."

I almost say I'll wait right here, but know that will come up as a big red lie to Isaiah. As I've always said, lies get more complicated when you try to elaborate on them. So, I decide to keep mine simple.

"I'll be right back," Isaiah tells me, his eyebrows raised as if telling me I'd better be here when he returns.

As soon as Isaiah phases, I run to my bedroom and grab my sword.

It doesn't take me long to drive to the cemetery. Once there, I immediately see Baal. He's standing beside Uncle Dan's grave. Since it's still winter, grass hasn't grown over the overturned earth, marking his grave until spring arrives.

Baal is dressed smartly in a grey herringbone-style sweater, black jeans, and black trench coat.

He smiles when he sees me. The dimples in his cheeks do nothing to make it look like much more than a leer.

"I see you found my note," he says in a friendly tone.

"Where is Chandler?" I ask, not seeing any reason to play nice.

"Oh, he's with Levi. After what Lucifer did to him, he felt like getting a little revenge."

"When will you things learn to stop messing with me? Whether you like it or not, Lucifer considers me a friend."

Baal laughs. "You're deluding yourself if you think that. Lucifer can't have friends. He betrayed his very best one. What makes you think you're anything special?"

"What do you want from me?" I ask, knowing Chandler's safety will depend on my cooperation.

"I want you to tell me what you are. The rock star is playing stubborn and not saying anything. I'll say one thing for you: You do seem to instill loyalty in your subjects, even when they're being tortured. It's a talent Lucifer could learn from you."

"What have you done to Chandler?" I ask, focusing on the one word Baal said which stood out: tortured.

"Take that sword off and leave it here," Baal orders. "Then I'll take you to your friend."

I unbuckle the baldric and lean my sword up against the backside of Uncle Dan's grave. I hold my hand out to Baal, and he phases us to Chandler's location.

CHAPTER 20

I hear the crack of a whip being struck.

I find myself in a place I've been before: Stonehenge.

I hear the sound of the whip again and look up.

Atop four massive stones composing one side of the large circle are three slabs of stone, pushed together to almost make a bridge-like structure. Levi, now pale with death and the first signs of decomposition, stands on top of the stone bridge. In the twilight of day, I see him holding what looks like a whip made from a bolt of lightning. It pulses with energy as he rears it behind his back and propels it forward, to strike a target I can't see. I feel something spatter onto my face and reach up to my cheek. When I look at my hand, I see blood, and begin to tremble. I know exactly where Chandler is now.

Levi finally pulls his focus away from his gruesome task

as he notices my presence. He looks down at me with so much hatred I can actually feel the heat of his gaze on my skin.

"Your friend refuses to tell me what you are," Levi says, rearing the lightning whip over his shoulder to strike Chandler again.

"Stop!" I yell. "I'll tell you what I am. Just stop hurting him!"

Levi looks down at me and follows through with the motion of the whip. I hear Chandler moan slightly. He must have passed out from the pain of Levi's torture a long time ago, since he isn't screaming. But he's still alive. That's the important thing, I tell myself.

Levi phases off the rock bridge and comes to stand in front of me. He holds the whip by his side. It crackles with energy.

"Tell me what you are!" he demands.

"If I tell you, what guarantee do I have that you won't just kill me and Chandler afterwards?"

"Oh, I won't kill you, if that's what you're thinking," Levi smirks. "I'll leave that messy little job to Lucifer. I would hate to deprive him of the pleasure to flay you alive after he learns your dirty little secret."

"And how do I know neither of you will torture more of my friends after I tell you?"

Baal shrugs. "Why would we? The whole point of this is to break your bond with Lucifer and get him thinking straight again."

I hear Chandler let out a moan of pain. It's killing me that I can hear him but not see him. I have no way of knowing how badly he's injured or how close to death.

"Fine," I say, not seeing any way out of this except to tell them the truth. "My soul is bound to …"

"Jess, run!"

Before I know it, Isaiah is tackling both Levi and Baal to the ground. I allow myself two seconds of shock at the unexpected rescue attempt before I fly up to the stone bridge to get Chandler. I barely have time to register what I see. The flesh on Chandler's back is covered with deep slash marks made by Levi's lightning whip. I gather Chandler in my arms, being careful not to touch the fresh cuts. Chandler moans and opens his eyes.

"I knew you'd come," he says.

"Put your arms around my neck," I tell him.

With a grunt of effort and grimace of pain, Chandler does as I ask.

Out of the corner of my eye, I see Baal and Levi holding Isaiah down on the ground.

"Isaiah, go!" I yell, not understanding why he isn't phasing to safety.

Baal looks up at me, the boy-next-door charm ripped open to reveal the monster underneath the handsome façade.

"He can't!" Baal yells up to me. "Not until we let him go. Tell us what you are!"

"Jess," Isaiah says looking into my eyes, silently telling

me he knows he's about to die, and there's nothing I can do to stop it. Levi squeezes Isaiah's throat tighter.

I feel a warm trail of hopeless tears stream down my face, because I know Isaiah is sacrificing himself to give me time to save Chandler. There's no way I can save them both. I have to make a choice.

"Fly!" Isaiah yells with his last breath.

Just as I propel us into the air, I hear Baal's cry of frustration, and see him turn Isaiah into a pile of black ash. As I fly up, I see Lucifer standing just outside the stone circle, staring up at me. Our eyes meet; his look surprised and mine are full of tears.

I fly as high as I can into the sky and veer off towards the setting sun. I fight back my tears of grief and concentrate on what needs to be done next. After flying for what seems like forever, I land us on a grassy knoll and lay Chandler down onto his stomach.

There's only one person who I can call on for help.

I close my eyes and picture him.

"Zeruel," I say.

My father instantly appears.

"My God, Jess," he says, kneeling down by Chandler. "What happened?"

"Can you heal him?" I ask, holding back a sob of grief.

My father looks at the damage done to Chandler by Levi's whip.

"No, I can only heal you."

My dad picks Chandler up easily and throws him over

his shoulder. He holds his hand out to me. As soon as our skin touches, we're in my bedroom.

We lay Chandler stomach-down on my bed.

"We need to get Rafe," I say, hoping his new power is strong enough to heal Chandler's wounds.

I fumble for my phone, pulling it out of my back pocket, and call Mason.

"Jess what's wrong?" he asks. "I felt your grief but couldn't pinpoint your location."

"Get Rafe and bring him to my house now," I tell him.

"On my way."

In less than a minute, Mason and Rafe are in my bedroom.

The look of horror on their faces when they see Chandler says it all. Rafe immediately goes to Chandler while Mason enfolds me in his arms. It's only within the safe confines of his embrace that I allow myself to completely fall apart.

Mason gently chastises me for not waiting for him to go with me to the cemetery, but I feel sure if he had, he would be dead too.

As we sit on the couch in the living room, Mason holds me close, letting me use him to cry out my pain over the loss of Isaiah and the damage that keeping my secret for so long has caused.

"Isaiah never came to get me," Mason tells me. "He probably knew you were lying and followed you to the cemetery. Then from there, he would have just followed Baal's phase trail to your location."

"I wish he hadn't," I say. "I would have just told them what they wanted to know and left."

"I seriously doubt they would have just let you leave," Mason says, not in a condescending way but as simple fact. "They would have taken you to Lucifer right then and there so they could gloat."

I hear the rocking of the chair on my front porch. I feel Mason tense against me.

"Don't go out there," Mason begs, holding me tightly to him. "He saw you fly. He might have already figured out what you are."

I wipe the tears from my eyes and pull away from Mason, who reluctantly lets me go. I stand up.

"I have to talk to him," I tell Mason. "I know what I have to do."

"Jess," Mason stands in front of me, "I'm begging you. Please don't go out there."

I wrap my arms around Mason's waist and look into his eyes.

"I need you to trust me about this," I say to him. "God said I would know when the time was right, and the time is right now."

Mason's eyes widen. "You're picking tonight of all nights to offer him back his crown? Have you lost your mind?"

I shake my head in the face of Mason's growing ire.

"How is it that I have more faith in God's judgment than you do right now?"

"It's not God I doubt. It's Lucifer's ability not to kill you."

"Jess."

I look over Mason's shoulder and see Michael.

"Are you going to tell me not to offer it to him too?" I ask.

Michael shakes his head. "No, I think you're right. I think it's time he knows about us. And it's time you offered him his way to salvation."

"Do you think he'll take it?" I ask.

Michael hesitates. "I don't know."

"What was Michael's answer to that question?" Mason asks.

"He doesn't know. But he feels the same way I do. It's time to tell Lucifer the truth."

Mason sighs in defeat because there's no way he can stop me now, not with Michael backing up my decision.

"Just be careful," he says, bringing my body closer to his and hugging me tightly.

I grab Lucifer's crown from its hiding place in my entertainment center. It's still wrapped in the small white hand towel I placed it in. When I walk out onto the porch, I find Lucifer rocking in his chair, hands folded in his lap. He doesn't look up at me, just stares at his folded hands.

I stand by the railing with his crown in my hands, waiting for him to speak.

Finally, he says, "When did you learn how to fly?"

Lucifer looks up at me. It's near dusk. Even though his face is partially hidden by shadows, I can see that it's a mask of controlled emotions.

"I learned how on the night your doppelganger tried to kill me on alternate Earth. That's how I escaped from him," I tell him.

Lucifer remains silent as he stares at me.

"What are you, Jessica?" he whispers.

"Can I trust you with my secret?" I ask. "Are you really my friend, Lucifer?"

Lucifer remains silent and just continues to stare at me, not willing to answer my questions but expecting an answer to his.

"Before my soul ever left Heaven, it melded with that of an archangel, and I became that archangel's vessel here on Earth."

Lucifer takes in a sharp breath.

"Michael," he whispers. I see him fully realize why he's been so drawn to me since we met. "That's why you can fly. You have some of his powers."

"Yes."

"And the others," Lucifer says, the pieces falling into place, "they're like you. They're vessels for the other archangels."

"Yes."

Lucifer sits back in the rocking chair and shakes his

head. "Why would you tell me this? Why give me such important information?"

"Because that's what friends do," I say. "They trust each other with their secrets. I'm trusting you with mine."

Lucifer looks away from me, still shaking his head in disbelief.

"Why would you want me as a friend?" he asks, and I hear the evidence of his self-loathing in his voice.

"Because I think you're worth it," I tell him. "You don't believe in yourself, but I believe in you. I know you can be better than what you allow yourself to be. I have faith in you."

"And how can I believe something so ridiculous?" he asks.

I place the crown on top of the rail at my back, and begin to take my bracelet off. Lucifer seems to notice its presence for the first time.

I walk over to him. "Give me your arm."

He hesitates but lifts his right arm, allowing me to clasp the bracelet around his wrist.

"What is it?" he asks, staring at the red and black bracelet with its silver angel charm.

I take hold of Lucifer's hand with both of mine. He doesn't pull away.

"Ask it to tell you what I feel for you," I tell him.

"Why?"

"Just do it," I urge.

"Out loud?" he asks.

"To yourself."

Lucifer grows silent. I know when he asks the bracelet to tell him what I feel for him because his grip tightens around my hand.

"That's not possible," he says, pushing my hand away. "You can't feel that way about me."

"I do."

"Why?" he asks, looking down at the bracelet still on his wrist, his voice hoarse with emotion.

"Because you're my friend, and friends have faith in one another."

I grab the towel-wrapped crown from its spot on the rail and begin to unwrap it. Lucifer's attention is drawn back to me by the motion, and I see his eyes glaze over with tears when he sees his crown.

"How did you get that?" he whispers.

"Your father repaired it and gave it to me. He told me I would know the right time to offer it back to you." I hold the crown out to Lucifer. "Please, take it and let go of your hatred."

Lucifer stands abruptly and walks up to the railing beside me, grasping it so tightly with both his hands I hear the wood begin to splinter. He takes in a deep, shuddering breath.

"You don't know what you're asking me to do," he says, shaking his head as if my request is an impossible task.

"Ask for His forgiveness, Lucifer. That's all He's ever wanted. He loves you."

I watch as Lucifer closes his eyes. "He can't still love me."

"Why?"

"Because of what I've allowed myself to become. How can He still love me?"

"Because He's your father. There's no greater love than that between a child and a parent. He can forgive you anything, but you have to ask Him for it."

Lucifer opens his eyes and looks at me. I see the shimmer of tears in his eyes.

"I can't," he whispers like a child.

"Yes, you can," I say, holding the crown out to him.

Lucifer looks down at the crown in my hands. Slowly, he loosens his grip on the rail and lifts one hand off, inching it closer to the crown. His breathing becomes labored, and it's almost like I can feel the war raging inside him. His hand trembles as it gets closer to his salvation.

I find myself holding my breath, praying he takes it and ends his own torment.

Lucifer lets out a guttural cry, and instead of grabbing the crown from my hands, he grabs me by the throat and pushes me against the porch post at my back, causing the house to shake.

He squeezes my neck so tightly I fear he'll break my neck. He stares into my eyes, seeming to search for evidence of his best friend inside my body. In one swift motion, he throws me off the porch onto the sidewalk, where I land hard on my side. The crown skitters out of my hands and rolls onto the front lawn.

I feel myself begin to cry. I don't cry for myself. I cry for Lucifer, and the opportunity of forgiveness he's willingly throwing away because of his pride. He's lost. He'll never ask for his father's forgiveness. He'll never stop his plan of revenge. He will never truly be my friend.

When I look back up at Lucifer, I see him trembling with rage.

"You and I are *not* friends," he says with finality. "I don't care how many archangels you have by your side. You will never be able to stop me. And tell my father He can keep that relic for all of eternity. I don't need His forgiveness. I never have. And the next time I see you, Jessica," he takes in a deep breath before saying, "I *will* kill you."

Lucifer phases, leaving me bereft of hope.

Mason rushes out the front door and pulls me to my feet. I collapse into his arms for the second time that night, sobbing out my anguish over Lucifer's missed opportunity. And I know in my heart Lucifer will keep his word.

The next time he sees me…he *will* kill me…

Mason holds me in the circle of his arms, trying to soothe my pain as you would an upset child. He attempts to calm my sobbing, but nothing he says, nothing he does, can stop the flow of my tears or heal the tear in my heart. With Lucifer's refusal to accept my friendship and his own redemption, my heart feels empty of hope, and an unending sense of loss fills my soul. The hollowness I feel doesn't solely belong to me. Michael's sorrow makes my heart feel like it has imploded inside my chest. We both had hope Lucifer would accept his chance at salvation. Lucifer's refusal of the crown, and perhaps last chance at forgiveness, isn't what upsets us the most. It's the fact that we both know he wanted to accept it that is tearing us apart.

"How could You do this to her?" I hear Mason ask someone, his voice filled with anguish over my sorrow. "How could You put her through this when she's already been through so much?"

"She was his best chance."

I force myself to stop crying and turn around. Lucifer's crown still lies where it fell, on the brown grass in the center of my front lawn. Standing behind the crown is God. He looks at me with the anguish only a heartbroken father can hold in His eyes. I know His sorrow isn't only for Lucifer's missed opportunity but for my pain as well.

He holds His arms out to me, and I don't hesitate to go to Him. When we embrace, I feel a sense of calm infuse me, filling the holes in my heart left behind by Lucifer.

"You did your best," He tells me, holding me tightly in His warm embrace. "It was him who failed you, not the other way around."

"He wanted to take it," I say, trying to prevent myself from sobbing but failing miserably. "I know he wanted to. I could feel it."

"He's always been his own worst enemy," God says with a deep sigh. He rests His chin on top of my head as He continues to hold me. "Now you know the pain I've felt since the moment he chose his pride over his love for Me."

"How do You live with the loss?"

"I choose to remain hopeful that one day he'll see his way through the darkness he surrounds himself with and find his way back to Me."

"I don't think I'll live long enough to see that happen," I tell Him.

"No, but I promise when it does, you'll be by My side to welcome him home."

"What do I do now?" I ask, seeking His guidance.

"Stop him."

"What if I can't?" I lift my head and look into God's eyes.

"You must," He tells me unequivocally. "And you will."

I lay my head back on God's chest, finding strength in His faith in me to find a way to stop Lucifer. I close my eyes, allowing myself to breathe, safe in the knowledge that whatever might happen from this point on, Lucifer will not win. I know I will defeat him, no matter the cost.

THE END

AUTHOR'S NOTE

Thank you so much for reading **Oblivion**, the third book in **The Watcher Chronicles.** If you have enjoyed this book please take a moment and leave a review. To leave a review please visit: Oblivion http://mybook.to/Oblivion-3

Thank you in advance for leaving a review for the book.
Sincerely,
S.J. West.

THE NEXT IN THE WATCHER CHRONICLES

Ascension,
The Watcher Chronicles, book 4

Get the third book in the series today, and continue Jess & Mason's story.

It's available at Amazon & Free on KU.

http://mybook.to/Ascension-4

ABOUT THE AUTHOR

Once upon a time, a little girl was born on a cold winter morning in the heart of Seoul, Korea. She was brought to America by her parents and raised in the Deep South where the words ma'am and y'all became an integrated part of her lexicon. She wrote her first novel at the age of eight and continued writing on and off during her teenage years. In college she studied biology and chemistry and finally combined the two by earning a master's degree in biochemistry.

After that she moved to Yankee land where she lived for four years working in a laboratory at Cornell University. Home-sickness and snow aversion forced her back South where she lives in the land, which spawned Jim Henson, Elvis Presley, Oprah Winfrey, John Grisham and B.B. King.

After finding her Prince Charming, she gave birth to a wondrous baby girl and they all lived happily ever after.

As always, you can learn about the progress on my books,

get news about new releases, new projects and participate on amazing giveaways by signing up for my newsletter:

FB Book Page: www.facebook.com/SJWestBooks/
FB Author
Page: https://www.facebook.com/sandra.west.585112
Website: www.sjwest.com
Amazon: author.to/SJWest-Amazon
Goodreads:
https://www.goodreads.com/author/show/6561395.S_J_
West
Bookbub: https://www.bookbub.com/authors/s-j-west
Newsletter Sign-up: http://eepurl.com/bQs0sX
Instagram: @authorsjwest
Twitter: @SJWest2013

If you'd like to contact the author, you can email her to: sandrawest481@gmail.com

31058771R00173

Made in the USA
Lexington, KY
14 February 2019